"Excuse me."

Standing in front of the kissing booth was a beautiful stranger—so cool and in control. In an instant Jason knew he'd love to be the one who fractured that control.

Beside him, his sister stirred. "May we help you?"

Jason never took his attention off the woman before him. "It's only obvious," he said solemnly. "She's afraid she missed her chance."

Then he gathered her in his arms and kissed her. He felt the thrill all the way to his toes. He wanted to stand there kissing her for the foreseeable future, but if he didn't call this off fast, he was going to lose the humor of the situation.

So he stood her up straight again, lifted his mouth reluctantly from hers. She blinked as if she wasn't sure quite what had happened.

"Honey," Jason said, "that kiss was way too nice to charge you for it." Digging around in his pocket, he pulled out a five-dollar bill and dropped it in the coffee can. "My treat," he announced.

Then with a tip of his hat, he sauntered off, leaving the stranger staring after him with a gaze so sharp he felt it between his shoulder blades like a knife.

ABOUT THE AUTHOR

Ruth Jean Dale lives in a Colorado pine forest within shouting distance of Pikes Peak. She is surrounded by two dogs, two cats, a husband (her one and only) and a passel of grown children and grandchildren. A former newspaper reporter and editor, she is living her dream: writing romance novels for Harlequin. As she says with typical understatement, "It doesn't get any better than this!" (Actually, proud to be a country girl at heart, she said, "It don't get no better…" but we cleaned it up.)

Books by Ruth Jean Dale

HARLEQUIN SUPERROMANCE
678—KIDS, CRITTERS AND CUPID
687—THE CUPID CHRONICLES

HARLEQUIN TEMPTATION
579—THE CUPID CONSPIRACY

HARLEQUIN ROMANCE
3441—RUNAWAY HONEYMOON
3465—BREAKFAST IN BED
3491—DASH TO THE ALTAR

Don't miss any of our special offers. Write to us at the following address for information on our newest releases.

Harlequin Reader Service
U.S.: 3010 Walden Ave., P.O. Box 1325, Buffalo, NY 14269
Canadian: P.O. Box 609, Fort Erie, Ont. L2A 5X3

CUPID'S REVENGE
Ruth Jean Dale

Harlequin Books

TORONTO • NEW YORK • LONDON
AMSTERDAM • PARIS • SYDNEY • HAMBURG
STOCKHOLM • ATHENS • TOKYO • MILAN
MADRID • WARSAW • BUDAPEST • AUCKLAND

ISBN 0-373-70788-6

CUPID'S REVENGE

Copyright © 1998 by Betty Lee Duran.

This book, and all the other CUPID books
past and future, owe their existence to Jane Robson.
If I'm the mother of the Camerons of Colorado,
she is surely the godmother.

CHAPTER ONE

SO MANY WOMEN...so little time.

The tall string bean of a cowboy quoted those damning words with a kind of friendly malice, adding after a significant pause, "And that's what Jason Cameron said, sure as I'm standin' here. He damned well meant it, too!" The cowboy looked around the bachelor herd with an emphatic nod as if to make sure everybody grasped the full significance of this revelation.

"Sounds just like something he'd say, damned if it don't," redheaded Jimmy Mosely concurred with glum disapproval. "I don't know about you fellas, but I'm gettin' a little fed up with the way ol' Jason monopolizes all the women around here."

All seven of them turned as one to stare balefully at the perpetrator of such melancholy. Jason Cameron stood across a street crowded with people, just outside the kissing booth at the First Annual Spring Fling of Cupid, Colorado. Waiting his turn as prime kisser, he noticed the attention of his friends and gave them a friendly wave.

A groan swept through their ranks.

"He ain't such a much," Jimmy announced.

"Damn women! For the life of me, I can't understand what they see in him."

"Whatever it is, I wish I could bottle it." Tap Wilson, the string bean, grimaced. "The way the women flock around him, you'd think he walked on water."

The little knot of bachelors settled into a miserable silence, but they were the only unhappy group in evidence on this first day of May. The town, all decked out for the inaugural event in a series of community fund-raisers to benefit Cupid Elementary School, bustled with an air of holiday excitement.

Since early morning, Main Street had been closed to vehicular traffic from Lover's Lane on the north to the Y on the south, where the two streets converged again in front of the dark and shuttered Hideout Saloon. Concession booths featuring everything from burritos to hot dogs to barbecue, and from pies to homemade cookies to cotton candy, stretched from one end of Main Street to the other. Interspersed were games—ringtoss, fishing pole and similar time-and-money-wasters—and booths that sold Cupid T-shirts and cookbooks and doodads galore.

The dunk tank hadn't opened yet but would; the kissing booth had gotten under way first thing with Miss Cupid, Melody Stroud, doing the honors for male customers and Jason Cameron set to do the same for the women.

Town officials could breathe easy over the weather, which was a picture-perfect seventy-some degrees of golden sunshine and balmy breezes. Colorado weather was chancy at best; May Day was almost as likely to produce snow as blue skies, but nobody had wanted to wait on the weather to launch the year-long fund drive. Judging by foot traffic on the temporary pedestrian mall, Cupidians, as they'd been labeled by the local newspaper, were turning out in full force to support their schoolkids.

The biggest man in the group of sore losers scuffled his cowboy boots on the sidewalk. At six foot two, he had the bulky shoulders of a bulldogger and the goofy grin of an eternal optimist. "Yeah, women," he said as if he'd just caught up with the conversation. "But Jason...he's a good ol' boy. Are you guys mad at him or somethin'?"

"Ah, hell, Beau—" Jimmy exchanged a quick glance with Tap "—nobody's mad at him...exactly."

Beau heaved a great sigh of relief. "That's good, 'cause Jason's a friend a mine."

"Jason's a friend of all of us," Tap said impatiently. "That ain't what's at stake here. Just because we like him is no reason for him to—" A pretty young woman with long brown hair hurried past and he changed conversational directions abruptly. "Hey there, Mary Lou!"

"Hi, guys." She tossed them a quick smile but didn't slow down.

"That's what I'm talkin' about." Tap looked after her with self-righteous indignation. "I went out with that gal a time or two. Then Jason Cameron quit rodeoin' and come back to town to stay, and now she won't even give me the time a day."

"Same with me'n Courtney Lewis," Jimmy agreed. "What's so all-fired special about Jason Cameron anyway? He puts his pants on one leg at a time just like—"

"You guys crack me up!"

At the sound of the laughing, feminine voice, they swung around en masse to confront Lorrie Anderson, blond and big-haired ex-wife of local rancher, Tom Purdy. Lorrie, a good-looking woman somewhere in her thirties, was wedged into a pair of undersized jeans and a plaid shirt one button shy of shy.

"Nobody's talkin' to you, Lorrie," Jimmy said.

"Oh, no?" She planted her hands on ample hips and raised both eyebrows. "I thought you were tryin' to figure out what's so all-fired special about Jason Cameron. Obviously, you need a woman to explain it to you. But if you're too pigheaded to listen…" She turned away, but a chorus of disclaimers brought her back around. "Okay," she gave in with alacrity, "but I'm only gonna say this once." She took a deep breath, which they appreciated. "For starters, Jason Cameron's just about the cutest thing ever to come down the trail around here. I swear, I didn't think he *could* get better-lookin', but since he's turned thirty, it's Katy-bar-the-door! On top of that, he's tall—"

"Beau's taller," Tap cut in.

Lorrie rolled her eyes. "Godzilla is taller, too—no offense, Beau."

Beau just gave her his goofy grin and shrugged.

She went on. "All that thick black hair and those gray eyes...mmm! Sexy as hell." She licked her lips. "It doesn't hurt any that he's a rodeo star, either."

"*Was.*"

"Whatever. He's got that devil-may-care attitude that draws women like flies to honey."

"That's all it takes?" Jimmy sounded contemptuous.

"No, that's not all it takes!" Lorrie glared at him in a good-natured way. "That Jason could charm the birds out of the trees. He is one sweet-talkin' cowboy, let me tell you. He comes on all...all *luscious* and slow and easy. He never pushes—"

"Never has to," Tap said in a sullen tone.

"That's right," Lorrie agreed. "He never has to. But when you're with him, you feel all...special, like you're the only woman in the world."

"Kinda mushy," Beau said.

Lorrie patted his bristled cheek. "That's why Jason's fightin' the girls off with a stick while you boys stand around bitchin' and moanin'," she informed them. "You can't argue with success. Now if you'll all just move aside, I want to get in that line before it stretches all the way to the Hideout."

Nobody asked which line she meant because the only line in sight led straight to the kissing booth.

And inside the kissing booth stood Jason Cameron, preparing to do his duty.

"Well, I'll be damned," Tap said suddenly.

His friends regarded him with surprise.

"Will ya look at that?" Tap pointed to a placard tacked up on the false front of the kissing booth. The new sign covered the previous one that had announced the going rate for kisses: a buck. The price for a lip-lock from Jason Cameron had been raised to five dollars.

"D'you believe that?" Jimmy turned away in disgust. "Talk about inflation." He ground his teeth in frustration. "I've about had it with that guy," he burst out. "We gotta *do* something or we're never gonna get the women back!"

A buzz of impatient accord greeted this pronouncement. In the silence that followed, Beau's voice sounded loud and plaintive.

"But what, Jimmy? *What?*"

JASON SHOVED HIS HAT back on his head and groaned. He'd gone along with the five-bucks-a-kiss proposal as a joke, figuring there'd be few takers, which meant less work for him. Boy, had he been wrong. The line of eager kissers stretched from the kissing booth in front of Cupid Elementary School almost to the newspaper office.

Which reminded him of his twin sister, Julie, editor of the *Cupid Chronicles* and the reason he was standing here feeling like an idiot in the first place.

This was all her fault. She'd tricked him into it. Hell, it was probably her idea to raise the price.

For a woman who didn't have any kids of her own, she sure had gotten herself involved in this school fund-raising effort. And when one Cameron got involved, the entire Cameron clan got involved.

Thinking of his twin, Jason tried not to scowl. Anyone who paid five bucks for a kiss deserved a smile along with it. Taking a deep breath, he got back down to business. Time was, after all, money.

"Howdy, Lorrie." He winked at Lorrie Purdy— check that, Lorrie Anderson again since the divorce. He spared a quick, surreptitious glance around. Tom was nowhere in sight, which was a damned good thing. The man had a jealous streak a mile wide. He might no longer be married to Lorrie, but he acted as if he were.

Lorrie offered Jason a five-dollar bill and a sexy smile. "Lay one on me, cowboy," she commanded. Without further ado, she reached across the narrow counter, grabbed him by both ears and pulled his face down to hers.

By the time she let him come up for air, he was gasping. "Jeez, Lorrie, how'd Tom ever let you get away?" he wheezed, feeling a little wild-eyed.

"He's an idiot," she said airily. "Thanks a bunch, Jason. I've been wantin' to do that since you were about sixteen years old—and it was worth the wait, cowboy!"

Jason gave her a weak smile and slumped across the counter, dragging in great gulps of air. He noticed a cluster of men nearby, all of them his buddies, and gave them a rueful smile.

"Jeez!" he muttered. "I've kissed so many women I'm losin' my pucker."

Jimmy Mosely sneered. "Pore thing."

Jason laughed. "Nah, I mean it. Kissin' can get to be real work if the circumstances aren't just right." He looked at the line, knowing his friends would make him suffer before they let him live this down. Wait 'til he got his hands on Julie!

Courtney Lewis stepped forward with a big smile. "You call this hard work?" she challenged, waving a five-dollar bill under his nose.

He plucked the money from her fingers and returned the smile. "It *would* be hard work if it was anyone but you, Courtney, darlin'. Lean over here, hon, so I can put my heart and soul into my work."

Only after he heard a grunt of disgust from the peanut gallery did he remember that Jimmy had dated Courtney there for a while. Well, Jimmy would understand that it was all for sweet charity....

JASON THOUGHT HIS TIME in the kissing booth was *never* going to come to an end, but of course, it finally did. Still, those in charge didn't take pity on him until he'd spent nearly two hours on the firing line, so to speak.

When relief appeared, it was in the form of his sister.

"Sorry, ladies, but time's up," she announced, waving her arms around officiously. "Don't let anybody in line behind you, Amy, 'cause this attraction is about to close. He'll be at the dunk tank later so anyone else can get to him there.'' She winked and laughed. ''Be sure to come back to the big Independence Day street fair and we'll give you another crack at kissing this big galoot.''

This was met with a chorus of laughter from the four women still in line. Jason kissed fast, then watched them depart with relief.

''Thanks, Jewel.'' He gave her a jaundiced glance. ''But if you think—''

''Don't call me Jewel!''

''You're going to get me inside this kissing booth again, you're out of your ever-lovin' mind.''

''It's for a worthy cause,'' she reminded him. ''We all have to do what little we can. I write editorials for the *Chronicles*, you kiss women.''

He swiped the back of one hand across his mouth. ''Yeah, and if you think that was fun, you're a sadist. Sure, it looks easy enough. Just pucker up and let 'er rip. But I got the feeling that some of those women were offering more than five bucks.''

''So when you gonna take one of 'em up on it?'' Julie, blunt as always, swung on her brother. ''Don't you think it's time you picked one and settled down? You're not getting any younger, brother dear.''

''You should know, since we're the same age.''

''Not anymore.'' She grinned. ''I'm twenty-nine and holding. You're thirty and getting set in your ways.''

"The hell I am! That's thirty, not eighty." But she'd struck a nerve.

He *was* becoming set in his ways, and he'd begun to worry about it...a little. Every morning for breakfast, rain or shine, he ate a bowl of oatmeal, four slices of home-cured bacon, two slabs of toast with grape jelly—always grape, never strawberry—and exactly three cups of coffee.

Every Wednesday night, he ate dinner at his sister-in-law's Rusty Spur Café, ordering the meat loaf with extra mashed potatoes and a big wedge of pie. But he didn't much care what kind of pie, he argued with himself. Didn't that show he wasn't set in his ways? On second thought, all Betsy's pies were great so maybe that didn't prove anything at all.

He used to go to the Hideout every Friday night with his friends, but since the saloon had closed, they'd taken to playing poker at one house or the other. Sometimes he'd take a date along, but more often he didn't. Saturday night was "date night" but the truth was, he'd just about run out of potential girlfriends, at least of the serious persuasion.

Hell, he *wanted* to get serious; he wanted to get *married.* He glared at Julie, who was all unconscious of his feelings as she counted the money in the coffee can. He wanted what she had with Max Mackenzie, what their sister, Maggie, had with Chase Britton, what older brother, Ben, had with the beautiful Betsy. But it wasn't as if Jason could put in an order: *Please send me one wife. Must be gorgeous, sexy, funny, feminine, self-sufficient and hardworking; must love children and ranch life and me.*

In the meantime, it wasn't as if he didn't have a life. He did, and a damned good one. In the year since he'd given up rodeo on a regular basis, he'd used a goodly portion of his savings to build a house of his own in Paradise Valley. He'd chosen the location with care, delighting in its remoteness while still being a part of the Camerons' Straight Arrow Ranch in the Rocky Mountains.

At first, the family hadn't understood his need to be on his own instead of living in the main house with the rest of them: Ben and Betsy, their three kids, and Grandma Cameron. Maggie lived with Chase in Aspen, where he owned and operated one of that resort city's most elegant restaurants; Julie and Max lived here in town in a house that belonged to Max's uncle, Gene Varner.

Gene had retired as owner, editor and publisher of the *Cupid Chronicles* a while back, leaving the weekly newspaper in the capable hands of his nephew—who was also the town marshal—and niece-in-law. Gene had bought a recreational vehicle and taken off for parts unknown. The last Jason had heard, Gene was in Missouri and heading south.

So why was Jason determined to build his own house and live alone? Ben, especially, had a hard time with that question. The oldest boy and head of the family, he'd taken the defection seriously. To this day, Jason didn't know if Ben really understood the burning need to get out from under the shadow of an older, almost revered brother.

Jason had loved Paradise Valley since boyhood. He'd stocked it with cattle and a dozen head of buffalo—the latest family venture—then settled down happily to the life of a rancher. Together the Cameron brothers were making big improvements in the Straight Arrow Ranch.

Only Jason was alone—although not by choice, he told himself. He was a victim of circumstances. If the right girl ever came along—

"Who," Julie exclaimed, "is *that?*"

Jason followed her pointing finger. "That's Tom Purdy," he said, wondering what she was so excited about. "He's probably looking for Lorrie."

"Not Tom. I mean that woman—right there. He just stepped in front of her."

Jason shrugged. "We were hopin' to get a few out-of-towners to come to this shindig," he said reasonably. "Probably somebody from—"

At that very moment, Tom moved. Jason saw the woman and his jaw dropped in stunned amazement.

"I think I'm in love," he said.

"Yeah, right." Julie gave him a dirty look, then glanced at her wristwatch. "You've got ten minutes to get over for your shift in the dunk tank."

"Yeah, sure." He kept staring.

"You mean you're not going to whine and complain about that? I thought you said—"

"Yeah, yeah, whatever."

Julie frowned, raised a brow, followed his gaze

and then laughed. "Well, what do you know?" she marveled. "Next time I want you to do something, I'll just run a pretty face past you and get you all tied up in knots before I hit you with it." She straightened. "Now don't forget. Dunk tank—ten minutes."

"I won't forget." Jason leaned his forearms on the counter and sighed.

Whoever the woman might be, she wasn't from around here. Everything about her proclaimed it, from the top of her head to the tips of her high-heeled shoes. While everyone else wore boots and sneakers and denim and chambray and cowboy hats, she wore a long-sleeved white shirt tucked neatly into tailored navy blue trousers.

But it was her hair that arrested his attention, hair that glowed bright as a flame in the intense mountain sunshine. For the first time in his life, Jason understood how a moth could be pulled inexorably into the fire. She half turned to speak to a young man at her side—Jason hadn't realized until that moment that she wasn't alone—and then her glance lifted unexpectedly and locked with his.

For a moment, their gazes held and he thought he saw a questioning flicker in hers. Then the throng shifted again, moved between them, and she disappeared from his sight.

Well, hell! That was the most interesting thing that had happened to him in a coon's age. An interesting new face was just what he needed. And although she hadn't been close enough for him to actually see all the details, he knew that "interesting" was the least of what he'd sensed about her.

She'd be beautiful. She'd be different. She probably loved kids and she might even learn to love—

"Excuse me."

The crowd parted and she stood there in front of him, her head cocked slightly and her no-nonsense hazel eyes level and questioning. The young man— a kid in his teens, actually—stood beside her, his youthful face petulant.

But after a cursory glance, Jason wasn't looking at the kid but at her, so cool and in control. In that instant, he knew that he'd love to be the one who fractured that control.

Beside him, Julie stirred. "May we help you?"

Jason never took his attention off the beautiful stranger before him. "It's only obvious," he said solemnly. "She's afraid she missed her chance."

And leaning across the counter, he reached for her.

CHAPTER TWO

JASON TUGGED HER FORWARD into his embrace, marveling at the way she fitted into his arms even with the narrow waist-high counter between them. Knowing perfectly well that she hadn't approached him for a kiss and equally aware that if he gave her half a chance she'd run, slap his face or both, he covered her mouth with his. Surely she'd go along with the joke—after the fact.

He caught her so far off guard that she didn't have a chance to resist. All she had time to do was stiffen, and then her lips parted as if to issue a protest. Not one to miss a golden opportunity, he slipped his tongue into her mouth with ease. This he hadn't done with any of the dozens of others—not even Lorrie, who had obviously been dying for him to try something.

He felt the thrill all the way to his toes. Damn, she was sweet, and he reveled in the heat of her mouth and the resilience of her upper arms beneath his hands. He wanted to stand there kissing her for the foreseeable future, but if he didn't call this off fast, he was going to lose the humor of the situation.

So he stood her up straight again, lifted his mouth reluctantly from hers and grinned down at her. She blinked as if she wasn't sure quite what had happened to her. Her long lashes fluttered up to reveal astonished eyes awash in shades of green and gold and brown.

"Honey," Jason said, "that kiss was way too nice to charge you for it." Digging around in his jeans pocket, he pulled out a five-dollar bill. With a flourish, he dropped it in Julie's coffee can, amused anew by the shock on his sister's face. He turned back to the stranger and winked, aware for the first time that the teenage boy was choking back laughter. "My treat," he announced.

With a tip of his hat, he sauntered off to take his place at the dunk tank, leaving the woman staring after him with a gaze so sharp he felt it between his shoulder blades like a knife.

DIANA KENNEDY had never been so insulted in all her thirty years—and it didn't help any that her stepson was practically hysterical with laughter. Since the obnoxious cowboy had ambled away before she could gather her wits, she turned her displeasure upon the young woman standing frozen behind the counter.

A sister, obviously; they had the same black hair and wide, long-lashed eyes—his gray, hers velvety brown. They also shared the same strong features, although the woman's were more delicate.

Diana's jaw tightened. "Of all the nerve! Who does he think he is, grabbing me that way?"

"Oh, dear!" The pretty young woman grimaced.

"Please let me apologize for my brother. I think he's kissed so many women in the past two hours that he's on automatic fast-forward." She stuck out her hand. "I'm Julie Mackenzie. Welcome to Cupid."

"I'm Diana Kennedy and this is my stepson, Ryan." She realized she'd spoken brusquely and tried to calm down. Her pulse pounded and she felt a hot flush stain her cheeks, brought on by the depredations of that uncouth cowboy. And she'd thought he'd looked so nice!

Okay, he still *looked* nice if she went only on outside appearances instead of actions. She'd seen him first from across the street and been impressed by his height and the breadth of his shoulders, his easy smile and the way his carefree laughter rang out so infectiously.

So she'd decided to ask him for directions, and what did she get for her trouble? Manhandled! His assault had been so unprovoked that she hadn't even been able to mount a defense. It was sexual harassment, plain and simple.

Julie looked uneasy. "Uh...my brother's not usually such a lout. Actually, he didn't even want to do this—"

"Do what, accost women?"

"Sell kisses. I kind of forced him into it. I think by the time it was over, he was a little slaphappy. I mean, how much fun would it be, on display and kissing half the female population of Cupid?"

Diana responded coldly. "He seemed to take to it like a duck takes to water. I, on the other hand, would rather slit my wrists than make that kind of public exhibition of myself."

"Yeah, well...I don't think anyone noticed." Julie edged away. "I really am sorry. I'm sure he'll apologize when he gets the chance."

"He'll get no more chances with me."

"I can see that." With a hesitant little wave, which was actually just the wiggling of a few fingers, Julie turned with her coffee can tucked beneath one arm and disappeared into the crowd.

By which time Ryan finally had control of himself. "Don't be such a grouch, Diana," he teased. "If you could have seen your face!"

Diana groaned. "You're not helping things a bit, young man. If I ever get that cowboy in my sights, he'll rue the day he—"

"Put up or shut up."

Ryan pointed and Diana turned to look in the direction he indicated. Sure enough, there, at the end of the block, stood the arrogant cowboy next to a metal contraption with a wire-mesh cage above a five-foot-deep tank of...*water.*

Above the water was suspended a seat that had a spring designed to dump the unfortunate individual sitting on it into that very *cold*-looking water. The same cowboy who'd humiliated her with his unwarranted attentions approached the ladder leading up to that seat. He stood there shaking his head as if debating the wisdom of proceeding. A busty blond woman sidled up next to him and engaged him in conversation.

Diana was far more interested in the metal contraption. "A dunk tank," she said softly. "Perfect."

Even as she watched, the cowboy tugged off his boots without pausing in his friendly banter with the blonde. Dropping the boots, he placed his big cowboy hat on her overteased hair. Next he pulled his shirttail from his jeans and ripped it over his head in one smooth motion.

He was one fine sight. From the sloping muscles of broad shoulders to a washboard stomach, his narrow torso gleamed in golden ripples in the sunlight. Diana's mouth went dry and she swallowed hard, putting that condition down to the lack of humidity in this dry-as-a-bone state. After living with the humidity of Texas, the air here seemed to suck the moisture right out of her body....

And the breath right out of her lungs.

"Jeez, Diana," Ryan drawled, "you gonna just stand there and stare or do you plan to get even? If you were such a hotshot softball pitcher in high school, now's your chance to prove it."

It certainly was. Maybe it wouldn't get her off on the right foot with her new neighbors, but she suddenly felt reckless and uncaring for the consequences. Normally even-tempered and calm, dispassionate and unflappable, she'd somehow let that stranger do the unthinkable: bull his way right through all her defenses.

For that, he'd have to pay—big time.

A quick glance around located the ticket booth. Perhaps a half-dozen people waited in line, laughing and talking and letting broad gaps develop between them and the middle-aged woman handing out the tickets from a pink roll before her in the booth.

Without hesitation, Diana marched straight to the head of the line and plunked down a ten-dollar bill. "Excuse me," she said to the surprised man whose place she'd just usurped, "but I'm in an awful hurry." To the woman inside, she added, "Three tickets for the dunk tank, please."

Tickets and change firmly in hand, she marched toward the crowd queuing up to toss baseballs at the small target that would dump the cowboy, now edging his way onto the trick seat, into the drink.

"Excuse me. Excuse me, please," Diana repeated courteously, even while she elbowed her way to the head of the line. Mostly men and boys were gathering to heave baseballs aimed at dunking one of their own, while the women and girls congregated around the tank to call encouragement to the "victim." But everybody seemed to sense the importance of Diana's mission because they parted before her like the Red Sea parted for Moses. Something big was afoot and they all seemed to know that.

And relish it.

"Hey, Jason," a tall string bean of a man hollered, "you shoulda wore your wet suit! This little lady is loaded for bear!"

Jason looked around and his face lit up at the sight of her. "Hey, you followed me!" he yelled, grinning broadly. He waved.

She waved back. "I sure did. Are you ready?"

"Honey, your chances of dumping me into the drink are slim and none," he hollered, playing to the crowd with his boasts. "Heck, I coulda left my boots on. Do you think we should let her move a little closer to the target, boys? It's not fair for a—"

Smiling, Diana wound up and let fly with the first baseball.

Bingo!

Jason, still talking and joking with his friends, hit the water with a tremendous splash. He came up choking and gasping to a thunderous ovation. Diana ignored the noise and catcalls, waiting impatiently for him to climb up the ladder and regain his seat. Back on his perch with water cascading around him, his smile seemed a tad less certain. "What we got here?" he appealed to the crowd. "A ringer?"

"Beginner's luck," she assured him. Taking a careful windup, she heaved the second ball. It hit the target with a satisfying metallic *twang*. The seat swung aside and she had a glimpse of Jason's star-tled face, saw his lips form an exclamation lost in thunderous applause: *Uh-oh!*

He hit the water again and disappeared beneath the surface. Coming up, he wiped his streaming face with both hands before doggedly heading for the ladder once more. By the time he was back on his perch, his arrogant smile had become a puzzled frown.

"Can't we talk this over?" he asked plaintively. "You got me all wrong. How much is one little ol' kiss worth…?'' His voice slid up on the final word, even as his body plunged down.

He came up choking and sputtering for the third and final time, at least at Diana's hands. She waited until he'd regained his feet and was looking directly at her before she spoke.

"Now," she said with her sweetest smile, "I'd say we're just about even, cowboy."

Collecting eighteen-year-old Ryan, she turned and marched away. Somebody *else* could give her directions to the Hideout.

JASON MIGHT BE A NOVICE in the kissing booth, but he knew his way around a dunk tank. As a result, he'd come prepared. After an hour spent climbing out of icy water and onto his perch only to be knocked off again in the name of charity, all he could think about were the dry clothes he'd stashed in Julie's office at the *Cupid Chronicles*. He watched the second shift arrive with gratitude, then scooted around on the narrow seat to reach for the ladder.

"Just one more shot!" Jimmy Mosely pleaded, brandishing a baseball. "C'mon, Jason! Be a pal!"

"Being your pal is dangerous to my health," Jason retorted. "You've already ducked me at least—"

One more time than Jason had been about to acknowledge. Jimmy's pitch hit the target and Jason hit the water. He sank to the bottom and wished he could stay there. What the hell was eating Jimmy anyway? He's been slamming balls into the target as if it was personal.

Finally out of oxygen, Jason stood up to thunderous applause. Taking a mocking bow, he climbed out of the tank to make way for Bob Mays, sports editor of the *Chronicles* and on everybody's shit list since he'd written an article several months ago that was critical of the local recreational basketball league. Bob, a puny half-pint of a guy, looked a little leery about what awaited him, but he climbed gamely up to take his precarious seat above the water tank.

Gathering his boots and shirt and slapping his Stetson on his head, Jason sprinted barefoot down the block toward the newspaper office. First, he had to get dressed.

Second, he had to find that woman.

"HER NAME'S DIANA KENNEDY and the kid's her stepson," Julie said. "She was mad as a wet hen over the way you grabbed her, and I, for one, don't blame her. That's all I know."

"Ah, hell." Jason, fully dressed and dry again, rubbed damp hair with a paper towel. "You don't know where she's from or where she's going?"

Julie shook her head.

"How about you, Max?" Jason turned toward his brother-in-law.

Max sat on a desk with his booted feet on a chair, watching the interplay between his wife and her twin brother. He wore a crisp tan uniform as befitted the law in Cupid, and sported a shiny town marshal's badge on his chest. He looked exactly like what he was: a big, tough lawman who'd been tamed by a pretty woman with a mind of her own.

"How about me—what?" Max said.

"Did you see her?"

"Hell, no!"

"What kinda marshal are you anyway? It's your job to check out strangers in town," Jason pointed out. "That woman's a stranger—trust me. If she's ever been within a hundred miles of Cupid before, I'd know."

Max shrugged without offense. "Town's full of strangers today, in case you hadn't noticed. I haven't seen a single redhead, though. Sorry."

"You should be sorry," Julie agreed on a gust of laughter. "She really put old Jason in his place— and she did it for the entire world to see. I thought I'd die laughing when she let fly with that baseball and dumped him in the drink that first time."

Jason grimaced. "Where's your family loyalty, Jewel? Besides, it was no big deal. I musta been dunked fifty times."

"But the first time's always the best," she taunted. "Right, Cosmo?"

Cosmo was Max's middle name, but nobody dared use it to his face except his wife. He gave her an indulgent smile. "Lighten up on him, will you, hon? The boy needs understanding after what he's been through. I bet he's single-handedly made more

money for the school today than any other dozen
fine citizens put together.''

"Yeah," Jason said darkly, "and what thanks do
I get from my own sister?'' He tossed the paper
towel into a trash basket and smoothed his hair back
with both hands. "Either of you seen Chase?''

"I don't think he and Maggie are here yet," Julie
said. "They'll make it, though. Blair's thinking
about spending most of her last summer before college at the ranch. She'll make sure they get here so
she can check it out, see what kind of bargain she
can strike with Ben.''

Jason groaned. His eighteen-year-old niece, although pretty and smart as a whip, was a real handful under any circumstances. Having her around for
any length of time always led from one family crisis
to another. Only Ben, toughest of the Cameron siblings and boss of the Straight Arrow Ranch, seemed
to have the knack of keeping her in line.

"Why are you looking for Chase?'' Julie added.

"Because," Jason said, "I've decided to make
him a business proposition he can't refuse. I'm
gonna let him put up the money so I can buy the
Hideout.''

"Let him?'' Julie gave a snort of laughter. "I
can't believe you're still talking about that.'' She
waved through the large front window at a group of
teenagers walking past. They waved back; everyone
in town knew the Camerons. "I thought—''

"You thought wrong if you thought I'd forget
about it. I was just trying to figure out a way to

finance it without asking for help. Since I can't come up with the money on my own, Chase is the logical one to bring in.''

"Yeah, the one with the bucks.'' She cocked her head. "But what would he want with that old honky-tonk bar and restaurant when he's got that chichi place in Aspen?''

"Nothing, I hope. I want to run it myself. He'd just be a sort of...you know, a silent partner.''

Julie laughed and Jason had to admit that the possibility of a silent Chase was pretty far-fetched.

"Hey,'' he argued, "it's a great business opportunity. This town hasn't been the same since the Hideout closed.''

Max nodded. "I'll vouch for that. Been awful quiet around here, if you ask me. Not much for me to do.''

"Jason,'' Julie said, "you're nuts. What do you know about running a bar? You hardly even drink anymore, not since—''

"Let's don't go into that,'' he interrupted sharply. "That wasn't my finest hour.''

"I don't know,'' Max drawled. "Some people would think that a shotgun duel at twenty paces survived by all the participants—''

"Knock it off, will you?'' Jason groaned in embarrassment. "That was a long time ago.'' He'd been drunk as a skunk or he'd never have accepted Johnny King's challenge, and he didn't like to be reminded of his feckless youth.

Julie took pity on him but not enough to give up

the argument entirely. "I thought you had your hands full managing the buffalo herd and helping Ben with the cattle. Where would you find the time to—"

The front door opened and old Ethan Turner entered, his grandson, Beau, at his heels. The two men, one at least ninety and the other barely thirty, were dressed alike in Wrangler jeans and boots and Western shirts with identical white Stetsons tilted at an identically jaunty angle. But there the resemblance ended, for Ethan was small—no more than five-five—while Beau was enormous—at least six-two and more than a hundred pounds heavier than his grandpa.

"Howdy, all," Ethan said, politely removing his hat. When Beau just stood there grinning his broad, dopey grin, the old man drove a sharp elbow into the younger man's gut.

Beau let out a *whoosh* of surprise, then snatched his hat off to cradle it against his broad chest. "Howdy, all," he echoed.

"Ethan, Beau." Max nodded. "Come on in and sit a spell."

"Much obliged, but we're on our way to meet up with some folks," Ethan said in his soft, self-effacing voice. "I just dropped by to mention that somethin' may be goin' on at the Hideout. Thought you oughta know, Marshal."

Max's heavy eyebrows rose. "Something going on like what?"

"Like somebody's got inside and is moving

around the place," Ethan said. "What with all the strangers in town, they might be up to no good, don't you know." He lifted his hat in a farewell salute and turned back toward the door. "Good day to you all."

"Good day to you all," Beau echoed, following his grandfather out.

Max looked at his wife and sighed. "I guess I'd better take a stroll on down and see what's going on there. Probably just kids. If they haven't done any damage, I'll just give 'em a good scare and throw their butts out." He swung his feet to the floor and stood up, rearranging the heavy leather gun belt around his waist.

"You're such a pussycat," Julie said with beaming approval. "If the bad guys only knew!"

"Yeah, right." Max glanced at Jason. "See you later, hotshot."

"Not a chance." Jason wedged his hat back on his head and squared his shoulders. "I'm going with you. If anybody's messin' around inside *my*—"

"It's not yours yet," Julie interrupted, following the two men to the door. "Talking everybody's ear off about it for months doesn't make it so."

"I'm done talking," Jason said. He paused at the open door. "My mind is made up. I want the Hideout. When I decide I want something, I go after it."

"Yeah," Julie called after him. "And you always get it. But sooner or later, Jason Cameron... Sooner or later..."

CHAPTER THREE

INSIDE THE HIDEOUT SALOON at the end of Main Street, Diana Kennedy surveyed the entryway of the establishment she'd purchased a mere six weeks ago, sight unseen. The minute she'd caught her first glimpse of the weathered log building with the tall false front, she'd felt sure it was everything Gene Varner had told her it would be.

Standing face-to-face with a stuffed buffalo stationed before the partial wall screening the entryway, she realized it was even *more* than Gene had promised.

She couldn't have been happier.

"Ryan!" she called, excitement making her voice tremble. "Come quick and see what I've found!"

Ryan scuffed through the open door, out of the blazing sunlight into the dark and dusty interior. "What?" he asked, sounding bored.

"A buffalo!" She pointed. "This is wonderful. It gives me chills, thinking about the Old West as it must have really been."

Ryan put out a tentative hand to pat the bulky creature. A puff of dust rose into the still air, making them both cough. "It's not real," he pronounced. "It's just a moth-eaten piece of junk."

He turned and she saw his face, illuminated by sunlight streaming through the open door. He looked unhappy, almost...distraught.

"Let's get out of here, Diana," he burst out. "Screw the Old West! Let's go home to Dallas and pretend none of this ever happened."

"You know we can't do that. I've sunk everything we have into this move." She stepped toward him, reaching out a beseeching hand. "If you'll just give it a chance... It'll be wonderful, wait and see. But you've got to try, Ryan. If only..."

He was no longer there. He'd simply turned and walked past her and deeper into the gloomy interior.

Sighing, she stood there for a minute to regain her poise. Did he think it had been an easy decision for her to turn her back on everything she'd ever known? To uproot herself and her stepson and risk everything by traveling all the way from Dallas to this little Colorado town in the Rocky Mountains in hopes of a better life?

If he did, he was dead wrong. It was just that with the approach of her thirtieth birthday, she'd realized if she ever planned to make a break with city life, it was now or never.

Then as if it had been fate, out of the blue appeared Gene Varner. He'd been introduced to her by mutual friends, and when he'd learned of her background in food services, one thing had led to another and he'd ended up telling her about this little saloon and restaurant tucked away in the Colorado Rockies....

Two years earlier, it would have meant nothing to her, but two years earlier she'd had a husband as well as a son. When Gene came into her life, all that had changed. Paul was dead, victim of a fatal heart attack at the age of forty-four. Only six weeks before meeting Gene, she'd received the final insurance payment. With it had come an unreasoning terror that if she didn't use it to ensure their future, the money would be frittered away.

Buying the Hideout represented the kind of gamble she'd always longed to take but had never been able to work up sufficient nerve to act upon. So she didn't know all that much about running such an establishment; Paul had been a chef and she'd worked for a food wholesaler, so she wasn't completely in the dark.

And she was so very unhappy and restless and fed up with life in the big city. She'd lived in Dallas all her life and she longed for something both more and less: less hectic and dangerous and crowded, more slow-paced and safe and...and *solitary*.

Now, despite unprovoked sexual harassment by that obnoxious cowboy, she felt great relief that her new challenge was exactly as it had been represented by both Gene and the real-estate agent.

This will work, she told herself. *I'm sure of it.*

It had to work, for Ryan as much as for herself. She squared her shoulders, took a deep breath and followed her stepson. Stepping out of the entry and into a big room, she stopped short.

Through dust motes dancing past grimy windowpanes, she could make out a magnificent antique bar running the length of the far wall. Beyond a motley assortment of tables and chairs lay a wooden dance floor—the biggest dance floor in this part of Colorado, Gene has boasted, complete with bandstand.

Ryan stood in the middle of that dance floor, a lonely figure in the gloom. He clenched his fists at his sides.

"I want to go home," he said in a ragged voice. "This is the pits—I told you it would be."

"It's not the pits at all, sweetheart." She took a few steps toward him, wanting to offer comfort but unsure how to proceed. She supposed she was a terrible mother, might even have been a terrible mother if she'd borne this child herself instead of "inheriting" him when he was twelve. But regardless of her parenting deficiencies, she did love him and want him to be happy.

"What are you—blind?" He jerked his head back and glared at her. "Look at this place. It's a mess."

"We'll clean it up," she said.

"*Who* will?"

"We—you and me. All it needs is a little bit of elbow grease."

"It needs a lot more than that."

"Whatever it takes, we'll provide."

"All by ourselves? I don't think so."

"I *do* think so." And she meant it. She was used to doing for herself and she would drag him with her through sheer force of will, if she had to. "Give it a chance, Ryan."

He made a little exclamation of disgust. "I promised you I'd stay for the summer but that's all. If you think I'm going to come back here once I get to UT, you're crazy."

"The University of Texas is hardly at the ends of the earth," she said. "Of course you'll come home for holidays and breaks—"

"No chance." His voice came out flat and certain. "If you want to see me, you better head back to Texas where we both belong. I do *not* intend to bury myself in some crummy little town in the middle of nowhere."

"But Ryan—"

"My mind's made up." He stared at her hard. "Looks like yours is, too."

She sighed. "We'll talk about this later."

"Whatever." He sounded somewhat less than sincere.

"In the meantime, let's look around and see what we've got here." She forced a cheerful note into her voice, but she didn't feel cheerful at all. How could she be happy if her son refused to give Colorado even a try?

Paul, she thought, *I'm letting you down. I'm not up to this.*

But what she said was, "The kitchen's got to be back there someplace. The electricity was supposed to be turned on today, but since it hasn't been, let's go see if we can find any candles. Then we'll explore."

They did better than that; they found not only

candles but a flashlight that still worked. Even then, it was impossible to see much more than broad details.

"We'll get the electricity turned on tomorrow," Diana promised, pointing the flashlight toward walls covered with…something. Mounted animal heads— but she couldn't tell what kind of animals—and memorabilia of some sort. She swept the beam of light across the mirror behind the bar. "In the meantime—"

She let out a shriek and dropped the flashlight. She'd seen the outline of a man reflected in the mirror.

"TAKE IT EASY, MA'AM." The deep male voice echoed through the huge room. "I'm Marshal Mackenzie and I just dropped by to make sure everything is all right."

"*Jeez!*" Ryan's disgusted voice came out of the dark. "I thought you'd stepped on a snake, Di."

Diana's racing heart slowed a notch or two. "Good grief," she said plaintively, "you *scared* me!"

"Sorry about that," the marshal replied, his voice polite but implacable. "I got a report that somebody had broken in here and I'm just checking it out."

"I didn't break in. I have a key."

"Swell," the marshal said. "Let's go outside and you can show it to me. This way, folks."

There was nothing to do but follow the marshal's orders. Once outside, she squinted against the strong sunlight to see him. A man in his mid-thirties, Marshal Mackenzie looked quite capable of handling anything that might come along, including anyone brazen enough to break into the Hideout in broad daylight in the middle of a community festival.

That thought gave Diana considerable comfort. She offered her hand. "I'm Diana Kennedy."

"I know." He took her hand in a grip so firm she winced.

"How...?"

He grinned. "Got a good description. That hair is a dead giveaway."

"I see." She did, too; he must know the cowboy she'd tangled with. As marshal, he probably knew everybody. "This is my stepson, Ryan."

Ryan, hanging suspiciously in the background, said a sullen, "Hi." He looked greatly out of place here with his baggy denims, long, sloppy shirt and a cap pulled around with the bill in back.

The marshal acknowledged the boy, his eyes narrow and assessing. "You wouldn't happen to be a badass, would you, son?"

Ryan's eyes flared. "You've got no right to—"

"Yes or no." The marshal's voice crackled with command.

"No," Ryan snarled. "Not that it's any of your business."

"Everything that happens in and around Cupid is my business," the man replied easily, "not to mention my jurisdiction. Now about that key, ma'am..." He swung his attention back to Diana.

She dug into her pants pocket and offered it to him without a word. She realized who he was now: Gene Varner's nephew. Gene had spoken of him with great pride and affection.

He took the key, examined it, handed it back.

"And you got this key from...?"

"A real-estate agent, when I bought this place. I'm the new owner of the Hideout, Marshal Mackenzie."

His eyes, the greenest she'd ever seen, went wide. Then he started to laugh. "In that case, welcome to Cupid, Diana Kennedy. You are purely gonna love living here."

And he laughed some more.

"JEEZ, BLAIR, are you comin' or not? I don't have all day!"

Jason, with Beau Turner waiting patiently by his side, glared at his niece. She'd swung away from their course down the middle of Main Street to stop at a booth selling snow cones. Damn, from here he couldn't see what was going on at the Hideout for the crowd.

He gritted his teeth with annoyance over the delay. This was all Maggie's fault. When she'd grabbed him in a big hug, that damned Max just kept right on moving. Then before Jason could make his getaway, Beau had come loping up.

"The marshal catch them thieves yet?"

"I'm on my way to find out just as soon as Maggie turns loose of me."

"Think I'll trail along with you. Grandpa's hooked up with his lady friend."

Maggie's stepdaughter, Blair, chimed in, "Me, too!" But since everything in her life was a melodrama, they'd made little progress toward their goal even after they'd gotten away from Maggie and Chase and their three-year-old son, also named Chase but called Dusty. Every kid they passed had to be acknowledged; every booth and display was an invitation for Blair to digress.

Now she glanced back at him over her shoulder while she waited for her treat. "Hey, mellow out, Jason." She fished change from her pocket. "And don't you dare go on without me or I'll tell Grandma on you," she added for good measure.

Blair, always a lippy kid, had grown into a lippy girl.

A helluva good-looking lippy girl, Jason realized, waiting with exaggerated patience for her to rejoin them. Jeez, he hated the thought of spending the entire summer fighting boys off with a stick. He supposed that now she was about to graduate from high school and get ready for college, she'd think she was all grown-up and ready to handle her own love life.

Hell, she'd thought that last summer and the summer before. He and Ben were both in *big* trouble.

She accepted her snow cone—a blue one—and trotted back to join him in the street. She had legs all the way down to the ground, and they were on display big time in those khaki shorts. Long, silky brown hair swirled around her shoulders and a strand stuck to moist pink lips. She flicked it away with natural grace.

"So Uncle Max thinks someone's breaking into the Hideout," she said, taking a sip from the paper cone.

"How come he's 'Uncle Max' and I'm just 'Jason'?"

Beau apparently saw a chance to look good. "'Cause Max married her aunt Julie," he explained with ponderous efficiency. "That makes him her uncle...right?"

"Well, for—" Jason caught himself in time to keep from hurting the big man's feelings. "I'm Julie's brother, so what does that make me?"

The intricacies of that relationship were too much for Beau. He frowned. "A twin?"

"Right!" Blair patted him on bulging biceps and made a face at Jason. "Forget it. You're not gonna win this one. You're too young to be my uncle."

"I'm thirty damn years old. That's old enough to be your *father*...practically."

"Okay," she said, unusually agreeable, "you *act* too young to be my uncle. How's that? Mom says it's time you grew up and got yourself a wife—if you could find anyone who'd have you—and settle down and act like an adult. Mom says—"

"Mom," Jason said grimly, "should mind her own business." Mom, Blair's stepmother and Jason's sister, Maggie, had always been more judgmental than was good for her.

"Yeah," Blair agreed with a chuckle. "I keep

telling Pop that, but he loves her anyway." She had to run to keep up with him and Beau. "Hey, slow down! I'm sloppin' this blue stuff all over my T-shirt. Uncle Max is on the case. It's not like you already own that place or anything."

"Maybe not, but I intend to." He could see the front of the Hideout now, but not a sign of Max or anybody else. The door, however, stood open.

Out of the clear blue, Blair said, "Dad told Mom that as soon as you asked him for the money to buy the Hideout, he'd give it to you."

Jason stopped short. "When did he say that?"

"Months ago." She tossed her head and the straight brown hair went flying again.

"And you didn't tell me? Nobody told me?"

"He said not to." Damn, she looked smug. "He said you had to ask, that everything came too easily for you and he wasn't gonna be a party to making you any more conceited than you already are."

Beau guffawed. "She's got you there, Jase."

Jason gave Beau a dirty look and started walking again. "Chase actually said that—conceited?"

"Well..." she hedged, trotting along one step behind the two men. "I guess he didn't actually use that very word, but that's what he meant. Everybody knows how conceited you are, Jason. Just because you're cute and all the girls chase after you—"

"That's *Uncle* Jason to you, kid," he practically roared. "I swear to God, my own family treats me—"

At that moment, three people walked around the

corner of the Hideout and Jason forgot all about Blair and Beau and everything else. For first in line was Max Mackenzie and second was Diana Kennedy; Jason never got to third.

Diana Kennedy, she of the flaming red-gold hair and major-league arm.

He stopped so short that Blair ran up his heels. The wet coldness of melted blue snow cone splashed between his shoulder blades. She gave an annoyed grunt, which might have included an apology.

He didn't even care, he was so busy grinning at the prettiest woman he'd ever seen. He spared a quick, delighted glance at Max. "Caught 'em red-handed, did you, Marshal? Since they're strangers in these parts, maybe you'll give 'em another chance."

"Maybe I will at that," Max said, laughter edging his voice. "Diana...Ryan Kennedy, I'd like you to meet three of Cupid's finest. This guy grinning like a Cheshire cat is my brother-in-law, Jason Cameron."

Jason swept off his Stetson and made a low bow. "I am mighty pleased to meet you," he said with a world of sincerity.

Diana's expression never changed. She might have been looking at a blank space in the landscape for all the animation she showed. Max noticed, shrugged and went on.

"That good-looking girl in the middle is our mutual niece, Blair Britton. She lives in Aspen, but she's here with her family for the big street fair."

"Blair." Diana's smile transformed her face. She inclined her head in a friendly greeting.

Blair murmured hi, but her attention was on Ryan, not his stepmother.

Ryan didn't say anything, either, but he was looking plenty. *Where's that stick now that I need it?* Jason had to wonder.

Max pressed on. "Last but never least, I'd like you both to meet Beau Turner. Beau's family has ranched around here for a long time."

Beau snatched his hat from his shaggy head and scuffed his feet in the dirt of the parking lot. "Howdy, ma'am," he mumbled. "Mighty glad to make your acquaintance."

"We're pleased to meet you, Beau." Diana dazzled him with her smile.

Why didn't she look at me *that way?* Jason wondered dourly. "Just passing through, are you?" he asked, hoping the answer would be no, even if she was about as friendly as a rattlesnake.

The answer *was* no. But almost before the word was out of her mouth, she turned to Max. "I meant to mention it to you before this, but I met your uncle Gene."

"You're kidding." Max shook his head in amazement. "Where'd you run into him? Last we heard he was in Missouri and heading south in that mini-motor home he's so fired up about."

"We were introduced in Dallas by mutual friends. The Dawsons—do you know them?"

Max shook his head. "I'm from California, so

Gene and I tend to know different people, except the ones here in Cupid.''

Jason had to get in on this. "Was it Gene's idea for you to visit Cupid on your way to...wherever?"

At last she looked straight at him—or through him, as the case might be. "Not exactly," she said, her voice chilly as ice chips.

Jason was getting damned frustrated by her attitude. Couldn't she take a joke? Dragging information out of her was like pulling teeth. "Then you have friends here?" he guessed.

She shook her head. "I don't know a soul, except the four of you, of course."

He was on the verge of yelling, *Then what the hell are you doing here?* Fortunately, Max took pity on him.

"Diana's just bought the Hideout," he announced, a sharp note of warning tingeing his words for those who knew him well enough to discern it. "I'm sure we all want to welcome her to Cupid. Diana, anything I can do for you, just look me up."

Max tipped his hat, gave his brother-in-law a cautionary glance, then strode away. He left behind one dumbfounded cowboy.

CHAPTER FOUR

JASON CAMERON looked stunned.

Diana couldn't imagine why, unless the Hideout had some fatal flaw of which she was blissfully unaware. Maybe it had closed for reasons other than those she'd been given: that the previous owner, Peggy Morse, had developed respiratory problems that necessitated moving to a lower elevation.

"You have a problem with that?" Diana asked. "I bought the place all nice and legal, so if you know some reason I shouldn't—"

"No, no, nothing like that." He clapped his hat back on his head. "I was just...surprised." He seemed to pull himself together. "Like Max says, welcome to Cupid."

"Thank you. Now if you'll excuse me..." She turned and headed for the door.

He was at her side in an instant. "Why don't I just hang around and see if there's anything I can do to help out?"

"Thank you again, but that's not necessary." She paused in the doorway, reluctant to have him enter. Ryan, Blair and the big man called Beau were engaged in a conversation of their own and showed no interest in coming inside. Diana certainly didn't want to be alone with Jason Cameron. Couldn't he take a hint?

He grinned, his mouth making a sensual curve in his lean face. Damn, the man was good-looking. Or maybe it wasn't so much a matter of facial features as it was the humor that sparkled in his gray eyes. He pushed back his hat, and dark hair spilled over his forehead, lending him a rakish air.

"I think it's necessary," he disagreed.

Hooking thumbs in his belt loops, he rocked back on his boot heels. She couldn't help noticing the huge silver buckle that anchored his heavy, engraved leather belt around flat hips.

This guy was a hunk, and he knew it. Her mouth curled down in disapproval.

"How can they possibly do without you at the dunk tank?" she inquired with innocent malice.

His groan made him seem unexpectedly human. "I'm lucky I didn't catch my death climbin' in and out of that ice water," he said. "That's some arm you got there, by the way."

He lifted his right hand and Diana took a hasty step back, which was ridiculous. Somehow she'd thought he was about to touch her arm to test his own judgment.

He gave her a quizzical look, which told her he'd noticed her reaction, and reached past her toward the light switch on the wall.

"I've already checked the electricity," she said quickly. "It was supposed to be on by today but—"

Light flooded the room and she blinked at the unexpectedness of it. "What in the...?"

Jason shrugged. "Looks like the power guy woke up."

"Better late than never."

"He's not late, since it's still today. You're just in too big a hurry." He had a smile brilliant enough to stop traffic. "Slow down, Diana."

"I don't have time to slow down, but don't let me keep *you*." She glanced pointedly at the door. "You must have more important things to do than—"

"I don't, not thing one." He began heading around the entry's guardian buffalo. This time, he did touch her, just a light hand on her waist to guide her along. She started from the contact just the same.

They rounded the corner and she said a soft "Oh!" of pleasure.

The rough plank walls were covered with a profusion of mining and cowboy paraphernalia, maps, stuffed birds and animals. Brass fixtures gleamed dully behind the bar; even the kick rail was brass. There were no bar stools. Apparently, the serious drinkers just bellied right on up to the scarred wooden surface.

"Great, isn't it?"

His soft voice just at her ear made her jump with surprise and tension. She managed a nod of agreement.

"This place has been a big part of community life

around here for a long time," he went on. "When Peggy closed it down, everybody felt the loss."

"A bar?" She cast him a dubious glance.

His grin was irresistible. "A *family* bar," he elaborated. "At night, this place was all singin', dancin', drinkin' and once in a blue moon, fightin'. But during the day, it was for everybody, young or old. Peggy ran a real good kitchen with the best hamburgers in these mountains. You'd find kids to grannies to whole families in here—but rarely after seven o'clock. After that, the big kids took over."

"I see."

Diana walked away from him, away from the light touch of his hand at the small of her back. Crossing to the bar, she slid her palm over the dusty, scarred surface. But she wasn't thinking about that.

She was thinking about Jason.

This man, she realized with disapproval, had real star quality. She'd seen it at work earlier at the street fair, but up close like this, she actually *felt* it.

Part of it was self-confidence. Jason had so much he was doubtless accustomed to sweeping everyone along with him. He didn't seem to have a clue that at the present moment, he was wasting his time and effort.

He wasn't going to sweep Diana Kennedy *anywhere*, especially not off her feet. She neither liked nor trusted all that easy charm, and she certainly wasn't susceptible to it.

She'd lost her virginity to a charmer, but when she'd chosen a man to marry, he'd been a workaholic: a chef who dreamed of having a place of his own and was willing to work night and day toward that end. Diana had been the perfect wife for such a man. Self-contained and solitary by nature and training, she'd been completely happy to spend most of her time on her own pursuits or caring for Paul's son, Ryan.

As the only child of equally self-contained parents, she'd learned at an early age to control her enthusiasms. Only once, when she was nineteen, had she fallen for a man with more charm than character and she'd sworn she'd never do that again.

As even-tempered as Jason was volatile, she had *always* been in control of her feelings and her actions—with that one exception. Older and wiser now, it would take more than a handsome cowboy Romeo full of superficial charm to change that.

But it was kind of fun to watch him try to worm his way past her natural defenses, especially when eight feet of floor separated them.

She turned, pressing her back against the bar. "Thanks for the history lesson," she said in a noncommittal tone. "Now you really must excuse me."

"Must I?" Deep, attractive creases appeared in his cheeks when he smiled. It was…disconcerting.

She didn't suppose he did much at the request of others, although they probably did plenty for him.

She straightened away from the bar, all business. "I've got a lot to do," she said, stating the obvious.

"You mean here? That'll wait until tomorrow.

Why don't you let me show you Cupid's first annual Spring Fling—''

''There's no such thing as a 'first annual.' That's a misnomer.''

He grinned. ''Details. A rose by any other name... I can introduce you to folks you need to know.''

''There's plenty of time for that.'' Where was Ryan? She'd forgotten all about him. He must be out front flirting with that pretty little Britton girl.

He sighed. ''You're sure I can't tempt you?''

He could tempt her plenty if she didn't have a will of iron. She shook her head mutely, shocked by her thoughts.

''In that case...'' He took a dragging step, the very picture of reluctance. He gave her a narrow, assessing look. ''In that case, I guess I'd better apologize and get it over with.''

It was the last thing she expected. If he'd intended to apologize, he should have, would have, done it right away.

Wouldn't he? She frowned. ''I beg your pardon?''

He gave a dramatic groan. ''It meant so little to you that you've already forgotten? You cut me to the quick!''

She had to laugh a little at that. ''I don't think anyone could cut you to the quick, at least not with words.''

''You only say that because you don't know me,'' he countered. ''I'm really a sensitive soul.'' He walked toward her, not toward the door.

"I don't intend to know you." She edged to one side, sliding along the front of the bar. "As far as your tender sensibilities are concerned, that's your problem."

"That's what *you* think."

He stopped before her, his tall, lean body seeming to hem her in without touching her or the bar against which she pressed. His smile was whimsical, charming.

"I'm trying to apologize for grabbing you and kissing you the way I did," he said. "It was...Julie called it uncouth."

"Julie was right." She felt breathless, as if she'd been running and he'd been chasing. "What would you call it?"

He seemed to consider that carefully. He licked his lips. "I suppose I'd call it...just having a little fun for a worthy cause."

"You call self-gratification a worthy cause?"

He looked wounded. "I call remodeling the gym at Cupid Elementary School a worthy cause."

She hadn't realized the purpose behind the street fair. But that didn't change a thing.

"What do you call making a public display of yourself?"

"Hey," he said, "I was among friends. Friends make allowances for worthy causes." He cocked his head, peering at her closely. "It doesn't look like I've convinced you, Diana Kennedy."

"All I know," she said, "is that I would *never* sell kisses, not if—not if somebody held a *gun* to my head. I'm a very private person. You're a very public person, obviously. There's no middle ground.''

He shifted to one side. Putting a big, capable hand on the bar next to her, he leaned against his stiff arm. The move brought him considerably closer to her while she just stood there wishing he'd go away but incapable of moving—make that determined *not* to move, not to let him manipulate her on her own turf.

"There's always a middle ground," he said softly, his gaze locked with hers. "I'm sorry we got off on the wrong foot. I want to help you, make you welcome in Cupid, make you glad you came. This is a nice little town if you give it, and us, a chance."

"I don't need any help, but thank you just the same."

Now she did move, out and away from his intimidating nearness.

He drew back, his expression puzzled. "Everybody needs help sooner or later."

"Not necessarily."

If he wouldn't leave on his own, she'd show him the way. She started toward the front door. He followed. She might as well have been a carrot on a stick.

"But who'll handle the heavy stuff?" he argued. "A little thing like you can't—"

"If I need someone to do the heavy stuff, as you call it, I'll hire someone."

"But—"

"Good day, Mr. Cameron!"

"Jeez!" He stared at her, his expression perplexed. "It was only one little bitty ol' kiss. What am I going to have to do to live it down?"

She was spared a reply by Beau, trotting through the open doorway.

"Hey, Jase, they're callin' for you! Time to go to jail!"

A fitting place for him to end up, Diana thought. The man was a menace to society, at least the female half.

"Well, hell." Jason glanced from Beau to Diana. "I forgot all about that."

He really was a one-man, money-for-charity machine, apparently.

"Duty calls," she said. "Feel free to answer."

"I don't suppose you'd like to make a donation to help me raise bail?" he inquired hopefully.

"Is that how it works?" She'd never attended any event even vaguely like Cupid's Spring Fling. These people had more silly ways to raise money than she'd ever imagined.

Jason nodded. "I gotta sit in that cage on Main Street until my friends ante up enough bucks for the school fund to post my bail."

"A fitting conclusion to your fund-raising activities," she said very tongue in cheek. "Thank you for your good wishes—and goodbye."

This time, he finally went, Beau trotting behind him like a faithful dog. Only when he'd slipped out of sight in the crowd did Diana remember to look around for Ryan.

She found him sitting on the steps next to a concrete ramp leading up to the back door, talking to Blair. The girl smiled and Diana smiled back.

"Ryan," Diana said, "think you could come in and give me a hand now?"

"Ah, Di—"

"I'll come, too," Blair said quickly, jumping to her feet and brushing off the seat of her khaki shorts.

Sure, why not? Diana thought, leading the way inside. But as Ryan followed along behind, she didn't like the realization that this time, Blair was the carrot on the stick.

LIFE, AS WELL AS the Hideout, looked a great deal brighter once the electricity had been turned on. With the two teens to help her, Diana made short work of the first chore facing her: making sure they had a place to sleep tonight.

Many of their things were in storage, waiting to be shipped. She'd packed only what she thought they'd need right away: bed and bath linens, clothing and personal items, a little food. She knew from the real-estate agent that there was a small apartment in the back on the abbreviated second floor. She and Ryan would use that until they had an opportunity to find more suitable accommodations.

Although the agent had stressed the word "small," Diana was still shocked at how tiny the two-room apartment really was. The bedroom was barely large enough to hold a double bed, a small dresser and one wooden chair. The sitting room, as she supposed it might be called, was crowded with a love seat that pulled out to a bed, one easy chair, a coffee table made from a log flattened on one side with four stubby legs on the other, and a bookcase. An equally minuscule bathroom was situated between the two rooms.

That was it. Not even a kitchen—but of course, the logic behind that was the full kitchen available downstairs.

Only Blair was enthusiastic.

"It's darling!" she declared, dropping an armful of sheets and pillowcases on the small sofa. "Like a doll's house."

"It stinks." Ryan didn't drop his armful of blankets; he heaved it. Blankets landed on the floor in a heap.

Diana gave him a warning glance. "It's not the Ritz but it'll do," she said firmly.

While Blair helped make up the bed, Ryan went, with much grumbling, to fetch the suitcases from the car. Blair grimaced and shook her head.

"Just like a man," she said. "They're always complaining about something."

Diana shook out a sheet, amused by the girl's superior attitude. "You think so?"

"I *know* so. Take my uncle Jason, for example—oops!" She covered her mouth with one hand.

"What about your uncle Jason?" Diana lifted the mattress corner to tuck in the fitted fabric.

"I don't suppose I should talk about him." The girl leaned down to tuck in her own corner.

"Why not?" Diana couldn't resist asking.

The girl's eyes were clear and untroubled. "Because you're mad at him, right? That's what Ryan said anyway. Because Jason kissed you."

"I wouldn't exactly say I'm mad." Furious, yes; insulted, yes. But mad...?

"That's a relief. I *thought* Ryan might be exaggerating. I mean, what's to get mad about? Jason's hot—all the girls are after him." Blair frowned. "Something wrong with that sheet?"

Diana realized she was standing there crushing the top sheet between her hands and hastily shook it out over the bed. Blair grabbed hold of an edge and pulled it toward her.

"Besides," she chattered on, "it wasn't Jason's idea to do that dumb kissing booth anyway. Aunt Julie pushed him into it."

"He didn't seem to mind."

"He's just a good sport. All the Camerons are."

Don't start asking questions about the Camerons, Diana warned herself. You'll find out all you need to know about these people without...

"How many Camerons *are* there?"

"A bunch." Blair started for the door between the two rooms. "Which blanket do you want?"

"The blue one."

The girl returned with the blue blanket without missing a beat in the conversation. "Grandma Cameron is head of the family. I don't know how old she is but pretty old."

To a teenage kid, thirty probably seemed old. Diana stifled a smile.

"My mom's next—she's not really my mom, you know. She's only been married to my dad for five or six years but she's okay. I have a little brother named Chase after my dad—he's three—but everybody calls him Dusty because he usually is."

"Big family!" Diana had no concept of that.

"You ain't heard nothin' yet. Uncle Ben comes next. He runs the Straight Arrow Ranch and he's married to Aunt Betsy, who's a sweetheart. They've got three kids. Aunt Betsy is part owner of the Rusty Spur Café and she bakes just about the best pies and cakes and bread in Colorado."

"I see." Diana made neat, square corners, wondering why this recitation seemed so fascinating.

"Ryan said you met Aunt Julie, and Uncle Max is the marshal—he was with the Los Angeles Police Department before he moved to Cupid." For a moment, her good cheer left her. "They don't have any kids."

"They're young," Diana said. "They've got lots of time."

"I suppose. Personally, I wouldn't find not having a kid much of a hardship, but Julie seems to."

Diana waited. Blair didn't go on, just finished making up her side of the bed and then sat down on it as if awaiting further orders.

"Uh...that's everybody?" Diana couldn't believe she'd said that.

"Isn't that enough?" Blair's expression was incredulous. "Yeah, that's all—except for Jason and you know him. He used to be a professional rodeo cowboy, but a while back, he just quit and came home to stay. He lives in his own place way out in Paradise Valley. He helps Ben with the cattle and ranch chores and he's brought in a few head of buffalo."

"Whatever for?" Diana was astonished. "I thought buffalo were practically on the verge of extinction." She thought of her own buffalo, stuffed and guarding the entryway. Hard to believe he had real live brethren out there in the mountains somewhere.

"They were, a few years ago. They're making a comeback." Blair gave Diana a sly smile. "They're not really buffalo, you know. They're really American bison. A buffalo is a water buffalo like...like in Africa."

Diana did know, but she simply laughed as if it was news to her and sat down on the bed across from the girl. "You certainly seem to be an expert on the subject, whatever you call them."

"I should be. When Jason gets a bright idea, he gets everybody into the act. We've heard him carry on about bringing buffalo to the Straight Arrow for years and—and other stuff." She glanced away evasively. "When Jason gets excited, believe me, everybody's just swept along with him."

This was easy for Diana to believe.

Blair let out a sudden peal of laughter. "Have you ever heard of cattle barons? You know, big ranchers?"

Diana nodded.

"Jason wants to be a buffalo baron. And what Jason wants, Jason gets."

Diana felt a chilly shiver run down her backbone. Jason would be a formidable foe. Fortunately, she had nothing that he wanted.

She would damned well keep it that way.

She patted Blair's hand where it lay against the blue blanket. "What do you suppose is keeping Ryan? Let's go see—"

"I'm here, and look who I caught coming in the front door."

Diana knew before she looked.

Sure enough, there stood Jason, smiling, holding a cardboard box with paper cups inside. "Thought you might like something to drink," he said cheerfully, "and *a little help*."

Was he going to leave her any choice?

"Jason! Did you break out of jail or what?" Blair's face was an open book; she obviously adored her uncle.

But then, Diana thought with an uneasy feeling, who didn't—including the man himself?

CHAPTER FIVE

DIANA THOUGHT she'd never get rid of the Camerons, which included Blair, even if her name *was* Britton. They were obviously a large and close-knit group, which in itself was intimidating.

All Diana wanted was to be alone with Ryan. It had taken a while after her marriage, but they'd grown so close that now she felt as if he really were her own flesh and blood.

But Jason Cameron had insisted on bringing in a big bag of hamburgers before he'd leave for good. He wouldn't take no for an answer, which seemed to be the way he approached everything.

"You've got that look on your face," he said, "the one you women get when your mind is made up and you're not going to be confused by facts. If I left before bringing food into this place, you'd probably starve that poor kid to death." He jerked his chin toward Ryan, hovering over Blair, who didn't seem to care one way or the other.

"We've got stuff in the car," Diana said, feeling crowded by his insistence. "Half a loaf of bread, some tuna, a few cookies—"

"Sounds delicious, but why are you looking a gift horse in the mouth?" He resorted to rhetoric. "Can't you just say 'Thank you, Jason,' and let it go at that?''

Actually, she couldn't, not without a great deal of effort. She hated to be beholden to anyone for anything, even something as minor as a bag of burgers.

Calling upon that great deal of effort, she managed to say a very sweet—a saccharine sweet—"Thank you, Jason."

He gave a satisfied nod. "That's better. You're welcome."

She opened the bag. A hot, greasy aroma assaulted her nostrils; the hamburgers smelled wonderful. But she hadn't forgotten what this was all about. "You're leaving now, right?"

"Oh, yeah." He looked startled, as if he thought he'd distracted her to the point of forgetfulness. "Right." He raised his voice. "Blair, time to go. I told your folks I'd make sure you got back to the ranch."

"I'm ready." She stood up with an impersonal smile for Ryan. She's playing him like a violin, Diana thought, more amused than apprehensive.

Jason turned to leave. "I'll drop by tomorrow or the next day to see how you're doing, Diana."

"There's no need to do that. I'm perfectly capable of handling anything that comes up...but thanks for the offer."

"Diana!" He looked and sounded gently exasperated. After a moment, he added, "You are a stubborn, stubborn woman."

She feigned surprise. "If that's true, why are you the first to mention it?"

As if he was. As if she cared to what conclusions casual acquaintances might jump.

Casual. The key word was *casual*. She had important business ahead of her, making a new life for herself and her stepson. She couldn't allow herself to be distracted by a big, good-looking cowboy who kissed first and asked questions later.

THE NEXT DAY, a Sunday, was wonderful. Nobody disturbed her, nobody dropped by—particularly not Jason, although she found herself expecting him to appear at any moment. He'd said he'd come. She wondered why he didn't—with gratitude for his absence, of course.

Diana spent the day resting and getting acquainted with the Hideout, but there was little she could actually do until Monday, when she'd swing into high gear. First order of business would be turning on the telephones so she could locate workers to handle the cleanup, spruce-up jobs she couldn't, while starting the quest for permits and licenses. Next she'd need to collect supplies for the cleaning and sprucing up, and finally, she'd have to decide on the best way to begin the hiring process for cooks, bartenders, waitpersons and busboys.

Ryan slept most of the morning, then borrowed the minivan to make a tour of the community. He returned in a deep funk, insisting that the town wasn't much more than a wide spot in the road.

Diana translated: he hadn't seen Blair or any other good-looking girls. In fact, he reported, most of Cupid, except for the churches, closed down tight on Sundays.

They made a dinner of peanut butter sandwiches and apples and went to bed early, Diana giving Ryan the tiny bedroom while she slept on the pullout bed. She could barely wait for morning, so eager was she to tackle what lay ahead.

She'd just stumbled into the kitchen on automatic pilot when a sharp knock on the back door startled her into reluctant wakefulness. She found Jason Cameron standing on the back porch with a big grin on his face and another cardboard box in his hands.

"Brought you some breakfast," he announced cheerfully, walking in without waiting for an invitation. "I picked this up at the Rusty Spur so I can guarantee it'll be good." He pulled a brown paper bag out of the box. "I got coffee and cinnamon rolls, along with orange juice."

The tempting aromas of hot coffee and cinnamon made her mouth water. She groaned. "Jason, you're incorrigible! I told you, I can take care of myself. I'm perfectly capable..." She sniffed appreciatively. "It does smell good," she admitted with reluctance.

He pried the lid from a foam cup and offered it. "I brought sugar, sweetener and packets of that phony cream, if you want any."

"Nothing. Just coffee." She sipped cautiously. "This is really very nice of you but—"

"Yeah, yeah," he cut her off impatiently.

"You're a big girl and you can take care of yourself. I'm goin', but I think I better warn you first."

"Warn me about what?" She lounged against the countertop, holding the warm container between both hands, watching him. He was, unfortunately, as good-looking as she remembered.

He also looked big and bold and accustomed to having his own way. His presence was so strong that she felt almost insignificant in his shadow.

"You're going to have company," he said.

She straightened. "What do you mean? How do you know? Who...?"

He shrugged. "People. Everybody, sooner or later. It's that kind of town." His gray eyes narrowed. "And if you want to make a success of this place, you might want to think twice before you throw anybody out."

So she *had* hurt his feelings. "Jason, I didn't mean to imply—"

"Sure you did." His sudden smile took any sting from his words. "But don't worry. I can handle rejection. At least, I think I can."

He gave her a suggestive wink, turned and walked back out the door. Smiling ruefully when she should have been righteously indignant, Diana reached for the bag of cinnamon rolls.

Jason Cameron was going to be big trouble, but he *wasn't* going to get under her skin.

HE'D CALLED IT RIGHT.

Her new neighbors started dropping by at nine

o'clock and never stopped. They looked around with bright, eager attention to see what she was doing while offering greetings and assistance and gifts of food and drink: cans of soda, pitchers of lemonade, home-baked cookies, even a pie.

She accepted the greetings and—reluctantly—the food, while turning down the assistance. She and Ryan were doing just fine, thank you very much.

It was true. By noon, she had telephone service and could really get to work—or so she thought. With so many people wanting to meet her, she found it impossible to work upstairs in the office and finally set up temporarily with a phone behind the bar where she could make calls between visitors.

At one o'clock, a pretty blonde with curly hair and big blue eyes arrived with lunch.

"I'm Betsy Cameron," the newcomer explained, opening a paper bag and smiling at Ryan. "Welcome to Cupid, Diana. Jason said you two might appreciate a little lunch, since you're so busy."

"Appreciate" was a word difficult to get around. "We do," Diana said, "but—"

"Hope you like meat loaf sandwiches," Betsy interrupted cheerfully, offering a huge wrapped package to each of them. "It's on my homemade bread."

"Wow!" Ryan ripped off the wrapping of his sandwich. "I'm starving. This looks great." He took a big bite, his eyes lighting up. "Better than great!"

Betsy beamed. "If there's anything else I can do to help out, please let me know, Diana."

"You've already done enough," Diana said,

made uneasy as always by this outpouring of goodwill. "Here, let me pay you for the lunch." She reached for her purse beneath the bar.

Betsy took a quick step back and her smile turned into a frown. "Certainly not. This is just my way of saying welcome."

Diana sighed. Didn't these people get it? She wanted to do this herself! Now she was forced to say, however reluctantly, "In that case, I thank you. You're very kind."

Betsy's sunny smile returned. "Well, Jason said..." And she was off on a paean to her brother-in-law.

No wonder Jason was conceited.

Betsy left and Diana got back to work on the telephone, nibbling at her sandwich between calls. This wasn't proving to be as easy as she'd expected. She needed carpenters, a cleaning crew, landscaping—

The door squeaked, announcing yet another arrival. She groaned. At this rate, she'd never get the Hideout ready to open. But as Jason had pointed out, these people were not only her new neighbors but potential customers. It wouldn't do to offend them. Shoulders slumping with resignation, she watched two newcomers round the entryway.

They were a real sight: two attractive old folks who looked to be in their eighties, maybe even older, Diana realized as they came closer. But judging from their upright carriages, they hadn't given in to their years and didn't intend to.

The woman was tall, taller than Diana and taller

than the man at her side. She wore jeans and a denim jacket over a plaid shirt, and her feet were booted. A white cowboy hat rested on a head of dark hair liberally streaked with white strands. Her face was only lightly lined, although her skin had that fragile look common to the aged.

She smiled and stuck out a veined hand with gnarled knuckles. "Howdy," she said. "I'm Etta May Cameron, but most folks call me Granny. This here is Ethan Turner and I won't tell you what most folks call him."

Ethan looked pained but made no objection. Dressed almost identically to the woman, he was whipcord lean with a full head of white hair and a luxurious mustache on a weather-beaten face. His blue eyes had a squint that even Diana, no expert on things Western, recognized as pure cowboy.

He nodded gravely and said, "Howdy, ma'am. Welcome to Cupid."

Diana was enchanted with these two oldsters. "That's very kind of you both," she said with more sincerity than she'd felt toward any of the others. "Mr. Turner, are you by any chance related to Beau Turner? I met him the day of the street fair."

He practically swelled with pride. "Beau's my grandson," he said. "Me'n him run the Lazy T north of town."

Diana turned her smile on the old lady. "And you're related to all the Camerons, I would guess."

She let out a hearty laugh. "Maybe not all of 'em,

but the ones around here anyway. How many of 'em you met?''

"Well, Jason, of course.''

"Of course.'' Etta May's smile was indulgent. "Very few pretty girls get past that boy.''

Diana had already guessed that. "Betsy brought lunch and I met Julie, although we only spoke for a few minutes.'' And that was spent debating the merits of her twin, but Diana wouldn't bring that up now. "I suppose you could call Blair and the marshal Camerons by marriage,'' she concluded.

"Camerons by marriage!'' Etta May hooted with laughter. "That's about right. You've got a good start there, but you still got a few more Camerons to go. Well, we just wanted to wish you well and now we have.'' She glanced at Ethan. "You about ready to hit the road? This child obviously has a lot of work ahead of her and we're just in the way.''

"Oh, no!'' *Now why did I say that?* Diana wondered, although it was too late to take it back. In fact, she didn't want to take it back. "Would you like to sit down for a while? I have some cans of soda if you'd like something to drink.''

Etta May waved her off. "No, no, we won't get in your way any longer. If there's anything we can do to help you, just let us know. Coming, Ethan?''

"Coming, my...'' The missing word—*love*, or maybe *dear*—hung in the air. The old man dropped his gaze as if embarrassed.

Etta May just laughed and reached out to slip her arm through the crook of his. "In that case—''

"Grandma!" The strident voice came from across the room and Diana knew instantly that Jason had arrived. "What the hell are you doing?"

He crossed the room with long, determined strides. When he came close, Diana saw that his face was tight, and harder than she'd ever seen it. What in the world was the matter with him?

Etta May watched his approach without obvious concern. When he stomped to a halt, she said, "I came to welcome this young lady to our fine community. You got a problem with that, Jason Cameron?"

"Hell, no!" His tight gaze flicked over Ethan. "You know what I got the problem with."

Etta May smiled sweetly at her grandson. "And you know I purely do not give a hoot in hell about that particular problem." Her voice dripped honey. She reached out and patted his cheek with her gnarled fingers. "Mind your own business, boy," she said. "Ethan, shall we go?"

Ethan looked as if he wanted to say something to Jason himself, but he didn't. He just tucked Etta May's hand beneath his elbow, gave it a little pat and led her from the Hideout.

Jason watched them depart, steam practically shooting from his ears. Mystified, Diana tried to figure out what his problem might be. He obviously hadn't been happy to find his grandma with old Ethan, but why? Surely there wasn't a Grandpa Cameron at home.

"How long were they here?" he asked sharply.

"Only a few minutes. Why are you so angry?"

"I'm not angry...exactly."

"You could have fooled me. Why don't you sit down and I'll get us both a soda and you can tell me all about it." Damn, she shouldn't have said that. Sharing problems came perilously close to offering friendship.

For a minute, he just looked at her. Then he nodded curtly. "Okay, someone's bound to tell you sooner or later. Might as well get it over with."

"This isn't sounding very good." She reached into a cooler filled with ice and withdrew two cans of soda, which she set on the bar.

"It isn't." He shook his head with evident frustration. "Why's she doing this?" he asked plaintively. "She's old enough to know better."

"Maybe she's old enough to know better than *you* do. Mr. Turner seemed like a very nice man."

He gave her a disgusted glance. "Have you ever noticed how people are always saying things like that about mass murderers? 'I can't imagine why he killed forty-four innocent bystanders. He was such a *nice* boy.'"

She had to laugh. "Okay, if Mr. Turner killed forty-four people, I'll withdraw the 'nice' comment. Did he?"

Jason grimaced. "No."

"Then what *did* he do?" She popped the tab from her can of soda.

"He robbed banks," Jason said. "He went to prison for it. Did you ever hear of the Outlaw

Grandpa? Well, that's Ethan Turner—and I don't want him messin' around with my grandma!''

HE'D FINALLY CUT THROUGH all her brusque impersonality, Jason saw with no small degree of pleasure. She stared at him with her lips slightly parted, her eyes wide with amazement.

Finally, she said, "I don't believe it!"

But he saw she did, really. He nodded emphatically. "It's the God's truth. Happened a few years back and it was quite a scandal. He got out of jail on good behavior and probably because he's older than God. Then he came back to Cupid and wound up right in the middle of a big horse-rustling ring."

She gave an incredulous laugh, and it occurred to him that she didn't laugh nearly enough. On a beautiful woman, a laugh was like perfume...infinitely enticing.

As if he needed more enticement where she was concerned.

"No," she said, shaking her head. "Horse rustling in this day and age? I don't think so."

"It happened."

She still looked dubious. "Was he guilty? If he was, why isn't he in prison now?"

"Because he *wasn't* guilty, at least that time. It was Beau mixed up in the rustling. He's still on probation because of it."

"Good grief. And he looked so..." She darted him a faintly teasing glance. "Dare I use the word 'nice'?"

"Yeah," Jason grumbled, "Beau is nice. He just has this habit of falling in with bad company."

"But now he seems to be following *you* around, so what kind of trouble could he get into?" She said it lightly, teasingly.

If she only knew.

"We're not talking about Beau. We're talking about Ethan. He's not the kind of man I want my grandma running around with."

"Are you sure?"

"Hell, yes, I'm sure!"

"Slow down and think about what you said, Jason. I don't think you want your grandma running around with any man. I think no matter who she might be interested in—"

"Interested! She's not interested, not the way you mean."

"Why not?"

"Why— Why— Because..." He sputtered to a halt. It was so *obvious*.

Diana filled in the blanks. "Because she's old?"

"She is that," he agreed grimly. "Why can't she act her age?"

"Jason! She's old, not dead!" She leaned across the bar and punched him in the shoulder. It was the first time she had ever deliberately touched him, and if it kept her touching him, he'd let her pound on him all day.

The light blow effectively cut through the tension and he grinned. "Now what'd I miss?"

"You wouldn't like any man your grandmother

was seeing," she informed him. "Mr. Turner has paid his debt to society."

"He's still an old crook," Jason grumbled. "He's not good enough for my grandma."

She made a sound of disbelief. "Few men are good enough for the women who fall for them." She stifled a smile. "I think you'll have to let your grandmother be the judge of that."

"Maybe so and maybe not. Let's change the subject."

He could almost see her pull back although she didn't move so much as a single muscle.

"I know," she said, "you came to offer help, see what it is the poor little city girl doesn't know how to handle this time. Well, I'm sorry to inform you that I'm handling everything just fine."

"Good for you." He set his can of soda back on the bar. "Have you located a good carpenter to do the repairs around here?" He gestured toward the sagging trim around the big bar mirror as an obvious example.

"Well, no, but—"

"And someone to clean? I don't think you'll want to do the grub work yourself."

"Well, no, but..." She looked at him with lips pursed. "I am having a little trouble. There doesn't seem to be anyone here in Cupid who does that sort of thing, so I'm calling people in—"

"Of *course* there are people in Cupid. You just don't know who they are."

"I checked the phone book," she defended herself.

"And it didn't do you a bit of good, did it? Here, give me that telephone." He reached for it.

"I'll do it myself!" She yanked the instrument beyond his reach.

"Fine. You can call Dwight Deakins about the carpentry. Dwight was marshal here before Max. After he retired, he started doing repairs and sorta developed into the best handyman in these parts. For cleaning..." He thought for a minute. "Call Mary Davis. She cleans the *Chronicles* office and the bank and several more. She's real good and real reliable."

"And their telephone numbers are...?" He gave them. She wrote them down, then hesitated before finally giving in. "Okay, I'll call them. Thanks for the help, but I'd have figured this out for myself!"

"Sure you would," he said jauntily. "I'll let you get on with it, then. Just remember, if you need anything—"

"I'll remember," she said hastily. "I'll remember. But the answer is still no!"

CHAPTER SIX

DWIGHT DEAKINS LOUNGED against the bar at the Hideout, shaking his head with seeming regret. "I'd like to help you out, little lady," he said, "but I promised Doc Kunkle I'd take care a his roof before I did anything else. Then Nancy Wyatt's been after me for a coon's age to help her with a remodel on that addition she had put onto her house last year. Some big outfit from Denver come in and made a real mess of it."

Diana could hardly believe her ears. It had taken days for the punchy ex-marshal to even come by to *talk* to her and now he was blathering on about roofs and remodels when her livelihood was at stake.

She hated to sound desperate but supposed she was. "Mr. Deakins—"

"Call me Dwight," he invited. "Everybody does."

She sucked in a steadying breath. "All right, Dwight. I'm really in a bind here. If I'm going to reopen the Hideout on schedule..." She swallowed hard. "I'm aiming for June 1."

He pursed his lips thoughtfully. "Never happen."

"But—"

He shook his head decisively. "And it's not just

me," he went on. "There's too many loose ends for you to tie up. Gotta get your liquor license in order, hire help... Have you looked into that yet?"

"No, but the last owner said—"

"Far as the repairs are concerned," he talked over her, "I could get everything taken care of by..." He considered. "My best advice is to aim for a July 1 opening."

"But I don't want..." She clenched her teeth and got hold of herself. "I'll take your advice under consideration."

"Good enough. Let me know if you want that work done."

"I will." But only after she'd exhausted every other possible avenue. Who did he think he was anyway?

On his way out, he passed Julie Mackenzie coming in. "You gonna help fix this place up?" she asked.

He shrugged. "Don't look like it. I'm pretty busy already—only come in here as a favor to Jason. Now it seems I won't be needed after all."

Julie approached Diana, frowning. "Dwight's the best handyman and fixer-upper around," she said. "You should have grabbed him."

"His schedule didn't fit mine. I'll find someone else. So what can I do for you, Julie?"

The editor waved her reporter's notebook in the air and smiled. "I'm looking for a story," she announced. "Folks are interested in your plans for the

Hideout, and in you, too. Think you can spare a few minutes to talk to me?''

Diana sighed. This was the last thing she wanted—to spill her guts before a lot of strangers. But it wouldn't be wise to offend the local press. "Sure," she said. "Let's sit down and I'll tell you anything you want to know, although I should warn you that I'm pretty dull.''

"I doubt that.'' Julie pulled out a chair before one of the round tables, laid her notebook on the scarred surface, opened it and held her pen poised for action. "Okay,'' she commanded, "tell me everything! Let's start with how you found out about the Hideout....''

So Diana told her: about meeting Gene Varner, about speaking to the real-estate agent, about seeing pictures of the place.

"So now that you're here, are you disappointed?'' Julie asked.

"Not at all!'' Diana tried to keep her grin from stretching ear to ear. "It's even better than I anticipated. The minute I walked in, I knew I'd made the right decision.''

"Not the *very* minute!'' Julie spoke in a light, teasing tone.

"Yes, the very minute.'' Diana nodded her head for emphasis. "I saw that buffalo standing in the entryway and it was love at first sight.''

"Old moth-eaten Bill?''

"Bill?'' The name, which should have been obvious but wasn't, delighted Diana. "*Buffalo* Bill? I love it!"

"Legend has it that particular critter was actually shot by *the* Buffalo Bill. Don't know if it's true, but I suppose it's possible, since Bill Cody spent a lot of time in Colorado. He's even buried on Lookout Mountain west of Denver, but that's another story."

"*I* believe," Diana said. "That buffalo just sort of epitomizes this whole venture for me—the Old West and the new, my old life and my new one. In fact, I've been thinking about moving him to a spot of honor somewhere inside—maybe on the corner of the bandstand. What do you think?"

"He's been standing guard over that door for a long time. Why bother moving him?"

"The truth?" Diana stifled a smile. "I'm afraid someone will walk in, fall in love with him like I did and cart him away. That's silly, I know."

"I'll say it is!" Julie laughed heartily. "Why would anyone steal a stuffed buffalo?"

Diana shrugged. "I think I'd try if he wasn't already mine, and if I couldn't buy him, of course."

"I guess Grandma's right when she says there's no accounting for taste." Julie picked up her pen, all business again. "So the place didn't disappoint you. That's good. Was it difficult leaving Dallas? You say you lived there all your life?"

"That's right." Diana didn't like treading so close to personal revelations. "But after my husband died, it wasn't the same. I was ready to try something else."

"And Ryan?"

"Not quite so enthusiastic, but he'll come around." Diana leaned forward. "How about you? Have you lived in Cupid all your life?"

"Yes, except for a few months I was in California with Max. Then Dwight retired and Max got the job as marshal and we came back home. We're never going to leave again. About your husband—judging from Ryan's age, he must have been a few years older than you."

"A few." Try sixteen. "He was a chef, by the way, and I worked for a food wholesaler. That's how we met."

"And you never had children of your own?"

"Ryan is my own."

"Of course. I didn't mean—"

"I didn't take offense. Ryan's nearly thirteen years younger than I am and that created problems at first, but we're long past that."

"That's good."

"You like kids, don't you?"

Julie blinked in surprise. "Doesn't everybody?" She sighed, her expression changing to one of guarded sadness. "I don't have any of my own, unfortunately."

"There's time," Diana said softly, remembering Blair's reaction when she'd said her aunt and uncle were childless.

Julie let out her breath slowly. "Of course there is. Only...we've been married for five years and it looks as if we may never..."

"You will if you want them," Diana said.

"Is that the opinion of Dr. Diana?"

"That's the opinion of someone who learned to love a child not her own. Have you thought of adoption?"

"We've thought, but that's about all at this point." Julie's brown eyes flashed. "It really irritates me, you know. My sister-in-law Betsy's got two kids—Ben already had Joey when they got together—and even Maggie's had a baby and she was well past thirty before she and Chase even got married. With them for an example, I thought it would be easy!"

"It's been my experience," Diana said with care to conceal her amusement, "that nothing is ever easy, especially not things that other people make *look* easy."

"You're right." Julie slapped down her pen. "And I'd be such a great mother!"

"I love your self-confidence," Diana observed wryly. "I'm mostly a lousy mother, no matter how hard I try. Seriously, though, I've known some wonderful adopted and blended families. There's a girl I went to school with..."

They talked, and the interview was apparently forgotten, to Diana's relief. She didn't like talking about herself but enjoyed the trials and tribulations of Julie, who occasionally tossed in a question as if to maintain the fiction of an interview.

Ryan walked through with an armload of old

cardboard signs he'd been sorting in the basement. "You two still at it?" he inquired with surprise.

Julie laughed and closed her notebook. "Yes, but I really do need to get a move on. Thanks for the interview, Diana. I'll try to keep my story straight." She stood up. "By the way, where are you two staying?"

"Upstairs." Diana rose, too.

"In that tiny little apartment?" Julie made a face. She swung her purse strap over her shoulder, then stopped short with an exclamation that sounded vaguely like "Eureka!" Before she could elaborate, Ryan interrupted.

"Jason's here!" he sang out from the entrance.

All Diana's easiness fell away and she stifled an exclamation of displeasure. It wouldn't do to reveal her negative feelings with his twin standing by, though.

Julie waited for him impatiently. "Jason, your timing is perfect. I've got this great idea."

He plucked off his Stetson and set it upside down on a table. "Run for the hills, everybody! Julie's got an idea."

"No, this one's really good. Don't you think Betsy's little house over on Lover's Lane would be just perfect for Diana and Ryan until they find something permanent?"

Jason's face lit up. "That's a great idea. Why don't I just—"

"What *are* you two talking about? The apartment upstairs is perfectly adequate for now."

Julie glanced at her watch. "I'm running late, Jason. Maybe you could take her over and show her the place. The key's under the mat, as always."

"Glad to." He turned one of those patented smiles on Diana, the ones that weakened women's knees—and minds. "Trust me, this is a good idea."

"But..."

"Oh, go *on*, Diana!" Ryan had returned and was listening. "*You* may like that cracker box upstairs, but I'm fed up with stumbling over you every time I turn around."

Julie shot him a look of caution. "Don't get the idea that this house we're talking about is a mansion because it isn't. It's only got one bathroom, I'm afraid, but there is a lot more room than here. Besides, once this place opens, nobody will get any rest upstairs. Have you thought of that?"

Diana had tried *not* to think of that. "I figured I'd worry about it when the time came," she said lamely, realizing that "Betsy's little house" might be the best thing that had happened to her since she and Ryan arrived in town.

"The time's come," Jason said firmly, taking her elbow. He added to his sister, "I'll take it from here, Jewel."

"Okay. And don't call me Jewel!"

Diana resisted the instinct to yank her elbow free of his grasp. "Want to come along, Ryan?"

"Not a chance." He turned and headed toward the kitchen. "I'm gonna fix myself a sandwich and then I'll get back to that stuff in the basement. Most of it's junk. It's just a matter of hauling it outside to the trash bins. You go on, and for God's sake, take it!''

Jason guided her toward the door. ''Guess you got your orders,'' he said.

''Guess I did,'' she agreed, figuring she might as well stop arguing and get this over with.

TO JASON'S DISGUST, Diana insisted on driving her own car and following his pickup while he led the way: left fork of the Y and onto Lover's Lane. Betsy's cottage was the last house on the left before the road made an almost square turn to lead back to Main Street. He pulled up into the driveway and stopped. She parked on the street and crawled out of the minivan.

He waited for her on the small porch, admiring her moves. The day was cool but brilliant with sunshine, and she wore a powder blue windbreaker over her Texas Longhorns T-shirt and jeans. A light breeze lifted strands of her strawberry blond hair and sent them wafting around her face; she brushed them aside impatiently and hurried on as if she had important business to attend to.

He'd never known a woman who kept such tight control of herself. She stepped up beside him on the covered porch.

''What a cute little cottage,'' she said. ''It's Betsy's?''

''Yep. She inherited it from her grandmother.'' Jason knelt, lifted one corner of the small rubber

Welcome mat and extracted a key. "Here goes nothing." Standing, he inserted the key in the lock and the front door swung open.

Diana stepped inside and paused to look around. Her expression gave nothing away.

Jason hadn't expected her to be overly impressed, but he'd hoped for more than this. Sure, it was a small house—not more than eight hundred square feet. But it had been built at least ninety years ago and it did have personality, or so Betsy always claimed.

The front door opened directly into the living room with the dining room to the left. The rooms were not only tiny but dark, as well. Reaching over, he flicked a switch on the wall and they were bathed in the illumination of one plain overhead glass light fixture.

The furniture was old, too, although nowhere near as old as the house. An overstuffed chair and old blue sofa faced a small stone fireplace. Jason recalled there had also been a rocking chair here once, but Betsy had moved it to the ranch.

He followed Diana through the rooms: dining room, barely large enough to hold an oak table and four chairs; and kitchen, possibly the largest room in the house, with space for a table and chairs in addition to the refrigerator and cookstove.

Diana led the way into a small hall.

"That's the bathroom." Jason pointed. "There's only one. That door on the left is the second bedroom. It used to be reachable only through the other bedroom and was more a sort of sitting room, Betsy says. But it's easier to rent with a separate entrance.''

"I see," Diana murmured.

He wondered *what* she saw; whatever it was, she wasn't sharing. ''The door on the right is to the main bedroom, if you can call twelve by twelve 'main.' ''

She opened the door and stepped through. After a moment's hesitation, he followed. He found her standing beside the bed, running her fingers over the wrought-iron bed frame. Looking down at the patchwork quilt that served as a bedspread, she smiled. Finally.

"So what do you think?" he asked as anxiously as if it mattered. If she didn't choose to live here, so what? It was nothing to him.

"I like it," she said. Turning her head slowly, she surveyed the remainder of the room: an old chifforobe with peeling veneer, a spindly bedside table. "How do you know Betsy wants to rent it?"

"Betsy always wants to rent it," he said. "Not too much call for rentals in Cupid, so when it's empty, she's always on the lookout for someone to move in and take care of the place. I guess you could say she has a sentimental attachment to it since it was her grandmother's last home."

"I see." Again, that smooth, beautiful, unfathomable expression. "I take it there's a furnace and a water tank?"

"Yep. In the basement, along with a washer and

dryer.'' He turned deliberately toward the door, not caring whether she wanted to live here or not.

Not much. He wheeled around, hoping his smile wasn't a dead giveaway.

"So what do you think?" he asked. "Is this the house of your dreams or what?"

OHH, JASON, DON'T DO THIS to me, she thought. Somehow he always managed to wiggle his way through defenses she'd thought were impenetrable.

The house was adorable—and so was he.

She gave him a cool glance. "Why are you going to so much trouble to be charming?" she asked with all the finesse of a sledgehammer.

He stared back at her as if aghast. "What makes you think I'm *trying?*" he countered. "Couldn't I just be a naturally charming sort of guy?"

"Yeah, right." She rolled her eyes.

"No, really." He looked as if she'd hurt his feelings again. "Maybe this is just the way I am. Hell, Diana, not too many people object."

"You mean not too many women object." She walked past him, down the hall and into the living room. "Does that fireplace work?"

"Yes, and don't try to change the subject."

"The subject *is* changed. I have no right to...to criticize you." She had no right to do *anything* with him and she didn't intend to.

"Nah, you started this." He stepped around in front of her, close enough to intimidate but not touching. "What did you mean with that crack about women not objecting?"

"They don't, do they?" She moved to a window to hold aside a dusty lace curtain.

"Why would they? Listen, Diana, I like women."

"There's a news flash." She turned to face him.

"I mean I *genuinely* like women, all women. I like old ones and young ones, big ones and little ones." He came toward her, his gaze intensifying the closer he got. "Some I like more than others, of course."

She drew herself up tight, almost as if she could somehow keep her distance from him regardless of his own intent. He stopped so close his booted feet extended on either side of her sneaker-shod feet.

"Most of all," he said with quiet intensity, "I like pretty, stiff-necked *Texas* women...and I didn't even know it until now."

If he touched her, she'd—she'd scream! No, she'd slap his face, that's what she'd do. Under no circumstances would she allow a repeat of what had happened the first time they'd more or less met. That kiss, that damnable kiss.

She dared him, she double-dared him to make a move. She was ready for anything.

Except for him to thrust his hands deep into his jeans pockets, hunch his shoulders and turn away. "It's up to you, you know," he said.

"W-what's up to me?" Get a grip, girl, get a grip!

"Whether or not you want this house." He looked puzzled that she hadn't followed his train of thought. "If you do, we can go to the Spur right now and give Betsy the good news. If you don't…" He shrugged as if he couldn't care less.

"I want it," she said, her voice surprisingly husky. "Thanks."

She sure was getting tired of saying that word to him.

THE DEAL was quickly struck in the hallway outside the kitchen of the Rusty Spur Café and sealed with a handshake. Betsy beamed.

"I'm so happy my little house will have someone living in it again," she said. "I hate when it stands empty."

"This is terribly kind of you," Diana said. "I'll take good care of it, I promise."

"I'm not the least bit concerned about that," Betsy said. "Now, let me ask you this—have you met my husband?"

Diana shook her head. "But I've heard about him. Ben, right?"

"Right. He's out front eating apple pie. If you'll come along, I'll introduce you."

Diana followed Betsy while Jason followed Diana down the short hall and out into the restaurant proper. Past a curving counter were booths and tables. A sign hanging over the largest proclaimed it the Liars' Table. Most appropriately, a rusty spur hung on a nail above the front door immediately opposite the hallway where they'd entered.

The place was busy, diners at nearly every table

and all the counter stools taken. Diana hadn't realized it was lunchtime already.

Betsy approached a big man seated on the end stool and leaned forward to kiss him on one sun-browned cheek—a dead giveaway that this was Ben, but by no means the only clue. He looked so much like Jason—or Jason looked so much like Ben—that it was eerie: the same unruly black hair and rebellious gray eyes. The Cameron men wore authority like a mantle, although Jason's was tempered with humor not readily apparent on Ben's face.

"Honey," Betsy whispered in his ear loud enough for everyone to hear, "this is—"

"Yeah," he said, his lean cheeks creasing when he smiled, "this is Diana Kennedy. I'd know that hair anywhere."

"How did you…?" Diana's hand flew to her hair, diverted from a handshake.

Ben grinned. "My little brother—"

"Shut up, Ben."

"Yeah, that one. He mentioned the hair."

Betsy intervened. "Diana's going to move into Grandmother's little house," she said happily. "Jason just took her by to see it."

"Good old Jason."

"Yes. Now I've got to get back to work before Nancy shoots me." She glanced at Ben's empty pie plate. "Want another piece of pie, honey?"

"Maybe Diana and Jason would like to join me."

"Diana and I haven't had lunch yet," Jason said

quickly, taking her elbow. "I see an open booth right over there."

She shook free of him with one expert move. "Sorry, but I don't have time for lunch. Thanks for everything, Jason. It was wonderful meeting you, Ben. And, Betsy, I can't thank you enough for letting me live in your house."

Diana turned and walked out the way she'd come, down the hall to the back door.

Jason figured you could have heard a pin drop in the Rusty Spur. Hell, they'd all been listening and they'd heard Diana turn him down like he was something the cat dragged in.

One old boy at the Liars' Table let out a howl of laughter. "You sure swept that gal off her feet, Jase!" he chortled.

"Yeah," yelled Jimmy Mosely, seated in a booth with Tap and Beau. "The Queen Bee's eatin' outa your hand! Way to go, Jason!"

More humiliated than he had any reason to be, Jason glared a warning at his friends before heading for the back door himself. Ben's steely tone stopped him in his tracks.

"What the hell are you doin' in town today anyway? I thought you said you'd move those cows in the east pasture."

Jason felt his hackles rise. Ben often had that effect on him. "So? There's plenty of time."

"Not if you're gonna run around mooning over a woman who won't give you the time of day," Ben said bluntly. "You've spent more time in Cupid this past week than you did all last month. Think you might get your mind back on business any time soon?''

''I *might,* but I won't unless you get off my back,'' Jason flared. ''You're my brother, not my boss.''

Damn, his palms itched to grab a handful of Ben's shirt. They hadn't had a knock-down-drag-out fight since...hell, he couldn't remember when. Maybe since the birthday party before Ben and Betsy even got married, when Ben had tossed Jason bodily across the room to land on top of Betsy's elegant cake.

For a moment, the brothers glared at each other. Then Jason muttered, ''I'm outa here!'' and was.

For a couple of minutes, the customers of the Rusty Spur sat in contemplative silence. Then Jimmy Mosely said, his voice cutting easily through the hush, ''Well, how d'you like that? If that Queen Bee keeps playin' hard to get, she could just end up takin' ol' Jason's mind right off the rest of the female population in these parts.''

Tap Wilson let out a great honking laugh. ''Hell, if he ever got serious about that gal, Cupid would *really* get revenge,'' he said.

Beau said, ''Boy, howdy!''

CHAPTER SEVEN

DIANA VOWED TO OPEN the Hideout June 1 if it killed her.

It was beginning to look as if it would. No matter how hard she and Ryan worked, they needed *help*, the kind of help you hired, not the kind everyone kept offering as a matter of course.

Mary Davis, at least, was a little ray of sunshine, even though she came in for her interview with her six-year-old great-nephew in tow. In her late fifties, she looked grimly determined, a no-nonsense sort of woman.

"I'm sorry about bringing the boy," she apologized brusquely. "His name's Mikey and he's my niece's—was anyway. Now he's mine, and until I can figure out what to do with him, I just bring him along to work with me. He won't get in the way."

Diana smiled at the little boy, who looked exactly like her idea of a young Huckleberry Finn or Tom Sawyer. Straight sandy hair fell over his forehead and freckles dotted his cheeks. Blue eyes stared back at her solemnly.

"Is that good for him?" she wanted to know.

Mary shrugged. "Can't be helped. Now about this job…"

Diana explained, keeping a watchful eye on Mikey. The little boy sat down on the floor beside his aunt, so close that his shoulder pressed against her leg. When he caught Diana watching him, he gave her an uncertain smile.

"...so that's what I need," she concluded. "Help to get this place cleaned up and ready to open, then someone to keep it that way. I understand you have several other clients, so perhaps it would be too much for you?"

Mary thought about that, chewing on her lower lip. "It would," she said finally, "except I have a friend who's lookin' to get into this line of work. Between the two of us, we could handle it."

"That's a relief." And it was. Finally, something was going right. Now if she could only find a handyman, several bartenders, cooks...

But first, she knelt to smile at the silent child. "What a good boy you are!" she said. "If your aunt Mary doesn't mind, I'll bet we can find you a treat...."

JULIE'S STORY ABOUT DIANA came out in Thursday's *Cupid Chronicles,* and at first Diana had high hopes it would make her task easier. She wasn't too crazy about the story's emphasis on her affection for Buffalo Bill, afraid that people would be laughing at her, but if that was the worst that came out of it...

It wasn't. A perfectly innocent quote was rocking the whole town and Diana didn't even know it.

I've never lived in a small town before, but how hard can it be? I may miss the cultural opportunities of a big city, the excitement and the challenge, but I've never needed to be the center of everyone's attention. I just want to do my job and give the people of Cupid the best darn saloon they've ever had.

Tap Wilson took that as a slam. "Sounds like a crack against Jason, that part about being the center of attention," he grumbled

"Yeah, and she knocked our cultural opportunities, too." That from Jimmy Mosely who wouldn't know culture if it spit in his eye.

Somebody else took exception to the "how hard can it be?" comment and somebody else interpreted the part about "the best darn saloon they've ever had" to be a slur against earlier versions and owners.

All agreed that for an outsider, she was talkin' a little too big for her britches.

When Julie heard, she exploded. "You guys are nuts! She's a perfectly nice woman trying to make it on her own and you people should be ashamed of yourselves for looking for things to pick at her about."

Yeah, but everybody knew that Julie Cameron Mackenzie was a hothead herself under most circumstances. She just didn't want to mess up her brother's chances—assuming he had any, which most of the town doubted. Still, the Queen Bee was taking up a whole lot of his time and attention.

And that was good, very good.

"WHADDAYA MEAN, you don't have time?" Jason frowned at Dwight Deakins.

Dwight paused with one foot on the ladder. He'd been on his way up to fix Doc Kunkle's roof when Jason had come roaring in. "I mean, I ain't got time," he repeated calmly.

"Ah, come on, Dwight." Jason tried wheedling. "She really needs the help. If you don't do it, how will I know it's been done right?"

Dwight frowned. "Excuse me for asking, but what business is it of yours? It's not your saloon, Jason. She beat you to it."

"I know that." Jason glared at the toe of his boot. "I'm...just trying to be a good neighbor."

"Yeah, right." Dwight started up the ladder again.

"I'd take it as a personal favor if you'd change your mind and help her out," Jason said.

Dwight paused on the third rung to look down on the morose cowboy. He frowned. "You know, I don't believe you've ever asked me for a favor before, boy. Even when I threw your butt in jail—"

"That's because I haven't," Jason cut in. He didn't like being reminded of his temporary fall from grace.

"You really are sweet on this gal." Dwight looked as if he could hardly believe it.

"Hell, no!" Jason shoved his hands into his jeans pockets and hunched his shoulders. "I'd do the same for anyone."

"But you're doin' it for the Queen Bee and she's gonna break your poor old heart," Dwight predicted. "She is one cold fish, m'boy. But if it means that much to you, hell, yes, go tell her I've changed my mind."

"You tell her," Jason said. "I don't want her to think I'm stickin' my nose in her business."

Even if he was.

Now who else did he need to talk to? And how could he find them all in a bunch, so he didn't have to spend the next month making the same pitch over and over again?

MEANWHILE, BACK AT the Hideout, Diana finally took pity on Ryan and Blair and gave them a half-hour break. They hurried out the back door, cans of soda in hand, to sit side by side on the steps.

Diana sighed and popped the top on her own soda can. Blair came practically every day to help and had since she'd graduated from high school and moved to the Straight Arrow for the summer. She had her own car, a new Jeep she'd received as a graduation gift, and apparently she pretty much came and went as she pleased, sometimes returning to the ranch and other times staying in town with Max and Julie. They had plenty of room in Gene's big old Victorian house on Lover's Lane.

Most of the time, the two kids spent hard at work.

They really *were* working, and if this place ever opened again—which Diana was beginning to doubt—it would be in good part because of their efforts. But they weren't within her purview *all* the time and they were both eighteen, a very vulnerable age....

Well, she'd worry about that when she had time. Thrusting such thoughts aside, she turned back to the grill, black with grease and age. Rolling up her sleeves, she went to work.

BEAU FOUND RYAN AND BLAIR sitting on the back step of the Hideout, shoulder to shoulder. He trotted over, a big grin on his face.

"Howdy," he said. "Whatcha doin'?"

The couple exchanged amused glances. "Nothing," Ryan said. "What are *you* doing?"

"Tryin' to avoid Jason," Beau said.

Blair took a swig of her soda. "Why? I thought Jason was your friend."

Beau nodded emphatically. "Sure is. My *best* friend. But he's twistin' my arm about helpin' out your ma, Ryan."

"He wants you to help her or he doesn't want you to help her?"

"He..." Confused, Beau lifted a booted foot to the second step and leaned on his bent knee. "Huh?"

"Just tell us what Jason said," Blair suggested.

"Oh, okay. He said I should go to work here, says everybody should. He says give her a chance. He likes her even if she don't like him." He shook his head in disbelief. "Everybody liked Jason before that Queen Bee came to town."

"Queen Bee!" Ryan and Blair laughed together and then Ryan added, "Who calls her that?"

"Not Jason!" Beau glanced around in alarm. He didn't think his hero would much care for that name. "Everybody else. She don't like him and they think it's funny, but I don't. I think...I think she's crazy. Why would I want to work for a crazy lady?"

Ryan shrugged. "She's not crazy. She just acts that way sometimes."

"Yeah, well..." Beau shook his head. "If she's not crazy, why don't she just sell out to Jason and go back where she belongs? She shouldn'ta grabbed this place out from under him anyway."

Ryan blinked in surprise. "Jason wanted to buy this place?"

"Sure," Beau said. "Everybody knows that." He straightened. "I gotta be goin'. See you kids around, okay?"

They watched him amble away. After he was out of earshot, Blair said thoughtfully, "Jason *is* acting funny. I wonder if he's..."

"What?"

"Never mind."

"Did he really want to buy this place?"

"Yeah, he said so anyway." She jumped up. "Time for us to get back to work. If my father could see me now, he wouldn't believe it."

She led the way back inside, Ryan trotting along behind her like a puppy dog.

"WELL, DAMMIT!" Jason surveyed the small crowd of gossipers on the loading dock in front of the Cupid Feed & Tack store at Third and Main Streets. They stared at him as if he were crazy.

"Well, hell," Charlie Gilroy retorted in kind, his heavy eyebrows almost meeting across his forehead when he frowned. "What else we got to talk about except that...that *girl* who thinks she's gonna come in here and teach us locals how it's done? Why should we go out of our way to help her when she's made it perfectly clear that she can do it all herself?"

"That's not what she said." Jason tamped down his irritation, but it was hard—real hard. "She's from a big city and she doesn't understand how it is with us small-town folks."

"She's just not friendly," Courtney Lewis complained. She'd stopped by to pick up a sack of chicken feed for her father and then hung around to talk to Jimmy Mosely. "She's got good manners but underneath—well, I think she thinks she's better than we are." She glanced around for support and got it.

"That's absolutely not true," Jason said flatly. "She's an outsider, that's all, and she'll never be an insider until we give her a chance. She may be a bit prickly but—but hell, *I* like her."

"Yeah," Jimmy said slyly, "she is a good-looker."

"That's not what I meant," Jason protested. "Listen, people, she's lookin' to hire help for the grand opening. Charlie, you used to tend bar at the Hideout. Why don't you go ask for your old job back?"

"I'm not sure I want it."

"You'll want it when the Hideout's a big success and somebody else has that job," Jason predicted. "You, Courtney, you used to wait tables at the pizza parlor. You could make a lot more at the Hideout."

Courtney sniffed. "I was among friends at the pizza parlor. Who *knows* who I'd be among at the Hideout?"

"Yeah, and what's it to you?" Jimmy demanded. "That Queen Bee bought the place right out from under you. Whaddaya want to help her for? If she goes under, you can pick up the place for a song."

"That does it!" Jason grabbed his hat off his head, slapped it against his thigh and put it back on. There was no talking to these people. "If you want to be responsible for driving her out of business before she even opens, I don't guess there's much I can do about it, but I damn sure won't be a party to this. She's down there now, working her bu—working her fingers to the bone to bring back the best meeting place Cupid ever had. And what're you all doing? Standing around criticizing her because she doesn't fall all over you." He paused for breath, belatedly aware that everybody was staring at him, even people who hadn't been part of the original discussion. Well, let 'em. "If you've got a conscience," he growled, "let it be your guide!"

He turned and jumped five feet off the loading dock to the graveled parking lot and strode away, his movements revealing his annoyance. Jimmy turned to Charlie with a long, low whistle.

"Ol' Jason's smitten," Jimmy said. "Imagine that. Hey, Courtney, let me throw that chicken feed in the back of your truck and you run along and take it to your mama. Us men got things to talk about." He exchanged a significant glance with Charlie.

Courtney resisted. "But I wanna—"

"Man talk," Jimmy said cheerfully, not in the least bit concerned with the political incorrectness of that remark. "Trust me, I'm thinkin' of Cupid's future."

DIANA DIDN'T KNOW what turned the tide, but all of a sudden, everything started to fall into place. She supposed that to be mostly the result of perseverance—her own.

Out of the clear blue, Dwight agreed to handle repairs and renovations; a man named Charlie Gilroy asked for his old job back as head bartender and offered to recruit other former employees; Courtney Lewis and several of her girlfriends came in asking for work as waitresses; Betsy Cameron recommended a couple of good short-order cooks.

Everything was coming up roses. Even Beau Turner, who'd already turned job offers down twice, sheepishly admitted he'd always wanted to be a bouncer and joined the team.

Time seemed to fly by after that. Jason was still dropping over more frequently than she'd like, but she was too busy to worry about it.

She and Ryan were settled more or less comfortably in the little cottage on Lover's Lane. The house was only a few blocks from the Hideout where they worked side by side from "can see to can't see," as Grandma Cameron put it.

Grandma and Ethan dropped in now and then and Diana was always delighted to see them. Somehow she'd developed an instant rapport with the old folks and was never too busy to spend a few minutes with them.

She'd bowed to reality and chosen her opening date—July 1—to coincide with the big Fourth of July street fair, again to benefit the elementary school. With a couple of days to get the operation organized, they'd be ready for the crowds expected for the holiday.

Liquor licenses, health inspections, employee training, ordering supplies, finding a suitable band— all was accomplished by June 30. Diana could hardly believe it. For so long it had seemed as if this day would never arrive, and now, here it was.

"Hey, Di!" Ryan stuck his head around the corner of the entryway. "Blair's invited me to the ranch for supper, and her aunt and uncle say it's okay, so I'm going."

Diana blinked out of her near trance composed of

equal parts anticipation and exhaustion. She felt almost light-headed at this stage of the game. "Betsy and Ben?"

"Yeah."

"Okay, have a good time. Mind your manners and don't be out too late."

"You got it."

"And Ryan?"

"Yeah?" His tone turned suspicious.

"Have a good time, sweetheart."

He gave her a startled smile and flipped her a quick salute before disappearing again. He'd been working so hard, and she knew she hadn't been giving him all the attention he needed and deserved. When things settled down...

If things settled down. But she was doing it for him as well as for herself. Moving behind the now gleaming bar, she filled a glass with ice cubes, added a shot of vodka from the array of bottles artistically arranged before the mirror and topped it off with tonic.

I'll celebrate, she decided. *One drink while I simply enjoy what I've accomplished.* Just a moment to savor all she'd achieved...

Walking to the center of the dance floor, she held out her glass as if in a toast. "Ladies and gentlemen," she began in a throaty, emotion-filled voice. She tried again, more calmly. "Ladies and gentlemen, they said it couldn't be done!"

She saluted the empty room, then took a sip of her drink before turning in a slow, dreamy circle.

They said it couldn't be done. See, Jason Cameron! I don't need you....

"Is this a private party," a husky voice inquired, "or can anyone join in?"

She wanted to groan. Jason Cameron, of course, as if conjured up by her imagination. She completed the circle until she faced him, standing just inside the entryway.

"Hi," she said, her voice slightly breathy.

He looked surprised. "Hi yourself." He didn't move, didn't approach her. His arms were behind his back as if he was hiding something. "Uhh...can I come in?"

"You are in," she pointed out.

"I mean..." He indicated the space between them.

"Sure."

He started forward, and sure enough, he had something behind him. It looked like some sort of low, flat cart. She frowned.

"What do you have there?"

"This?" He glanced back as if surprised to find it still there. "It's a buffalo cart."

"A what?" It was such a silly thing for him to say that she felt her mood lighten even more. "A buffalo pulls that thing?"

"No, a buffalo stands on that thing and *you* pull *him*. Julie said you were looking for a way to move Bill around. I thought—"

"Oh, Jason." She felt herself melting. "That's

the most thoughtful thing anyone's ever done for me."

He looked alarmed. "I seriously doubt that, but I'm glad you approve. I'm not sure the two of us can manage to get ol' Bill on this thing, but maybe tomorrow—"

"I'll put Beau in charge of moving buffaloes," she promised. "Did I say thank-you?"

"Not in so many words." Dropping the rope handle attached to the front of the cart, he crossed over to the jukebox next to the bandstand. Pulling a handful of change from his pocket, he glanced her way. "Mind if we have a little music? It's way too quiet in here."

She nodded, her attention on his broad back as he bent over the list of possible selections. He was a really well-built man, broad on the top and narrow on the bottom. She'd never seen him lose his cool or his temper. He knew exactly who he was and where he was going. God, how she envied him!

He'd reached her side before the music began, a slow country ballad that throbbed and moaned. He smiled.

"May I have this dance?"

Her gaze met his and clung. Breathlessly, she said, "Why don't you just have a drink with me and we'll sit this one out?"

"I don't drink much, in case you haven't noticed." He sounded suddenly serious. "Haven't since I got wiped out here at the Hideout one night a long time ago and ended up in a shotgun duel."

She laughed, saw he wasn't joking and said uncertainly, "Really?"

He nodded. "I thought you ought to know. Everybody else does. I didn't shoot anybody, but God knows I tried. He was a hoss thief, but even that couldn't keep me out of jail, among other trials and tribulations." His smile flashed sudden and warm. "I was a wild young fool in those days."

"But now you're older and wiser?" she finished the admission.

"God, I hope so." He held out a hand. "Dance with me, Diana."

"Oh, I don't—" His stormy gray eyes, deep as the sea, held her prisoner, causing her to change course abruptly. "See why not." She set her drink on the nearest table.

His smile drew her to him. "Just a little private celebration," he said against her hair. "I knew you could do it."

His praise sent a warming rush of pleasure through her. "Did you?" Her light, teasing voice sounded almost flirtatious and she sought to tamp down all the things she was feeling. "Sometimes I didn't know it myself."

"If that's true, you never let on."

He snugged his arms more closely around her and she let it happen, let him press her against him from shoulder to knee. Her hips fitted into the cradle of his; her thighs brushed against his. The unyielding wall of his chest pressing against her breasts sent little warning prickles racing through her. Entwined in each other's arms, they swayed to the music in perfect synchronization.

She couldn't seem to help dropping her head against his shoulder. "Maybe I'm not as tough as I seem," she murmured.

"Let's find out."

He stopped dancing but didn't release her. With one hand, he tilted her chin until her face angled beneath his. She stared back at him, nervously licking her lips while trying to dredge up some reason to resist.

None was forthcoming. She'd been feeling the warm glow of accomplishment when he'd appeared, right at the moment when she'd longed for someone with whom to share her triumph. *Oh, hell, tell the truth if only to yourself,* she thought with rash honesty. She wanted to share with Jason...wanted to share much more than triumph.

He seemed to know that. Leaning down, he brushed his mouth across hers. The jolt of that gentle contact made her gasp and stiffen in his arms, but not because she didn't like it—far, far from that. She liked it so much she didn't think she could stand it.

It had been *forever* since she'd been kissed, or at least it seemed that way. It felt so strange to be locked in a man's arms, but not unpleasant. Her breath came light and fast; his nearness overwhelmed but no longer intimidated her. Even when he caught her face between his hands, she didn't resist or even think about resisting.

For a moment, their gazes locked, his searching and hers, she supposed, helpless.

"Oh, hell," he said gruffly, "we're both dyin' to find out."

And this time, he *really* kissed her.

CHAPTER EIGHT

THE INVITATION IMPLICIT in her soft mouth jolted Jason into action. Coaxing her to yield, he teased the joining of her lips with his tongue. To his joyful astonishment, she opened to him with a sigh.

This was the way it was supposed to be, the way he'd sensed it could be the first time he saw her. So he was taking advantage of her unexpected vulnerability—so what? She should have realized from the beginning, as he had, that there was something between them that would have to break out sooner or later.

Okay, so it'd been later, but *later* was finally here. The minute he walked in dragging his little wooden platform, he'd known that this was the moment. Everything about her had been different, down to the air that crackled between them. For the first time, she'd been approachable...*hold*able.

He was not one to let an opportunity so eagerly awaited pass him by.

He'd been watching for his chance since the street fair, but she'd been as prickly as a cactus. He didn't know why he'd put up with it, didn't know why he kept coming back for more, unless it was the sheer challenge of her seeming indifference—which he'd never believed was genuine. But come back he had, again and again.

Tonight she was a different woman, responding to him the way he expected women to respond. There'd actually been something flirtatious in her manner, something vulnerable about the way she greeted him.

And danced with him.

He slipped his tongue into the sweet heat of her mouth and leaned into her. Still holding her face between his hands, he felt her arms slide around his waist. Her soft, almost inaudible moan electrified him, brought him to a state of instant arousal.

Nothing new there; he'd wanted her the minute he'd seen that silky red-gold hair, that stubborn jaw and challenging expression. But he'd only imagined what it could be like between them and he'd fallen far short of this reality.

She was like a flame in his arms, melting him, surrounding him, taking him into her mouth and promising much more. He knew what she was feeling because he felt the same thing. The oneness of that kiss, stretching on and on between them, sent shock waves right down to the soles of his cowboy boots.

At last he slid his mouth away, gasping for breath. Pressing little kisses on her cheek and up to her closed eyelids, he shuddered with the effort it took not to pick her up and carry her to the stairs in back, the stairs leading up to that dingy little apartment.

He drew his hands down, curving them to fit the

smoothness of her throat. With his thumbs, he explored the pulse thundering in the indentation at the base while he sought her lips again with his. This time, she surged to meet him.

Things might be moving a tad fast, he realized dimly, but it felt so right to touch the heat of her breast through the coolness of silk. He rubbed the nipple into tautness with his thumb, drawing a whimper from her. The sensual sound pushed him closer to the edge. Would this be—

"Diana! We had a flat tire and had to come—oops!"

Ryan's strident voice was the most unwelcome sound Jason could ever remember hearing, and that covered a lot of territory.

Diana leaped from his arms as if she'd been snakebit. For one glorious moment, she stood before him with wide, vulnerable eyes, a mouth softly swollen with his kisses, and her glorious hair a burnished tornado around her face and shoulders.

Then her eyes clouded over and her expression went blank. She straightened, reaching up with both hands to smooth back her tangled hair.

Why, he thought, she's embarrassed! She'd been married to the kid's dad and she's embarrassed to be caught like this.

Did Jason finally have a fix on this heretofore unfathomable woman? Hell, she was just shy. He could handle shy.

He'd *love* to handle shy.

DIANA WANTED TO DIE. Incredible as it was, she'd fallen into Jason Cameron's hands like a ripe plum. And if that wasn't enough, Ryan had caught her groping and being groped like some oversexed high school kid.

Like Ryan and Blair, perhaps? Diana stifled a groan.

Jason was staring at her as if she'd gone mad, which actually, she pretty much had. Exchanging passionate kisses with a man she didn't trust was completely out of character for her. She tried to speak and had to clear her throat before she could force out the words. "What were you saying, Ryan?"

"Uhh..." He glanced at Blair, who'd entered just behind him. "Mr. Cameron got a flat just at the edge of town and we came back to get it fixed. He'll be by to pick us up in a couple of minutes."

"I see." She licked her lips, not daring to even glance at Jason. "Would you like a soft drink while you wait? Come on in and—"

"Nah," Ryan said quickly, "we'll wait on the front steps. Okay with you, Blair?"

"Sure, fine." She cocked her head and looked at Diana, then Jason. A knowing smile hovered at the edges of her lips.

"All right." Frantically, Diana cast about for an explanation. "About what you saw—"

"I didn't see a damned thing," Ryan exploded. "Come on, Blair." Grabbing her shoulders, he pushed her out ahead of him. The door slammed behind them.

Jason caught Diana's hand in his as if he now had the right. "Don't worry about what they saw," he advised. "They know the facts of life."

"I don't mind their knowing as much as I mind giving them ideas of their own," she snapped, yanking her hand away. "I don't know what the hell got into me, but it'll never happen again, I promise you that."

"Never say never."

He caught her by the elbows, gave a slight tug and somehow propelled her right back into his arms. How did he do things like that? she wondered with irritation. Must be through long practice.

This time, she wasn't buying it. She stepped away. "That was a mistake," she said, glaring at him. "I'm not interested in any kind of relationship with you."

"Relationship. That covers a lot of territory."

"I'm including them all."

"Even friendship?"

She gave a short, impatient laugh. "Are you saying that's what you want?"

"For starters."

He looked surprised he'd said that. He didn't strike her as the kind of man who wanted a woman's *friendship*.

"Do you always go around grabbing your friends and k-kissing them? I thought that was reserved for strangers."

"Hey, I apologized for that!"

He gave her his charming little smile, and she was charmed all right—until she realized what he was doing to her. "Look," she said impatiently, "I appreciate all you've done..."

"Like what?"

"You know, like—like the buffalo cart to move Bill, and the food you brought when we first got here."

"Oh, that." He shrugged. "It was nothing."

"Then I'll forget it," she said sharply. "What I'm trying to say here is, I don't intend to get involved with you or anyone else."

"Too late." His smile disappeared as if it had never been. "We're already involved whether you like it or not. That kiss—"

"Was a mistake! Don't you hear what I'm saying?" Frustrated with her inability to make him understand, she clenched her hands into fists at her sides.

"I hear. I even think you believe it, but I don't. That kiss makes a liar of you, lady."

"The hell it does! You surprised me, that's all. That and the fact you're just too good at what you do." *Don't yell,* she cautioned herself. *Don't let him make you lose control. That's what he wants.*

The grin came back, creating fascinating creases at the corners of his mouth. "Yeah, I am," he agreed immodestly, "and I'm gratified you could tell by one little ol' kiss—two if you count the one

I paid five bucks for. But I'm here to tell you that you ain't seen nothin' yet.''

Sticking his hands into his jeans pockets, he leaned forward to place a chaste peck on her forehead before she could recoil beyond his reach. Then he sauntered out of the Hideout, leaving one very confused, very angry, very...*aroused* woman behind him.

RYAN AND BLAIR SAT CLOSE together on the top step at the Hideout, their thighs touching. Night had fallen but a streetlamp provided illumination—too much illumination, in Ryan's opinion. Nevertheless, he was just about to slip an arm around her waist when Jason stepped through the front door and paused to suck in a deep breath.

Ryan observed the newcomer in stony silence. He hadn't liked Jason Cameron before—hell, he watched Blair like a hawk, all the Camerons did—but Ryan liked the guy even less now. Finding him slobbering over Diana had been a helluva shock.

''So are you kids waiting for Ben to pick you up?'' Jason sounded amused.

Ryan didn't reply.

''Yeah,'' Blair said. ''Where you goin', Jason?''

''Home. Tomorrow's a big day.''

''What big day?''

Jason leaned down and ruffled her hair. ''Grand opening of the Hideout, what else? The whole town's gonna be here.''

She yanked her head aside. ''Yeah,'' she said

darkly, "or you'll know the reason why, right, Jason? I hear you're really leaning on people to make sure there's a good turnout."

"Why, Blair Britton, whatever are you talking about?" he asked in a light, teasing tone. "I'm just suggesting that everybody will have a real good time if they come and a real rotten time if they don't. It's up to them."

They watched him walk down the steps and climb into his pickup truck. He was whistling when he drove away.

"I don't like that guy," Ryan burst out. "He's too damned cocky, if you ask me."

"He's cocky all right." Surprised by his outburst, Blair glanced at him. "He's a good guy, though. Really he is. He just doesn't take anything too serious, you know?"

"Meaning Diana."

Blair shrugged. "I suppose—well, sure. He's not serious about her. He's never serious about any of them. He's just after a quick roll in the hay...and maybe the Hideout."

That last possibility startled Ryan. "You think he still wants this place?"

"Why wouldn't he? Nobody really thinks Diana can make a go of it. If she doesn't, she'll have to sell it to *somebody*."

Ryan frowned. "But he's helping her, trying to get people to come to the opening and all. Why would he do that if..." His eyes widened with understanding. "I get it. Nobody will be able to point a finger at him if the place bombs. And it probably will if he stops pushing it like he's been doing."

"Does Diana know?"

Blair was the prettiest girl Ryan knew and she looked even prettier with her face partially in shadow. He took her hand in his and she let him, although she allowed very little physical contact. Sometimes he wondered if she was...well, if she was frigid.

"Does Diana know he's helping her?" she asked again, more sharply this time.

"She doesn't have a clue." Which reminded him that she *really* didn't have a clue if she'd fall for that cowboy con artist's line of bullshit. He pressed Blair's acquiescent hand against his cheek. "Jeez, has she lost her marbles or what?"

"You know her better than I do. You tell me."

Her fingers curved beneath his hand and she stroked his cheek. He almost jumped off the step in reaction. "Hell—" He was having a hard time catching his breath. "Since my father died, she hasn't even looked at another man."

"She's not all that old, Ryan." Blair withdrew her hand and slipped it between her bent denim-covered knees. "She was bound to look at another guy sooner or later."

He felt bereft without her touch. "I suppose so."

"And Jason really is hot. I mean hot! And charming. Grandma says when he gets going, he can charm the spots off a pinto pony."

Ryan's head drooped. "I just don't see it," he

said plaintively. "I've never known Diana to go stupid before." She'd always been so levelheaded. He depended on that; she'd been his rock when his father died. Was she going to let him down now, over some dumb cowboy?

"You really love her, don't you?"

Blair touched his leg and again he jumped as if she'd done it with a branding iron instead of one soft little hand. "She's my stepmom," he said in a gravelly voice. He stared down at Blair's fingers, pale against dark denim. What would she do if he...

She squeezed his knee and withdrew her hand. "You love her," she said as if that settled it. "I like her, too. I'd hate to see him hurt her."

"Him?" Ryan was still thinking about that hand and missing it.

"Jason, who else?" She laughed at him, then stood up. "I think I see Uncle Ben coming."

Ryan rose to stand beside her, managing to brush his hand across the sweet swell of her backside. She moved away, not hurriedly, not as if she'd even noticed.

She peered at him through the shadows. "It would be a disaster if they got together," she said. "He'd break her heart."

Ryan, mesmerized by the outline of her lips, nodded. "We should do something," he agreed. "But what?"

DIANA FINALLY CLOSED UP the Hideout and went home to her rented cottage, but she hated to do it.

With so much riding on tomorrow, she could hardly bear to admit there was nothing more she could do.

Once inside the house, she made a pot of decaf and settled down before the cold fireplace, trying to calm herself. She'd done all she could do; she had. Going through the list of problems solved, she knew she had no reason to reproach herself.

It took a while to admit she wasn't worried about the Hideout at all. That was out of her hands in a sense. The grand opening would happen; it was inevitable.

Was a closer relationship with Jason Cameron equally inevitable?

Oh, God, why had that thought popped into her mind? She leaped from her chair and began to pace.

He had kissed her and she had let him.

No, she'd kissed him back. She had never tasted a kiss of such sweet passion before, not even from her husband. Paul had been like her, controlled and self-possessed. Nothing so unbridled had ever passed between them.

Eric hadn't even known the meaning of self-control, and caught by his charm, she'd forgotten, too. In another time, what he'd done to her would have been called "seduced and abandoned." After Eric, Paul had been the answer to her prayers.

She'd never expected to meet another man as charming as Eric—certainly hadn't wanted to. But she had, heaven help her, she had. And his name was Jason Cameron.

Dropping onto the sofa, she let out a despairing

moan at her own inability to face facts. Jason did exactly what he wanted, when he wanted, and he charmed others into going along with him. It would be up to her to stand her ground.

Well, she would—starting July 2. She had to get through the grand opening before rocking any boats. That shouldn't be so difficult; she'd be too busy for him to cause her any problems of a personal sort.

That was the answer, then. After tomorrow, he'd either play by her rules or she'd—she'd ban him from the Hideout for life. That implausible solution brought a smile to her face.

The front door opened and Ryan walked in. When he saw her, he stopped short. "What's the matter?" he asked.

"Nothing. Well, maybe I'm a little nervous."

"About Jason," he supplied, the corners of his mouth curving down.

She caught her breath in surprise. "Certainly not. About the grand opening tomorrow. This is it, Ryan—the big one. This is what we've been working for."

"Yeah. It's just that I thought…"

She waited for him to go on. He didn't, just looked uncomfortable. It was up to her.

"About what you saw…"

He turned toward her, his expression watchful. Guarded…wary…

Diana managed a weak smile. "Jason got carried away, that's all. You know how he is."

"I sure do." Too flat and hard for a boy's tone. "Do you?"

"What's that supposed to mean?"

"You're out of your class, Diana." Suddenly, the little boy was back. He dropped to his knees before her and covered her hands with his. "He's gonna make a fool of you."

"Not if I won't let him."

He scowled. "Famous last words. Just remember, after September, I won't be around to protect you."

His words pierced her to the heart: her little boy, the one she'd taken on when he was ten and she twenty-two, trying now to protect her. Tears, sudden and unexpected, sprang to her eyes and she willed them away.

"Ryan, thank you. Thank you for wanting to take care of me, but you don't need to worry." Leaning forward, she kissed his forehead. "I love you," she said, knowing she didn't tell him that often enough. "I also respect the young man you've become. But you needn't worry about me. I know how to handle Jason."

He looked unconvinced. "Blair says nobody knows how to handle Jason. She says—"

"He's her uncle," Diana pointed out. "She also happens to adore him. Speaking of Blair, how are the two of you getting along?"

"Okay." A very noncommittal answer. A shutter closed off all expression.

"You'll be careful, won't you, Ryan? Use good judgment...?"

A hot flush swept over his cheeks. "I don't need you to tell me about the birds and the bees," he said, standing up. "Blair's a real cold fish *that* way. Kind of reminds me of— Never mind. We're just friends, that's all."

Diana watched him go, realizing that he had been about to compare cold-fish Blair—thank you, God!—with cold-fish Diana. Or maybe that was *former* cold-fish Diana.

If Diana could fool her nearest and dearest into believing such a ridiculous and untrue thing, what about Blair?

Maybe at the age of eighteen, the girl didn't know herself. Just don't let Ryan be the one to teach her, Diana prayed silently.

CHAPTER NINE

GRANDMA CAMERON LOOKED at Jason with pity, her hands on her hips and a gleam in her gray eyes. "Boy, you look nervous as a cat in a roomful of rocking chairs," she announced.

"Huh?" Jason started, realizing only belatedly that she was talking to him. He turned toward her, away from the window next to the huge stone fireplace in the living room of the Straight Arrow Ranch.

"I said, you're a nervous wreck. You'd think you was the one responsible for what happens today at the Hideout."

He cast her an oblique glance, wondering how much she knew, deciding she was only guessing. "Not me," he said. "That's all up to Diana. Hard as she's been working, I expect everything will turn out fine."

"Especially since you been personally twistin' arms to get folks there," Granny said shrewdly. "Now, don't jump at me, boy. I like Diana. She's a nice girl and I want her to succeed. I'm not sure everybody feels the same way, though."

His antenna pricked up. "What's that supposed to mean exactly?"

"Just that not everybody's all that crazy about the girl. Like Dwight..." Again a knowing glance. "Busy as he is, lots of folks sure was surprised when he decided to do that work for her."

"Guess he had more time than he thought at first," Jason suggested, all innocence. He added more sharply, "But what do you mean, not everybody's crazy about her?"

"She's rubbed some folks the wrong way. There's some that think she's kinda standoffish. Stuck up—a Queen Bee, I heard somebody say."

Jason flexed his fists, outraged on Diana's behalf. What was the matter with these people? Maybe all those women's libbers were right. Maybe people really were threatened by a strong woman. Maybe his friends and neighbors weren't as good at judging character as he'd thought.

The whole bunch of them had just plummeted in his esteem. "They got her all wrong," he said. "Just because she doesn't throw her arms around everybody who drops by doesn't mean she's stuck up."

"Oh, I agree entirely." Granny crossed to the stairs leading up to the second floor of the ranch house. "I like her and so does..." Her eyes narrowed. After a deliberate pause, she added, "my gentleman friend."

"Now look here, Granny, are you still associating with Ethan Turner?" Jason had talked to her about that old reprobate after running into the two of them that day at the Hideout. Somehow he'd convinced himself that he'd gotten through to her. Now he realized he'd been fooling himself.

Granny laughed. "You think the town's got Diana wrong?" She threw the challenge in his teeth. "*I* think the town's got Ethan wrong, the town and most of the Camerons."

"If you think I'm going to stand by and let you—"

"When I want your opinion, I'll ask for it." She stopped him by dint of long practice. "Now if you'll stand aside, I gotta find out when Betsy and Ben will be ready to go into town."

Jason crossed to the hat rack near the door and plucked his Stetson from it. "I'm goin' on into town," he announced.

"Take Blair with you," Granny called after him. "She's in a big hurry to get there for some reason. I told her—"

Jason slammed the door, cutting off the rest of her command. Sure, he'd take Blair with him. What he couldn't take was his grandmother making a fool of herself in front of the entire town.

THE STRAIGHT ARROW RANCH lay north of Cupid, at the end of five miles of paved two-lane road followed by another seven of narrow, winding dirt road. A side road only a couple of miles from the Straight Arrow ranch house led to the Turners' broken-down Lazy T. It occurred to Jason that such proximity was perhaps not a good thing.

Blair gave him a glance filled with curiosity.

"What's *your* problem?" she asked with her usual bluntness. "You look like you're already in a bad mood and the day's hardly started."

"So who are you—Little Mary Sunshine?"

She laughed, placed an index finger to her chin and bobbed an exaggerated nod in his direction. "That's me," she agreed cheerfully, "and I see straight through you. You're mad because somebody else is opening up the Hideout today instead of you."

"Where'd you get a crazy idea like that?" Hell, Diana was doing a better job getting that saloon up and running than he ever could have. Sure, he'd wanted to give it a try, but after his initial disappointment, he'd quickly realized he'd trade that rundown old saloon for Diana's presence in his life any day.

"Everybody says so," Blair announced. "What I want to know is, are you putting the moves on her to get her to sell out to you, or do you really like her?"

"Oh, for..." Annoyed, Jason jerked the pickup onto the paved highway and glared at his niece. "What kind of jerk do you think I am? I don't use women that way."

"No?" She looked unconvinced. "I hope that's true because I really like her. She's...different. Not so boy-howdy-backslappin'-two-steppin' country."

"I thought you'd overcome that superiority complex you had when your big-city daddy married Maggie."

"That wasn't superiority, it was reality." She sighed. "You gotta admit, this is all kind of cornball." She changed subject with the speed of light. "Did I tell you my friend Libby and her family are going to Europe this summer?"

"Which has to do with what?"

"They invited me to go with them."

"And your pa said no."

"My pa always says no."

"Yeah." Jason laughed out loud. "I remember when you threatened to kill yourself or something if he didn't let you go to school in Switzerland. You can act like a real spoiled brat sometimes, kid."

She frowned, then brightened. "Thanks for calling it acting. There are those who believe it's the real me. It does piss me off, though. He never lets me do anything."

"Yeah, yeah, I've heard all this before. Bring on the violins."

"Jason, you're a jerk." She said it kinda friendly.

"I'm surprised you'd even want to go away, thick as you and Ryan Kennedy are getting."

"Thick? We're not *thick*." She gave him a disdainful glance. "We're friends. In the fall, I'm going off to CU and he's going off to the University of Texas. We'll probably never see each other again."

"You guys don't plan to have vacations or come back during the summers?"

She shook her head emphatically. "He's not. He hates it here. If Diana doesn't move back to Texas, he's staying there without her. He said he'd go to school year-round, work summers if he had to, but he's not coming back here.''

"No wonder you like him," Jason observed. "He's as pigheaded as you are."

"Sticks and stones... But if he had his way, Diana would sell tomorrow and the two of them would cut out of here never to be heard from again. He is *not* a happy camper.''

"In that case, it's even more important for you to keep..." How to say it? *Keep your legs closed and keep your clothes on?* He finished with a lame, "keep your wits about you."

"Oh, Jason!" She shook her head pityingly. "My generation knows all about sex, so you don't have to tippytoe around. You don't want me to have sex with *anybody*. All so-called adults take that attitude. 'Don't do as I do, do as I say!' Who's going to respect that?''

"Ryan better respect it," Jason said grimly, "or be prepared to have the holy hell beat out of him— which is the least I'd do for any niece of mine."

"Get a life." She rolled her eyes.

"I mean it. You've been warned."

"If Dad would just let me go to Europe with Libby, this conversation wouldn't be necessary."

"Manipulation, thy name is Blair." He pulled into the parking lot of Betsy's Rusty Spur at the north end of town. "So where you headed?"

She shrugged. "Here's fine. Don't worry about me. I'll hang around with the kids and meet the family at the Hideout at six, okay?''

"Okay," he agreed, perfectly willing to overlook the underlying seriousness of that last exchange. Hell, Blair was only eighteen, a little girl.

Of course, Jason had known a few hot-to-trot eighteen-year-olds when he'd been one himself....

ALL THE CAMERONS congregated at the Hideout by prearrangement at or near six o'clock. It took three of the small circular tables ringing the dance floor to accommodate them.

Almost all of them were there: Betsy and Ben and their three youngsters, Maggie and Chase with their toddler and teen, Julie and Max and Jason, who'd fought to keep from arriving earlier—he didn't want Diana to feel *too* sure of him.

Julie looked around the adjoining tables with a sharp glance. "Where's Grandma?"

"She asked us to drop her off at the hardware store," Betsy said. "I think she wanted to buy some new cup hooks. She said she'd walk on down after she got what she needed." She paused for a careful perusal of the room. "Doesn't this place look wonderful? Diana's done a great job."

Ben darted a pointed glance at his brother. "With a little help from her friends."

Julie smiled and nodded to an acquaintance across the room. "This is a nice turnout. Standing room only."

Ben's mouth quirked with amusement. "Yeah, it is. Wonder why?"

At that moment, Diana appeared. Despite the bor-

derline chaos around her, she looked cool and un-
ruffled. Jason stared at her, entranced. She wore a
navy blue skirt, perfectly plain and beautifully fitted,
and a soft white blouse with V neck and long, bil-
lowing sleeves. She really *does* look like a queen,
he thought. What a woman. Calm in the midst of
confusion, looking like royalty despite the long
hours of work and worry. Regardless of what the
rest of this town thought, Jason was *impressed*.

She smiled. "Hello, Camerons. Welcome to the
new Hideout. Has anyone taken your order?"

"Not yet," Julie said, "but we're in no hurry. My
goodness, you've done a great job here."

"Thank you."

Ben, one eyebrow lifting, glanced at Jason again
but fortunately did not add, *With a little help from
your friends.*

Diana went on in the same pleasant if impersonal
tone. "We're offering a limited menu tonight, since
we're just starting out as a team. Hamburgers and
French fries—a specialty."

Blair laughed. "French fries—yes!"

Thirteen-year-old Joey nodded enthusiastically.
"And a hamburger. Lisa Marie wants one, too.
Right, Lisa?"

Ben said, "Make mine well-done and Betsy's medium. Jason will want medium."

"Cosmo likes his rare," Julie offered, "and I'll
pass."

"Cholesterol," Max inserted. "Life's a bitch—"

"And then you die," Betsy finished his sentence

for him. "Grandma will be along in a minute and she likes hers well-done. Drinks. Let's see, the kids and Grandma like lemonade, white wine for me..."

Diana's eyes had glazed over. "Let me get you a waitress," she offered, glancing around. "Courtney, are you free?"

Courtney Lewis, who'd been streaking past, skidded to a halt in her high-heeled cowboy boots. All the wait staff wore jeans and colorful shirts and boots, some with hats to top off the cowboy look. "Hi, all," she said with a big smile. "Did you ever see such a mob? I can take your order, but don't hold your breath 'til you get your food. They are seriously backed up in the kitchen."

Diana frowned. "Please, Courtney, that's our problem, not our customers'." Again that coolly impersonal smile. "If you'll excuse me, I need to—"

A surprised buzz interrupted her, and she, along with all the Camerons and the loquacious waitress, turned toward the source of the sound. Around the walled-off entryway came the couple who had occasioned such shock.

And no wonder: it was Etta May Cameron and Ethan Turner, arm in arm.

"WHAT IN THE HELL!" Ben Cameron half rose from his seat at the table. His gray eyes narrowed dangerously.

Diana recoiled from the venom in his voice. The elder Cameron brother was obviously not a man with whom to trifle. Nor was the younger Cameron brother, who grabbed Ben's arm and yanked him back into his seat.

"Lighten up," Jason said in a low but commanding voice. "You don't want to air the family laundry in public, do you?"

Fresh tension tightened Diana's shoulders. As if she didn't have enough trouble, it looked as if the Camerons were ready to hit the warpath over Granny's choice of escorts.

There they all sat, taking up three of her best tables: big, good-looking men, pretty women and handsome children. Their very togetherness overwhelmed her. They seemed to read each other's minds, know each other's thoughts and intentions before a word was spoken.

More than a little scary and threatening to an only child of remote parents. She strove for a reassuring smile.

To no avail. The surprised buzz followed Etta May and Ethan as they approached the gathering of Camerons. Granny's smile was steely. "Got room for two more?" she asked in a tone that didn't betray so much as a note of embarrassment.

"We got room for one more," Ben said, his tone matching hers.

"Two." Blair jumped up and pushed her chair forward. "Mom, I want to talk to Ryan. Is he around, Diana?"

"In the kitchen moving supplies, the last I saw."

"Is it all right for me to go on in?"

"It is with me." Diana glanced at the girl's parents for confirmation.

Maggie nodded. Fortyish and the oldest of the Cameron siblings, she had a no-nonsense manner that Diana liked. A few strands of white marked her black hair, but her face was unlined. Her eyes, a velvet brown, revealed a lively intelligence.

"Don't get in the way," she called after the departing Blair. She patted the empty chair. "Sit here, Mr. Turner. We're glad to see you."

Ben let out an annoyed grunt but said nothing more. Knowing how Jason felt on this subject, Diana waited for him to add his two cents' worth but he didn't, just watched Ben as if expecting fireworks.

Max, who'd also been observing, leaned forward. His smile revealed a genuine fondness for the old gentleman. "I hear you got some new cows out at the Lazy T," he said. "How many head you running now, Ethan?".

"Oh, about—"

"Folks, I'm real busy here, so if you'd like to order, you got one chance and this is it." Courtney's plaintive voice cut across the chatter.

A murmur of apologies greeted her pronouncement, and once again, Betsy began to run through the order. Smiling when she felt like screaming, Diana edged away.

But not fast enough. Jason rose, almost at her side.

"Everything looks great, Diana."

"Thank you. If that's all..."

"It's not." His smile didn't waver. "When I came in, I noticed Buffalo Bill wasn't in his usual place of honor. Is he all right?"

That brought a genuine smile to her lips. "How could a stuffed buffalo not be all right? Not much chance he'd walk away."

"True." His gray eyes smiled at her even when his mouth was serious—his sensuous, sexy mouth.

She cleared her throat self-consciously. "Beau and some of the others got him up on that cart you built. He's hidden in the back, to be brought out during the ceremony." She grimaced. "I didn't want to, but Courtney and Beau and the others insisted I should say *something*."

"They're right."

"Yes, well, I'll do my best, but it's not the sort of thing I enjoy." Even as she grimaced, she knew it was exactly the sort of thing *he* enjoyed.

"You'll do great." He sounded absolutely certain.

"I'll settle for barely adequate." She should go on about her business, which seemed mostly to be circulating and handling crises. She didn't have time to stand next to him, shifting her feet and twiddling her thumbs like a kid.

"Is there anything—"

"Don't even say it." But she gave him a smile, surprising herself even more by reaching out to touch his forearm lightly. "When this is all over, Jason..."

"Yes?" A spark of expectation leaped into his dark eyes.

"We need to talk. There are a few things—"

"Yeah, there are. Just say when."

He sat back down and was instantly distracted by Julie, who leaned forward to say something. Diana turned away with a vague feeling that something had been lost in the translation. Something important...

SHE WANTED TO TALK TO HIM. That had to be good.

Jason smiled, nodded, answered questions, even argued, but his mind was definitely not on his rowdy family or the rowdy friends and neighbors swirling around him. And he thought about that kiss they'd shared just over there in the middle of a now crowded dance floor.

She'd felt so right in his arms, her slender strength somehow more than a match for his eagerness. He'd dreamed about that kiss, dreamed about where it might have led if the kids hadn't come in at the exact wrong instant.

Idiot, he derided himself. It wouldn't have led anywhere. She's not the kind of woman who jumps into bed the first time a man puts the moves on her. It will take time. *I'll have to woo her, court her...win her.*

He could hardly wait to get started.

"GOOD EVENING, EVERYBODY. My name is Diana Kennedy and I'm the new owner of the Hideout, for anyone I haven't had the pleasure of meeting yet."

At the sound of her amplified voice, the crowd split, shifted, moved off the dance floor. She took a deep breath and stepped down from the bandstand, accompanied by a drumroll. She darted the drummer a slightly confused smile of thanks.

She was incredibly nervous. Maybe no one else realized it, but it came through to Jason as loud and clear as if she'd shouted it.

But hell, she was doing a great job. He felt himself beaming like an idiot and tried to tone down his approving smile. He thought he'd succeeded until Ben glanced his way and let out a guffaw.

Diana continued, "Thank you all for coming here tonight to help me celebrate the realization of a dream. I hope that the Hideout will become what it was before, a favorite community hangout. I'll do everything I can to make that happen, so if you have any ideas or suggestions, I'd like to hear from you."

Jason led the applause. She waited until it had died down before going on.

"Now I'd like to present the mascot of the Hideout before we place him in his new spot of honor on the bandstand. Beau..." She turned, making a graceful gesture with one arm. The silky white fabric of her full sleeve fluttered gently.

From around the edge of the bandstand emerged Beau Turner, his hands on Buffalo Bill's rump for pushing purposes. Bill looked almost majestic on Jason's wheeled cart, which someone had painted red. The crowd burst into laughter, followed by more enthusiastic applause.

Jason wondered if anybody else was wondering, as he was, what she saw in that moth-eaten old relic. The delighted expression on her face left no doubt as to her feelings. For some reason, that critter meant a lot to her. A whole lot.

Damn, he itched to jump up and stand beside her and show his approval and support, for what it was worth. He could hardly keep himself in his seat.

When the crowd quieted, she went on, "I want to thank Jason Cameron for building the platform Bill's on, and my son, Ryan, and Blair Britton for decorating it. I want to thank—"

"Jason! Jason! Speech, speech, speech!"

Damned bachelor herd again, over by the bar making fools of themselves. But they'd given Jason the opening he needed. Leaping to his feet, he bowed right, then left. But instead of sitting back down, he crossed the dance floor to stand in front of Diana.

Who looked up at him in obvious confusion. Swallowing hard, she lifted the microphone to her mouth and began again, her glance holding a degree of warning. "I want to thank them—thank you, Jason—and I want to thank all of you, too, for coming here tonight to celebrate my grand opening. Thank you. Thank you all."

Jason's heart was just about busting with pride. She was wonderful and she was doing a wonderful job. He wanted her to know how great he thought she really was.

And in a sudden flash of intuition, he realized he

also wanted everyone to know that he was putting his claim on this beautiful woman. She might not be his now, but she would be.

In a rush of heady emotion fueled by pride and possessiveness, he caught her by her elbows and almost lifted her off the floor. "You're welcome," he said, and kissed her.

CHAPTER TEN

DIANA COULDN'T BELIEVE Jason was doing this to her—again! This man seemed to think he could grab her and kiss her anytime he wanted, public or private.

Nerves already stretched to the breaking point, Diana suffered his kiss because she had no choice.

He set her back on her feet and grinned as if he'd just done her an enormous favor. She struggled to maintain her dignity in the face of this totally unprovoked assault. What was he trying to prove, that his fabled charm had not deserted him?

His confident voice rattled what little composure she had left. "Let's all give the lady a great big hand for—"

"No," she said quickly, "let *me* give *you* a great big hand."

She lashed out as hard as she could with her right hand, catching him square across the jaw. If it stung him as much as it did her, the slap was successful.

She'd gone too far, she realized in the instant hush that fell over the crowded room. Jason was a big favorite of these people, most of whom he'd known all his life. She, on the other hand, was an interloper—practically a foreigner with her city ways and her reserved manner.

Now they would hate her for sure. On this, which should have been her big night, she'd lost control and ruined everything.

She stared at Jason, appalled at what she'd done. She'd hit him with all her strength and she could see the imprint of her hand burning a dark impression on his cheek and jaw. He'd be angry; this would be the end of his pursuit of her. This would probably be the end of *her* in this town. She braced herself for his retaliation, which was bound to come in angry words.

But he didn't look angry; he looked...bemused, as if he couldn't quite believe what had happened to him. Slowly and deliberately, he rubbed his jaw, never taking his attention off her.

His smile was completely unexpected. "I still say we need to give a big hand to the lady for all she's doin' for the fine town of Cupid, Colorado," he announced. "Folks?"

He began to clap with a deliberate cadence. Slowly, the audience joined in until the room rocked with the sound. Pulling herself together with a Herculean effort, Diana forced herself to smile at Jason, at the rest of the Camerons sitting nearby with a variety of disbelieving expressions on their faces, at the rest of the people crowded into the room.

When the sound died away, she said in a rush, "We'll be cutting the cake—"

"Don't let old Jason scare you away," a male

voice shouted from deep in the cluster of men around the bar. "You handled him just right. Hell, we can't afford to lose any more good-lookin' women around here."

Raucous laughter greeted this announcement, and Diana felt her cheeks burn. "Jason won't scare me away," she said with much more confidence than she felt. "I know how to handle him and a dozen more like him."

"Ain't no more like him. Praise the Lord!"

She joined in the general laughter, waiting until everyone had calmed down before going on more securely. "Why would I ever want to leave?" she asked rhetorically. "I've got everything I ever wanted here, including my own buffalo!" She stepped to Bill's side and draped an arm over his shaggy, moth-eaten neck. "Be sure to drop by to pay your respects to Buffalo Bill, everybody. As long as he's here, I'll be here, too."

Turning, she gestured toward Ryan, Blair and a couple of waiters hovering at the back of the room with their hands on a cart containing an enormous decorated sheet cake. "Now please join us in a piece of cake. Betsy Cameron baked it, so I know you won't want to miss out. Thank you again for coming and please come again."

With the cake the center of attention, Diana tried to melt into the background. Unfortunately, Jason was there, smiling at her, taking her elbow, speaking to her out of the corner of his mouth so no one else could hear.

"I'm gonna give this place the Cameron stamp of approval if it kills me," he muttered. "Now smile like you mean it and we'll duke it out later."

Suddenly aware that all the Camerons were watching, she did indeed smile at him like she meant it. Then again, maybe she did....

RYAN AND BLAIR SAT side by side on the back steps, paper napkins protecting their clothing from big slices of Betsy's cake. The girl used a forefinger to gouge a ditch through the chocolate frosting, which she then lifted to her mouth.

"Ummm." She looked to Ryan for agreement. "This is great. Wasn't it cute the way Betsy drew a picture of a buffalo in chocolate frosting?"

"Cute?" He rolled his eyes. "I'd have preferred a giant pie to all that *cake*."

She made a face at him that crinkled her nose. Blair was the most gorgeous girl he'd ever known, not to mention the most egotistical and unpredictable.

"Enjoy the cake," she advised, tearing off a corner with her fingers. "This is probably going to be the most exciting thing that happens here all summer."

Ryan looked at her, aghast. "You're kidding!"

"Only a little."

She'd managed to smear a bit of icing on her face just beyond the corner of her mouth. He found himself staring at it, mesmerized.

She went on, "We do have the big Fourth of July

community fair in a couple of days. At least that'll be something different.''

"Will it be like the thing that was going on the day Diana and I came to town?"

She nodded. "Exactly. Little kids and old folks seem to love it, but about all kids our age have to do is hang around and eat junk.''

"Bor-ing," he said.

"Yeah." She sighed. "It's going to be a long summer with nothing to do.''

They exchanged significant glances.

"I wish it was time to leave for college," she said wistfully.

"Yeah. Once I go, I'm never coming back here." He offered her his piece of cake since she'd finished her own.

She took it without a word of thanks, as if it was her due. "I had a chance to go to Europe, but my father said no."

"Hell, if he'd said yes, what would I have done all by myself the whole summer?"

"Found somebody else to bitch to?" She laughed. "We're stagnating, Ryan. If I was in Paris, London, Rome…"

"If I was back home in Dallas…"

"If wishes were horses…"

"If we had any guts…"

They exchanged significant glances once again. Since the very beginning, Ryan had felt as if they understood each other more perfectly than any two people, especially virtual strangers, had a right to.

"We need to shake things up," he said.

She nodded. "But how?"

He yielded to temptation and reached out to remove the smudge of frosting from her cheek, feeling the shock of touching her course all the way through his fingers and hand, past his clenching throat and into a gut gone wild. "I can't think about that when you're making such a mess with that cake," he said gruffly. He transferred the creamy sweetness from her skin to his tongue.

She caught her breath, and her beautiful hazel eyes went wide. "Ohhh," she whispered. Her tongue darted out to moisten full pink lips. "*Sexy!* Did you ever see that old movie where the guy lights two cigarettes and gives the woman one? The first time I saw that, I wanted to take up smoking."

He leaned toward her, just the tiniest little bit. "Blair, I—"

The back door opened behind them and they swayed apart as if they'd been caught at something. Which maybe in another thirty seconds they would have, Ryan thought through a red fog of disappointment. Blair was like smoke, easily seen but never there when he reached for her.

Behind them, Beau said, "What you kids doin'?"

"Not a damned thing." Ryan knew he sounded surly, but that was fair. He *felt* surly. "What are *you* doing?"

Beau inched past them on the step. He puffed out his massive chest and said pompously, "I'm doin' my *job*. I'm the bouncer. I look out for troublemakers. Somebody heard talkin' out here and I come to investigate.''

"Good for you, Beau." Blair nodded her approval.

The big man beamed. "That's what Jason told me to do, a real good job." He frowned. "But after Queen Bee hauled off and boxed his ears that way, I don't know why he gives a hoot."

Ryan laughed. "Sure you do. You're a guy. You know what he's after."

"The Hideout?" Beau looked as if he was struggling to understand.

Again, Ryan and Blair exchanged glances. *She* knew what he was talking about because she thought he was after the same thing from her. Only he wasn't. He wasn't trying to use her, he was totally crazy about her.

Totally.

"Yeah," he said at last. "Jason's after the Hideout, I guess." He sighed. "Beau, what'd you do around here for fun when they roll up the sidewalks at ten o'clock most nights?"

"Roll up the sidewalks—that's a good one." Beau considered. "We got a video store. I like movies myself."

Ryan groaned. "We gotta think of something to shake up the status quo around here."

"Great idea," Beau agreed enthusiastically. "Uhh...what's a status quo?"

DIANA MANAGED to avoid Jason, but she sought out other members of the Cameron family, anxious lest they resent her treatment of one of their own.

She needn't have worried.

Grandma Cameron dealt with that issue first thing, effectively taking it off the table when she said in a voice that carried like a siren, "Here's the champ! You sure give that boy whatfer and he doggone well deserved it."

"About that…"

Ben laughed at Diana's discomfort. "Everybody here's taken a swing at ol' Jason at one time or another." His look turned knowing. "A'course, he swung back on most of us."

Maggie, holding her sleeping child on her lap, grinned at her brother. "And sometimes he swung first, didn't he, Ben? You boys used to scrap more than you got along." She added to Diana, "Don't give it another thought. We all thought it was hysterically funny."

"Thanks." But it wasn't funny to me.

"Hate to break up this party," Maggie said, shifting in her chair to get a better grip on little Dusty, "but I think we'd better be heading back to the ranch. Chase?"

"Sure." He looked around. "Anyone know what became of Blair?"

"She was with Ryan a few minutes ago," Julie said. "She's having a good time, Chase. Let her stay. Max and I will take her home with us."

Chase and Maggie exchanged glances that began with questions and ended with agreement without a word being said. Diana was constantly astounded by the level of silent—and noisy—communication among these people.

Chase stood up and moved to Maggie's side. "Okay, Julie, but tell her that her mother and I expect to spend a little time with her tomorrow before we head back to Aspen."

Julie nodded; a deal was struck.

Chase turned the power of his smile on Diana. A handsome and charismatic man in his early forties, he had dark hair with a distinguished graying at the temples, and the same beautiful hazel eyes he'd passed on to his daughter. He also had a sophistication far beyond that of his in-laws.

"Nice opening," he complimented Diana. "Someday we'll have to get together and talk shop."

"I'd like that. I understand you have a restaurant in Aspen?"

He took Dusty from his mother's arms and cradled the toddler against his chest with such loving strength that Diana felt a lump rise in her throat. Here was a man who truly loved his family.

Only when the child was secure did he answer her. "Yes, but I have a real soft spot for the Hideout. I fell in love with my wife here. She taught me line-dancing."

Diana had no idea why all the Camerons burst out laughing. Apparently, you had to have been there.

Grandma Cameron also stood up. "I think it's time us old folks run along, too."

"Want a ride?" Chase asked. "We've got plenty of room."

Grandma glanced at Ben. "No need. Ethan can run me by."

"Grandma!" Ben started to stand.

Betsy stilled him with one small hand on his forearm. "Sit down, Ben," she said in her soft voice, but this time there was steel behind it. "Please don't cause another scene. I'd say the Camerons had done quite enough of that already without you getting into the act."

"Dammit, Betsy!"

"Yes, dear," she said sweetly. "You run along, Grandma. Nice seeing you, Mr. Turner."

"Thank you kindly, Mrs. Cameron." The old gentleman made a slight bow, then took Grandma's arm in a courtly manner.

Diana wanted out of all this family drama. "I also thank you all kindly for coming," she said. "I hope you'll be back soon."

All except Jason. If she never saw him again, it would be too soon.

FOR A WHILE IT LOOKED as if she'd get her wish, at least for the rest of the evening. From time to time she'd notice Jason across the room, but he didn't approach her, nor she him. She was grateful when the evening began winding down, relieved when closing time finally arrived.

"We'll be able to leave in a few minutes," she told Ryan. "I'll worry about the details tomorrow."

"Mind if I go on home now?" He gave a prodigious yawn. "I'm beat. I'll see you in the morning."

She watched him leave, wondering what was really going on in his head. He'd been incredibly gracious so far the past two months, but she didn't know how much longer it would be before he lost interest in...

Blair. Whom was Diana kidding? Ryan mooned over the girl like a dog over a steak bone. She sighed. Young love...

"Night—night, Diana."

"Good night, Beau. You did a great job. Thanks so much."

Others were leaving, too, as they completed their part of the closing routines still so new to all of them. The cook paused.

"We ran out of ground beef," he said apologetically. "The hamburgers were going like hotcakes, forgive the comparison."

"We'll get more tomorrow. Thank you, Perry. Everyone raved about the food."

"We'll get better," he promised. "Night, Miz Kennedy."

She was alone. Mary and her helper would be in bright and early with plenty of time to clean up for a 5:00 p.m. opening.

She'd survived. She should be ecstatic.

Maybe she would have been if not for the antics of Jason Cameron. With a final pat for Buffalo Bill, she went outside, locked the door behind her and walked down the steps. The night was still, the sky starry and far away. She paused beside her minivan, parked beneath a streetlamp because she'd known she'd be the last to leave.

The crunch of gravel brought her swinging around in panic.

"It's only me, Diana."

Only me. Only Jason Cameron.

"You just scared me out of ten years' growth," she said, pressing one hand above her pounding heart. "Haven't you caused me enough grief for one night?"

In the dappled light of the streetlamp, she couldn't see his expression clearly, although she had no sense of anger or any other strong emotion.

His sigh sounded plaintive. "Seems like all I ever do is apologize to you."

"That's because you keep doing such unforgivable things to me." She yanked open the door to her minivan, then hesitated, halfway waiting for him to grab her again. Ready for him to try it. Just try it!

He didn't, so she climbed inside. He stepped forward between the door and her, preventing her from closing it in his face.

"Diana," he said, "you're giving out mixed signals here."

"I am perfectly consistent in the signals I send out."

He shook his head. "You're not. After we danced

last night, after I kissed you, I thought...well, I thought we'd reached some kind of understanding.''

"Understanding! Are you mad? I don't understand anything about you.''

"You understand that you're driving me crazy. You understand that I'm going nuts trying to please you. You sure as hell understand that I want you. Of course, you don't understand how much, but how could you?''

He said all that with such calm, as if merely stating the obvious. She stared at him, mouth agape, only belatedly finding the wit to exclaim, "I don't understand any of that. All I want from you is to be left alone. You can't keep grabbing me like some— like some caveman. I won't stand for it, do you hear me? *I won't stand for it!*''

She gave him a shove, grabbed the door and slammed it shut. Hands shaking so badly she could barely fit the key into the ignition, she finally managed to start the van and go roaring out of the graveled parking lot.

Damn him! A glance in the rearview mirror told her he still stood there, a solitary figure looking after her. Damn him for daring to suggest they'd reached "some kind of understanding.''

All she understood was the same old thing. This man was her worst nightmare—someone who saw right past the front she presented to the world and straight into her traitorous heart.

"Some kind of understanding''? God, yes!

DIANA FELL into bed exhausted and lay there for most of the night, replaying everything that had happened at the grand opening. Every little mishap floated past her closed eyes like sheep jumping over a fence: the tray of glasses dropped by a clumsy busboy, the salad tossed not in the bowl but in a customer's lap, the Camerons in all their intimidating glory, Jason...

Not Jason. She wouldn't think about him. She had to go to sleep.

At last she did, but it wasn't the deep, peaceful slumber she so desperately needed. She awakened well after nine the next morning, groggy and disoriented. Ryan had already gone out, leaving a note. Grabbing a quick shower, Diana didn't even take time to prepare coffee before rushing out to make the short drive to the Hideout.

She had as much to do today as she'd had yesterday and the day before that. How could she have overslept?

But the opening really had been grand, she assured herself. Unlocking the front door, she hurried inside. At least, most of it had been grand, up until the point—

She stopped short. Something wasn't right. The hair on the nape of her neck prickled.

Standing in the middle of the dance floor, she made a slow turn, trying to figure out what was wrong. The cleaning team had done a great job; everything practically sparkled. All the liquor bottles lined up in brilliant array before the bar mirror; tables and chairs were in their proper places; the band had cleared out without leaving anything behind…

Her gaze zeroed in on the spot on the bandstand where her buffalo should be standing…but wasn't.

CHAPTER ELEVEN

FOR THE NEXT forty-five minutes, Diana turned the Hideout upside down. With panic growing by the second, she enlisted the help of everyone who walked through the door in her search.

Which wasn't many, since they wouldn't be opening for business until 5:00 p.m. for the next couple of days. Starting on July 4 just in time for the next big community fair, the Hideout would open for business at 11:00 a.m., which would be normal summer hours.

Eventually, Ryan wandered in with Blair in tow and both kids joined in the hunt. For all the good it did.

Buffalo Bill was gone.

Ryan patted his stepmother on the shoulder. "Don't take it so hard," he counseled. "He's bound to show up soon. I mean, where do you hide a stuffed buffalo?"

"That's right," Blair jumped in. "It's probably just a joke anyway."

"A joke!" Diana fought to control her roller-coaster emotions. "When I get my hands on whoever did this...!"

Ryan and Blair looked properly impressed with her fury.

Charlie Gilroy, head bartender, who'd come in to make sure his bar was in tip-top shape, shook his head in disbelief. "I thought I'd seen it all," he said, "but I have never even heard of anybody stealin' a stuffed buffalo." He frowned. "Or a live one, either."

Diana gritted her teeth. "I want my buffalo back!" Somehow her entire future seemed to come down to that specific point: someone had stolen something very precious to her, something that had come to symbolize all the things she was trying to accomplish. She couldn't let them get away with it! "I'm going to report this theft to the marshal," she decided. "I'll be back as soon as I've done that."

Charlie looked dubious. "You think that's a real good idea? Why don't you give whoever pulled this stunt a chance to bring ol' Bill back without gettin' in trouble with the law?"

"They deserve to be in trouble with the law."

"Jeez!" Ryan exchanged disbelieving glances with Blair and then he said, "Mr. Gilroy's right. This isn't the end of the world. We're talking about a moldy old buffalo, not the crown jewels."

Diana couldn't believe the emotion choking her. It was almost as if Buffalo Bill had come to personify everything she was trying to do to salvage her life and that of her stepson. She was going to get that buffalo back no matter what it took.

"I couldn't disagree with you more," she said

curtly. "Whoever did this is going to pay for it and that's a promise."

Wheeling about, she stormed from the room. The three watched her go with expressions of mutual concern.

Charlie Gilroy let out a huff of disapproval. "That woman sure does like to do things her own way," he complained. "Can't she take a joke? If she's not careful, she's gonna make the thieves mad and then she'll never get that buffalo back." Still shaking his head, he went back to restocking the bar.

DIANA WALKED the few blocks to the marshal's office, needing the expenditure of energy and the soothing brilliance of the July sunshine to help her calm down. Past the feed-and-tack store on Main Street, she turned right on Third, then left on Aspen Avenue.

Town hall took up a good part of the block between Main, Third and Aspen. Next to it, fronting on Main Street, was a hardware store. The marshal's office and jail stood behind that, fronting on Aspen. The office and printing plant of the *Cupid Chronicles* took up the rest of the block all the way to Second Street. The newspaper, the jail and city hall shared a parking lot at Aspen and Second.

Throwing open the door, she stormed inside. Lorrie Anderson stood behind the counter.

"Hi there, Diana." Her sunny smile slipped. "My goodness, you look mad enough to hunt bears with a switch."

"I am." Diana jerked her chin toward the door marked Marshal. "Is Max in?"

"Not exactly. He's—hey, where do you think you're going? Let me—"

"Sorry." Diana brushed past the startled woman. "This is important." With a quick knock to announce her intentions, she barged inside. "Marshal Mackenzie, I'm here to report a crime."

The tall broad-shouldered man standing at an open file cabinet in the corner turned slowly, a broad smile curving his mouth. But it wasn't Max Mackenzie. Oh, no! But why should it be? Nothing else had gone right today, so she shouldn't even be surprised to find Jason Cameron in front of her.

JASON HAD BEEN THINKING about Diana and now here she was. He figured his luck was holding, even if hers apparently wasn't.

"Good morning, Ms. Kennedy," he said in his best official manner. "Won't you have a seat?"

"I certainly will not." She looked around suspiciously. "What are you doing here? Where's the marshal?"

"He's in Denver for the day so I'm helpin' out." Jason took his time ambling over to the big, high-backed leather chair behind the desk. He sat down and adopted what he hoped was a professional manner. "What can I do for you?"

Plopping both palms flat on the desk, she leaned forward on stiff arms. He'd never seen her wear such an outraged expression. Her beautiful hazel eyes were stormy and her cheeks were pink.

"I've been robbed," she said.

"Holy...!" Jason surged to his feet. "I'm sorry, I had no idea it was something so serious. Is everyone all right? When...?"

"Everyone's perfectly fine," she said impatiently. "It happened some time between closing and about ten-thirty this morning, when I got in and discovered what had happened."

"How much money did they get away with? Jeez, Diana, I can't believe this." He shoved a hand through his hair in a distraught gesture. Who would do such a thing, especially to a woman alone and struggling to take care of herself and a kid?

"No money," she said.

"No...?" He frowned, trying to figure out where this was going. "Booze? Food? What else was in there?"

She sucked in a deep breath and he watched with fascination as her breasts rose beneath a silky turquoise-colored shirt.

"They took my buffalo, and I expect you—or rather the marshal—to find him *immediately.*"

He blinked, gave a little shudder of relief. "Let me get this straight. Somebody broke into the Hideout after you closed last night and stole a *stuffed buffalo?*"

"Exactly. And now I want to know what you're going to do about it."

He was having a helluva time keeping a straight face. "I'm going to..." He swallowed hard and smoothed out his expression. "I'm going to—"

"Jason Cameron, if you laugh at me..."

"I don't want to but I can't help it!" Sitting back down in Max's chair, he roared with laughter. By the time he regained control, she had, too. She looked as cold as ice and he found himself preferring her anger to this.

"If you're quite finished, I'd like to officially ask... No, I *demand* an investigation. And when you catch the guilty parties, I want them persecuted—"

"Prosecuted."

"That, too! I want them persecuted and prosecuted to the full extent of the law."

He wiped tears of laughter from the corners of his eyes. "Are you sure old Bill wasn't just rolled into a closet somewhere and left by mistake?"

"Quite sure. He's not anywhere inside the Hideout, I am absolutely certain."

"Any sign of forced entry?"

She looked surprised. "I don't know."

"Then I guess we better go take a look. Max will be handling the investigation—" he choked on the word, which seemed much too heavy for the crime involved "—but I'll try to pick up any evidence I can before everybody comes to work and messes up the..." It was hard to say "crime scene" but he managed to get the words out somehow.

She glared at him. "I don't find this the least bit funny," she flared. "My property has been stolen and it shouldn't matter to the law whether it was money or a car or a buffalo."

"You're absolutely right," he agreed, feeling

contrite but incapable of overcoming the basically ridiculous situation—not that he could blame her for being mad at him about it.

Her eyes narrowed to glittering, angry slits. "Did you have something to do with this? Is that why you think it's so funny?"

She couldn't possibly mean that. If he thought she did, he'd be downright insulted. It was the anger talking. "Diana," he said, "if everybody who laughs when they hear this is a suspect, the whole town's in trouble. Trust me on this—it's funny!"

"The whole town doesn't have a motive," she flung back at him. "You do."

This wasn't as funny as it had been. "Whaddaya mean, I do? What possible motive could I have to steal your dead buffalo when I've got a whole herd of live ones runnin' on my place?"

She lifted her chin and met his gaze. "You were angry at me for slapping you last night at the grand opening."

"Did I look angry?"

"No, but—"

"Did I act angry?"

"No, but that doesn't mean you didn't want to get even with me for embarrassing you, even if you didn't show it."

"I wasn't embarrassed."

A red tide swept over her cheeks and she half turned away. "I don't believe you."

"Because *you* were embarrassed."

"Any normal human being would have been."

She jerked around to confront him head-on. "Okay, we're even. You've had your joke. Now give me back my buffalo!"

For a moment, he just stared at her, wondering if she believed all this malarkey she was handing out.

Deciding reluctantly that she did, he sighed. "Believe me, if I had your buffalo, I'd do that very thing." He hitched up his jeans, trying to look all business. "If you don't trust me any more than that, maybe you'd prefer to wait until Max gets back to report this 'crime.'"

She chewed on her full lower lip. He'd kissed that lip and its companion. It deserved better than she was giving it. Finally, she said, "No, I think you'd better come over now. As you said, once people start arriving for work, the evidence could be destroyed."

"Right." Don't even smile, he warned himself. She's not in the mood. "Let's go."

He held the door for her and she walked through, careful not to touch him. Lorrie looked up.

"Sorry about that," she said, jerking her head toward Diana. "She wouldn't take no for an answer. You two goin' out?"

Jason nodded. "I've got me a crime to investigate," he said, trying not to sound too pompous and failing miserably.

Lorrie's eyes went wide. "What's happened? Somebody robbed the Hideout? Omigosh, what did they get away with?"

"They got away with Buffalo Bill—we got us a buffalonapping on our hands. Guess we'll have to look for a ransom note while we're at it. Just pray this isn't a serial crime."

Jason lost it then, and so did Lorrie. Diana, looking ready to kill them both, didn't even crack a smile.

BACK AT THE HIDEOUT, Jason re-covered all the ground they'd already been over, with one exception. Checking the doors for signs of forced entry, he found scratch marks around the lock on the back door leading outdoors from the kitchen.

"Makes sense," he said. "The ramp used for carting in supplies must be the way they got ol' Bill out of here."

"Yes," Diana said sarcastically, "with a little help from that nice cart you made for him. You know, the cart with all the *wheels*." She didn't know why she'd said that because she didn't actually think he had anything to do with her missing buffalo...really.

He frowned. "That attitude's getting a little stale," he complained. "I'm sorry I laughed but I couldn't help it. *No*body's gonna be able to help it."

"You're the only one with a motive."

"The hell I am." He looked disgusted. "Who d'you think you are around here—the Queen?"

She blinked. "What's that supposed to mean?"

"It means that you're not universally liked." She'd never heard him speak so bluntly. "I hate to be the one to tell you this, but not everybody thinks you fit in around here."

"Why, of all th-the..." She sputtered to a halt, remembering something. "Is that why they call me the Queen Bee?"

He groaned. "You heard about that, did you."

"Yes, but I didn't exactly get it."

"Simple. It means you put on airs."

She hadn't thought she was the Queen Bee, but she hadn't thought she was a pariah, either. That hurt. "Then you think someone might have taken my buffalo just because they don't like me?"

He shrugged. "They coulda done it to put you in your place, so to speak. Look, since we're talking frankly for once, maybe I oughta tell you—"

Charlie stuck his head through the kitchen doorway. "Hey, Diana, you want me to put all those extra cases of beer in the refrigerator or store 'em in the basement?"

"Use your best judgment, Charlie."

He looked surprised. "Okay."

She met Jason's level gaze. "You were saying?"

"Hey, Diana!"

This time, it was the cook. "Any place we can go to talk privately?" Jason demanded, once Diana had dealt with the interruption.

She hesitated, loath to take him upstairs to the small apartment but sure that was the only place they could be alone.

Alone with Jason Cameron in the vicinity of a bed. Dumb!

"Follow me." She led the way up the narrow stairs located just behind the bandstand. Throwing open the door, she walked inside, then turned to face him. "Say what it is you wanted to say." It sounded almost like a challenge.

"I *didn't* want to say it. That's the problem." He raked one hand through his unruly dark hair. "Once everybody gets to know you, they're gonna love you. But until that happens...well, I figured it couldn't hurt if I let everyone know I'm behind you one hundred percent."

"Which means what?" The very air in the small sitting room seemed to grow heavy with tension.

"Oh, hell." For the first time since she'd known him, he looked embarrassed. "I wanted to give you the...the Cameron stamp of approval, just like I said. I wanted everyone to know that we're behind you, and if they don't treat you right, they'll have the Camerons to deal with."

She stared at him with slowly dawning comprehension. "That's not what you mean at all."

"The hell it's not!" he flared.

She shook her head with certainty. "You don't mean the Camerons. You mean *you*. The Jason stamp of approval, because Jason Cameron is such a big man in this town." She watched him squirm and knew she'd hit that nail squarely on the head. "Why?" she burst out.

"Why what?"

"Why are you getting involved in my life and my problems? I've treated you the same—no, worse, far worse than I've treated anyone else. Yet you keep coming back for more."

"Damned if that ain't true—on both counts." His humor seemed to be returning.

"So tell me."

The air thickened. "You've got something I want," he said at last, his tone heavy with subtext.

Her body. She caught her breath. "I can't believe you said that to my face."

"Why not? You already knew it was true."

She turned her back on him. "I didn't—I don't." She whirled to face him again, breathing harder than she liked. "Why are you doing this to me? There are plenty of women chasing after you. Why don't you give them a break and leave me alone?"

"Maybe you just put your finger on it."

He stepped closer but didn't touch. Even so, she believed she could feel the heat of his body, the force of his personal magnetism drawing her to him.

She licked her lips. "I suppose that means you enjoy a challenge."

"Most people, male and female, enjoy challenges. Maybe that's the mistake I'm making with you."

"Your mistakes with me are too numerous to mention."

"Obviously. But maybe if I quit chasing you, you'd start chasing me."

"In your dreams."

His slow, meaningful "Yes" made her shiver with reaction. *Had* he dreamed about her? Actually *dreamed?*

"I'll never chase you, Jason. I'll never chase any man."

"How can you be so sure?"

His voice had dropped to a liquid purr that seemed to fill every part of her with a sweet warmth. "I...I can be so sure because I know myself," she said forcefully, trying to shake off the numbing effect he was having on her. "My feet are firmly on the ground and that's where they're going to stay."

"What a waste. You can miss a lot of good stuff that way."

"I can miss a lot of bad stuff that way, too. I like being in control of my environment, but also of my emotions and my life. You're not going to get anywhere with me, Jason, so you may as well give it up now."

He laughed, a smoky sound that surrounded her with an almost shocking intimacy. "I never give up. There's just no quit in me."

She took a quick step away, effectively breaking the intimate contact between them. "Why am I wasting my breath? You're supposed to be looking for my buffalo, not playing little games with me."

"I'm not so sure this is a game." Turning, he opened the door and stepped aside for her to precede him. He looked and sounded puzzled by what had just passed between them.

No more than she. Walking out into the hallway, she held herself stiffly erect. "So are you going to find my buffalo or what?"

"Ma'am," he said in a richly ironic voice, "I'm going back to the office right now to file my missing buffalo report. I don't think you have to worry, though. In a town the size of Cupid, there are only so many places you can hide a full-grown buffalo, even if he is stuffed.''

She started down the stairs. "When I find the guilty party, he's dead meat."

"I'd back off on the threats, if I were you."

"Why should I?"

"You want your buffalo back in one piece, don't you? You're in no position to call the shots."

At the foot of the stairs, she whirled to face him. "I'm not making threats," she said in a tight voice. "I'm making promises." A sudden inspiration occurred to her. "I'm also posting a reward. Then we'll see how long it takes to get my buffalo back."

She had no idea why he let out that long, drawn-out groan.

CHAPTER TWELVE

JULIE TOOK ONE LOOK at Diana's grim face and immediately invited her into the publisher's private office. Since the publisher was also her husband and the marshal, who was out of town in any case, she seated herself behind the desk and directed her caller to the other chair.

"You look like you've lost your last friend," Julie said cautiously.

"I've lost my buffalo," Diana corrected, "or rather, I didn't lose him. Somebody took him."

Julie blinked. "Took him where?"

"You tell me! Where does a thief hide a stuffed buffalo?"

"You don't mean...?"

"Julie Mackenzie, if you laugh, so help me I'll...!" Diana couldn't think of a threat bad enough to convey her warning.

Julie's laughter mutated into a kind of helpless groan, but her eyes sparkled with humor. "I'm sorry," she said when she could talk again. "I can see this isn't funny to you, but you've got to admit, it's not every day someone snatches a buffalo."

Diana's head drooped and she covered her face with her hands. "I'm so upset about this I can't think straight. I'm not going to let them get away with it!''

"Them? Do you know who did it?''

"I have my suspicions.'' Perhaps it wouldn't be wise to baldly accuse Julie's twin brother...yet.

"Have you reported the theft to the authorities?''

"If you can call your brother an authority.''

"Oh, that's right. He fills in for Cosmo sometimes.''

Diana rolled her eyes, overcome by skepticism. "Jason came over to the Hideout and looked around but he didn't find much. He said he'd write up a missing buffalo report—Julie, if you laugh, I'm going to clobber you—but that's not good enough.''

Julie was having a lot of trouble swallowing her mirth. "Is there something I can do to help, beyond putting the story in the newspaper, of course?''

"There certainly is.'' Diana gripped the wooden arms of her chair spasmodically. "I want to offer a one-thousand-dollar reward for the safe return of my buffalo and the apprehension and conviction of the thief or thieves.''

"Whoa, now!'' Julie recoiled. "Are you sure you want to do that before we give the law a chance to do its job?''

"How can the law do its job when it's too busy laughing?'' Diana was unable to conceal her bitterness.

Julie leaned forward earnestly. "Cosmo won't laugh, I promise you. He's very serious about crime.''

"Good. That makes one." Holy cow, was that a sniffle she choked back?

"Oh, Diana, I'm serious, too." Julie looked contrite. "But this *has* to be a joke. Why don't you give the perpetrators a chance to come clean and we'll all have a good laugh about it?"

Diana jumped up and started pacing. "Why does everyone keep saying that? *It's not a joke to me!* Will you announce the reward or won't you?"

"I'm...extremely reluctant to do that at this time."

"Why? Because the chief suspect is your brother?" So much for keeping her suspicions private.

Julie's eyes went wide. "Jason? You've got to be kidding! He's so goofy about you that he wouldn't dream of doing something guaranteed to piss you off."

"He's the only one with a motive," Diana argued. "But if you won't help me, I'll just have to find someone who will." She pivoted toward the door.

"Hang on a minute. I didn't say I wouldn't. I said I was reluctant. And the reason I'm reluctant is because of what happened the last time anybody offered a reward here in Cupid."

"Which was?" Diana paused.

Julie looked distinctly uncomfortable. "Has anybody told you about the horse rustling that was going on around here a while back?"

Diana nodded. "Jason told me that Mr. Turner

was falsely implicated but that Beau is still on probation for being mixed up in it.''

"That's right. Back before we knew Ethan was innocent, the *Chronicles* started a reward fund for the arrest and conviction—you know how that goes.''

"Did it work?''

Julie rolled her eyes. "What it did was get everybody in town all whipped into a frenzy. Then when I—when the paper turned out to be wrong about Ethan—''

"Julie Mackenzie! Are you saying you were behind the reward?''

A pained expression crossed Julie's face. "I was...hotheaded in those days,'' she said. "In retrospect...let's just say I'm not too proud of what I did. I'd like to help you avoid a similar mistake.''

"Especially when your brother may turn out to be the guilty party.''

"Will you stop saying that?'' Julie didn't sound angry or offended, simply annoyed by a ridiculous suggestion. "Jason's never stolen anything in his life.'' She gave a sudden short laugh. "Maybe a few hearts, but nothing else.''

"Even for a joke?''

Julie grimaced. "He does like a good joke, but in this case...'' She shook her head vehemently. "Not a chance. I'd swear to it.''

"In that case, you shouldn't mind putting a story in the newspaper about the reward,'' Diana pointed out. "I also want you to say that I intend to prose-

cute the perpetrator or perpetrators to the full extent
of the law.''

"Don't you think you're carrying this a little too
far?'' Julie's tone turned coaxing. "Face it, Diana.
Everybody in town's going to love this. To them,
it'll be a prank. Whoever did it will become an instant folk hero.''

"And I'll be the wicked witch who can't take a
joke, I suppose.'' Diana hadn't a doubt that was
what would happen but she couldn't let the knowl-
edge sway her. She was not the one in the wrong.
Someone had taken her buffalo and she had every
right—hell, she had a duty and obligation—to get it
back any way she could.

Julie shook her head doubtfully. "If you pursue
this with, uh, such vigor, I'm afraid that's exactly
how it'll end up.''

Diana turned again for the door. "I've been crit-
icized before and survived,'' she said. "I can't say
I care for it but I refuse to let public opinion sway
me when I know I'm in the right.''

Julie sighed; it was a sigh of surrender. "If you're
sure,'' she said. "But don't say I didn't warn you.''

"I won't.'' Diana's shoulders slumped with relief.
"Will you say your brother is the prime suspect?''

"Good God, no! He isn't, to anyone except you,
and he won't be.''

"All right, I can accept that. Time will certainly
tell.'' Diana reached for the doorknob. "When will
the story be printed?''

"I'm putting out a special Fourth of July issue

day after tomorrow. There's still time to get it in there.''

Diana let out a relieved breath. ''Thank you, Julie. I guess that's all I can do until your husband gets back into town.''

''That'll be late tonight. I'm sure he won't be able to get around to seeing you until tomorrow.''

''That's all right. At least now I feel as if I've done *something*.''

And that's what she so desperately needed, Diana realized on the walk back to the Hideout. She didn't like being out of control and that's exactly how Bill's disappearance was making her feel.

That and the constant pressure Jason Cameron put on her. *You've got something I want,* he'd said baldly.

And he wasn't talking about a stuffed buffalo, either.

MAX CAME AROUND the next day to talk to Diana about the theft, and as Julie had predicted, he didn't laugh. She'd calmed down by then anyway, at least outwardly.

''We'll find your buffalo,'' he promised her, examining the scratch marks around the back door. ''Can you tell me who has keys to this place?''

''Me, the two cleaners, the assistant manager. Why?''

He rose from his close scrutiny. ''Frankly, I don't know how they managed to get in this way without a key.''

"But the marks... Jason said—"

"Jason's a rancher, not a cop."

"As far as I'm concerned, he's also the chief suspect."

Max didn't laugh or try to defend his brother-in-law. "If he did it, his ass is grass."

They walked through the kitchen, just starting to gear up for that night.

"Still, even I could see the marks around the lock," she said.

"Could be just to throw us off. I'm not sure that old lock *could* be picked. Without a key, they'd most likely have had to smash it to get in." He shrugged. "Who knows? Stranger things have happened." He tipped his hat. "I'll keep you informed as the investigation moves along," he promised.

He sure would, she thought as she watched him leave. No way was she going to let this drop.

"SHE THINKS YOU DID IT," Max said.

"Well, son of a..." Jason snatched his hat off his head and slammed it onto Max's desk with a resentful glance at Blair, on whose account he resisted the terrible swearwords aching to be said. "After all I've tried to do for that ungrateful—"

"But you kept all that secret," Max pointed out reasonably. "Didn't want her to feel beholden, or so you said. You changed your mind?"

"No, I haven't changed my mind."

Blair darted him an oblique glance. "Did you do it, Jason?"

He opened his mouth, shut it again, then glared at her. "You've got a real smart mouth on you, kid."

"See, Uncle Max?" She gave him a taunting look. "He didn't answer the question. Maybe he *is* the guilty party."

"What possible motive could I have for stealing her damn buffalo? I got a whole herd of 'em already."

"Yeah," Max agreed. They both turned on Blair. "What have you got in mind?"

"Well..." She seemed to consider. "Okay, try this—he wants to piss her off so bad she'll sell the Hideout to him and go back to Texas."

"Not a chance," Jason said shortly. "I don't even want the damn place, now that I've seen how much time and effort it takes. Hell, I'm more interested in the owner than I am in that broken-down saloon."

"Okeydoke." She didn't look entirely convinced. Then she brightened. "How about this? You take her buffalo, and when you've got all the mileage you can out of that, you miraculously 'find' it and bring it back and then you're her hero. She's grateful—*voilà!* She's in bed with you before you can say Buffalo Bill."

"Blair!" Both uncles stared at her with disapproval.

She laughed. "Hey, I wasn't born yesterday. Jason's all hot to trot and here's this gorgeous babe who won't give him the time of day." She slipped off her perch on the corner of Max's desk. "That's probably never happened before."

"It's happened plenty," Jason blustered—although in truth, it hadn't.

"Yeah, right." She headed for the door. "I'd love to stay and chat but I'm meeting Ryan at the drive-in."

"Stay out of trouble," Jason yelled after her, "and keep your stupid theories to yourself!"

Her voice floated back to them, "As if!"

Jason glared at his brother-in-law, the only remaining target. "I'm gettin' real tired of this real fast," he complained.

"You'll get tireder when you see what Julie's printing in tomorrow's newspaper."

Jason groaned. "Now what?"

"Diana's offering a reward. Story's all there and she means business. She's also had a ton of reward posters printed up and they're gonna be posted all over town, just in time for the big Fourth of July street fair."

"And I suppose she's got my name smeared all over 'em."

"No. But Diana does tend to mention you in the same breath when she tells the tale."

"Well, that does it." Jason stood up, shaking his head furiously. Grabbing his hat, he slammed it on. "I've had it with that woman. Hell, I'm just throwin' good time after bad here. She thinks she's such hot stuff, let her make it on her own."

"That's what she claims she wants to do," Max agreed reasonably.

"And after I twisted arms to get people to go to her damned grand opening. What thanks do I get for that?"

"Hell, man, she doesn't know. Nobody told her. You said you'd kill 'em if they did."

Jason glared at the marshal. "She shoulda guessed. Now she's tellin' everybody I'm a damned thief. Well, I've had it."

"Which means what?"

"I'm through chasin' after her. There's plenty of fish in the sea. She can sink or swim all by her lonesome because Jason Cameron is *through* goin' where he's not wanted."

He meant it, too. That's why he said yes without a fight when they came after him to work the kissing booth again, although he'd decided earlier not to let them browbeat him into doing it ever again. He'd show the Queen Bee that there were women who'd stand in *line* to kiss him.

And not a one of them was going to slap his face.

EVERYBODY WHO WALKED into the Hideout on the Fourth of July seemed to be buzzing with speculation over Buffalo Bill's disappearance. Charlie Gilroy told Diana that half the folks seemed to think Jason had done it as a prank and the other half thought she'd done it herself.

"Me!" She stared at him in astonishment. "Why

on earth would I report my own buffalo stolen if it wasn't true?''

Charlie laughed. ''Hell, to stir up business. And it sure has done that.''

He was right; the place was packed and had been since the moment it opened.

Carrying out a tray of clean glasses, she overheard Jimmy and Tap discussing the subject.

''Bet you ten to one Jason did it,'' Jimmy said, whipping his wallet out of his hip pocket.

''You're on.'' Tap followed suit. ''Tom Purdy's holding the stakes. I hear it's runnin' even money, but all the ranchers haven't made it into town yet. They'll bet on Jason, sure.''

Diana was disgusted. This was serious. As soon as the *Chronicles* hit the street, they'd know how serious.

And as soon as the reward posters were spread all over town. Reaching beneath the bar, she pulled out the stack of fluorescent-colored pages. She glanced around, spotted Ryan and Blair talking at the edge of the room and worked her way toward them.

They'd give her a hand putting up the posters, and the sooner the better. While they were out, she could pick up a copy of the newspaper.

And see who—make that *what* was going on out there.

''LOOK!'' BLAIR POINTED through the crowd. ''There's Jason, and he's at it again.''

Diana didn't want to look but didn't seem capable

of resisting the pointing finger. Sure enough, there he was, in that damned kissing booth again.

As usual, the line stretched to hell and gone.

She grabbed the hammer out of Ryan's hand. "Are you kids here to help or to gawk?" Holding the nail and poster against a light pole with one hand, she used the other to raise the hammer and bring it down—

Right onto her thumb.

"God...bless it!" Dropping the hammer, she thrust her throbbing thumb into her mouth. It hurt like hell, which was probably why she felt like crying.

Ryan bent down to retrieve the hammer. "Calm down, why don't you? Jeez, Di, I've never seen you so freaked."

"I'm not freaked."

But she was—totally freaked. At that moment, she made the fatal mistake of glancing toward Jason again. Their gazes met, and then he insolently put his arms around the shoulders of two of the women surrounding him. He was hugging them and they were simpering up at him, but his gaze challenged Diana directly. *See? Just who the* hell *do you think you are?*

Blair peeled off a poster and held it against the pole. "You're freaked," she said as if her opinion settled it. "Why don't you go on over and see if the paper's out yet while Ryan and I finish this up. To tell you the truth, Diana, you're not much help."

"I—" she stifled a defense, realizing her position

was not defensible ''—appreciate the offer,'' she accepted, changing directions. ''If you're sure you don't mind...''

''Mind?'' Ryan secured the poster with one tap of the nail. ''We'd be grateful.''

''All right, then, I will. And thanks.'' She turned away but not before seeing Jason leaning over to kiss a short blonde with long arms—arms wrapping around his neck to hold him closer.

Diana hoped the very determined lady choked him.

THE HIDEOUT still overflowed with revelers when she returned with a copy of the *Chronicles* tucked beneath her arm. Julie had done an outstanding job with the story, even going so far as to place it on the front page. If nothing came of it, it wouldn't be because no one knew about the reward. Between the story in the paper and the posters nailed up all over town, everyone seemed to be abuzz with gossip.

Diana headed for the bar. ''Everything all right here?'' she asked Charlie when he had a moment.

''Yeah, thanks to Beau.''

''Beau?''

''I'm here, Miz Diana.'' The big man materialized beside her.

''You tell 'er,'' Charlie directed. ''I got work to do.''

Beau nodded enthusiastically.

Diana asked the question with dread. ''So what happened?''

Beau's chest swelled with pride. "I stopped us a fight is all."

Diana groaned. "Go on."

"Couple a'them ol' boys—" he gestured vaguely down the bar "—was arguin' about who took ol' Bill. One said it was Jason and the other said—beg pardon, Miz Di—anyways, the other guy said you done it your own self. One took a swing and the other'un took a swing back and first thing you know, punches was flyin' hot and heavy."

"Oh, Lord. Was anybody hurt?"

He beamed. "Nope. I stepped in purty quick and put an end to it. Told 'em they was both wrong as far as that went. You didn't do it and neither did ol' Jason."

He spoke with absolute certainty. Diana patted his bulging biceps. "Thanks, Beau. I knew you were the right man for the job."

"Yep, I shore am." He gave her a cocky little salute and turned away, obviously well satisfied with her praise.

What a lousy day, she thought, walking back to her office. Business was the only thing that was good.

Seeing Jason in the kissing booth had unsettled her more than she could have imagined; her thumb still throbbed where she'd banged it. Then to find that there'd nearly been a brawl...

She felt something beneath her foot and looked down at a piece of paper. Frowning, she picked it up.

CHAPTER THIRTEEN

JASON, STANDING at the end of the bar at the Hideout, didn't think Diana had even seen him before disappearing toward the office. Wedged in as he was between Melody Stroud and Lorrie Anderson, it was a wonder *he* saw *her*.

On the other hand, it wasn't all *that* surprising. She seemed to attract his attention like a bonfire attracted bugs. He choked on his beer at the thought. The lady sure as hell wasn't interested in being anybody's bonfire, especially his, even if she *did* treat him like a bug.

Lorrie ended his musings with an elbow in the ribs. "How ya doin', sugar? You look like you're in a daze."

"I'll survive," he said, meaning it in ways she couldn't know.

"Hey, Jason!"

Jason turned to find Dwight Deakins, the former marshal, standing behind him. "What's up, Dwight?"

The pudgy man waved a sheet of fluorescent green paper. "You seen this?"

"The reward poster?" Jason strove for a bored tone. "Sure. I saw her nailin' 'em up a while ago."

"Odds on the street are even that you're behind this buffalo thievery." Dwight shook his graying head. "Man, if I was still the marshal, your butt would be in a sling! You cain't go around stealin' a woman's..."

At that moment, Diana appeared at the back of the bandstand and marched across the dance floor. She was pale as a ghost and stiff as a poker and every other scary cliché Jason had ever heard. He stopped listening to Dwight, which was just as well because the guy was only trying to get a rise out of him anyway.

Despite all his best resolutions to butt out of her business and mind his own, Jason shoved away from the bar without a word to his companions and called her name in a tone that cut through all the general buzz of conversation.

Her head jerked in his direction and she changed course without missing a step, coming to an abrupt halt before him. Her eyes were wild, her expression stunned.

He caught her by the shoulders—damn, he wasn't supposed to touch her. "What *is* it? You look—"

"Take your hands off me, Jason Cameron."

"Sorry." He complied with an elaborate show. "I lost my head. You just look so...confounded. Tell me what it is."

"This!" She thrust the sheet of paper toward him, her eyes burning holes in his face.

He took it and smoothed out the wrinkles she'd made crushing it in her hand. They'd attracted attention. By the time he started reading aloud the words cut from a newspaper and pasted on the sheet, they were pretty much surrounded.

"'One million in cash by next Friday. Small nonsequential bills only or the buffalo gets it.'"

Into the stunned silence, Lorrie said in a hushed tone, "Why, it's a ransom note...a ransom note for a dead buffalo."

She started to laugh.

Melody joined in, then Charlie, then Tap. Soon the entire room rocked with an explosion of laughter. The commotion seemed to hit Diana like a series of blows and Jason wished he could wave his arms and turn it all off for her.

Unfortunately, he couldn't do that because it *was* funny as hell. When he could be heard again, he leaned forward and asked, "Where did you find this?"

She gestured behind her. "Shoved under the office door." Unexpectedly, she raised both arms and brought her fisted hands down on his chest. "Damn you, Jason! This is all your fault!"

Shocked by an attack he considered senseless, not to mention completely out of character, he caught her wrists and held her arms still. "Calm down, okay? I had nothing to do with it. In this mob, anyone could have snuck away for a couple minutes to leave the note."

"Nobody has a reason except you." Her eyes shot hot sparks at him.

Beneath his careful grip, he felt her flexing her muscles as if trying to find some way to escape. "I'll turn you loose if you'll promise not to start beatin' on me again," he said in a warning voice.

She grated out the words. "All right."

He released her. "Would you care to tell me why you're so all-fired determined to lay the blame for this on me?"

She grabbed the ransom note out of his hand. "Because...because..." She bit that luscious lower lip. "Because I'm not some kind of hysterical woman. I'm cool, calm and collected. *I never lose control.*"

He frowned. "Which has what to do with the fact that you think I'm a thief and a liar?"

"This horrible change in me is all your fault," she accused in a low voice that quivered with emotion. "You're out to get me, Jason Cameron, and you're using an innocent buffalo to do it."

He couldn't believe what he was hearing. The woman had gone around the bend, no doubt about it. There she stood, cute as a little speckled pup and trying like hell to find some way to make this out to be *his* fault after he'd moved heaven and earth to help her.

Disgusted, he shoved his hands into his pockets to keep from grabbing her and shaking her until her teeth rattled. "Well, hell," he said forcefully, "I'm innocent, but you're never gonna believe me so...so

I'll give you another damned buffalo. Anything to calm you down.''

"You're not going to put me off that way. I don't want another buffalo. I want Bill!''

He got right back in her face, matching her notch for notch on the "mad" scale. Her eyes flickered in reaction but she didn't flinch, just met his fury with her own.

"I *said*," he roared, "I'm *giving* you a friggin' buffalo whether you want it or not! I'll pick you up tomorrow at nine so you be *ready!*" Spinning around, he headed for the door.

"I will *not* be ready!" she called after him. "I won't even be out of bed by nine so don't bother—"

"Works for me," he yelled back, "especially the *bed* part. I'm comin' to get you so you do what you have to.''

He made his exit to general and enthusiastic applause.

SHE WAS READY.

No way would she let Jason Cameron come storming into her little house, banging through the rooms looking for her. She was ready for him, but it pissed her off big time.

The bottom line was, she couldn't let him set her off any time he chose. It gave him power. Every time she lost control, he took it. She wasn't sure why—didn't like the possibilities that sprang to mind, in fact. But for whatever reason, Jason Cameron knew how to push her buttons and he did it at every turn.

From now on, she vowed, things would be different.

When he banged on her front door promptly at nine o'clock, she took a deep breath and went to answer. "Look," she said as if continuing the conversation they'd started the previous day, "there's absolutely no reason for you to do this because I have no intention—"

"Me, neither. No intention whatsoever. You ready? Let's go."

"But—"

He opened the screen door and hauled her through. Why was he always touching her? Why was she beginning to anticipate that he would? Why was she still getting those little shivers every time he did?

"Wait a minute," she commanded. "I need my purse, at least."

"What for? Since I'm not gonna let you drive, you don't need your license. You don't need an ID because I know who the hell you are." Throwing open the passenger door, he grabbed her around the waist and hoisted her inside as if she were a sack of grain.

Each time he touched her, she felt another jolt. All these jolts were starting to wear her down. He slammed the door and she huddled against it to fasten her seat belt, still feeling the imprint of his fingers on her waist.

He loped around the front of the pickup and sprang in beside her. Fastening the seat belt with one hand, he simultaneously started the vehicle with the other. He gunned the engine.

"You ready?" He grinned wolfishly at her over one shoulder.

"For *what?*"

"Yep." He let out the clutch and hung a U-turn. "She's ready."

They drove north from Cupid on the two-lane paved road that ran through the heart of town. Diana, who hadn't been outside the city limits since she'd arrived in May, stared out the window with interest.

The rolling countryside glowed green and lush. Everywhere she looked, she saw animals both wild and domesticated. Several deer grazed among cattle in a pasture; squirrels and even a raccoon darted across the road ahead.

Jason turned west onto a narrow, winding dirt road. After they'd gone several miles, a surprise waited for her around a bend in the road. In the valley below, she saw several red-roofed ranch buildings, blending into their surroundings as if they were a natural part of the scenery. She caught her breath in appreciation. "What's that?"

He smiled, and all the tension that had been between them seemed to evaporate. "That's the Straight Arrow Ranch," he said, his tone heavy with pride. "That's gotta be one of the greatest sights in the world, at least to a Cameron."

"It's pretty great even to non-Camerons. Has your family been here long?"

"Since 1887. Great-Grandfather Robert Cameron was the first. He and his brother William settled here and started selling beef to miners and the Indian Agency. William eventually pulled out and made for Montana, but Robert stayed. That's how it began." The road curved alongside a little stream that marked the boundary of the ranch compound. "Horseshoe Creek," Jason told her.

They came to a small bridge spanning the creek and Jason slowed the vehicle. The road over the bridge led between a large corral on the right and smaller outbuildings on the left, heading toward the ranch house itself.

Everything looked solid and enduring. As it should, since it had been home to generations of Camerons.

This Cameron was driving on past.

"My place is up here a ways," he said, waving vaguely. "It'll take us another twenty minutes or so to get there. I told Granny we'd stop by to say hello to her on our way back, though. That all right with you?"

She gave him a jaundiced glance. As if he cared about her opinion.

On the other hand, she did like Grandma.

THEY TOPPED A RISE and a beautiful green valley spread out before them. "This," Jason announced, "is Paradise Valley. Home…"

She caught her breath on an exclamation of sheer delight. From towering pines to verdant meadows, she'd never seen or even imagined such a beautiful place. It all looked somehow...pristine, as if they were the very first people ever to discover its beauty.

The dirt road had gotten steadily worse and Jason maneuvered now with care. At the bottom of the slope, he turned right into the trees. Suddenly, they burst through and she saw his house, perched on the side of a hill. Ruggedly constructed of logs, it looked as if it had been there forever...and as if it belonged.

"Jason," she breathed, "it's perfect."

He gave her a startled glance. "You like it?"

"I love it," she said warmly, too warmly. She had to pull back. "I mean," she continued more sedately, "it seems to belong here in the middle of the wilderness. It's not a bit out of place."

"You sound surprised." He pulled up to the front steps and killed the engine.

Yes, she was surprised. She'd expected some kind of wild bachelor pad, or maybe a shack. She might still find that inside, she reminded herself. It was too soon to leap to judgment.

About the house, not the man. She shrugged. "Well, where are all those buffalo you keep talking about?" She glanced around but all she could see was a corral with several horses, and another log building that must be a barn.

"They're out doing what buffalo do—eating and running their fool legs off."

"Oh." Somehow she felt almost disappointed. "Then the trip was for nothing."

"Nothing, hell." He threw open his door. "From here on, we travel by horseback."

"But..."

He wasn't listening. She, Texas native though she might be, had never been close to a real live horse in her entire life. Apparently, that was about to change because she'd be *damned* if she'd wimp out now.

HE PUT HER ON TOP OF a fat old red mare named Gladys.

"You haven't got a thing to worry about," he assured her, adjusting her stirrup. He guided her foot into it, his hand warm upon her ankle above her sneaker. "As far as Gladys goes anyway. I should have told you to wear boots."

"I don't have any boots except the snow kind." She wiggled her bottom deeper into the saddle. It wasn't exactly like sitting in a rocking chair but it wasn't bad. Since she didn't intend to become a cowgirl, what difference did it make what she wore on her feet?

Jason swung into the saddle of a big gray, the movement so fluid and graceful that it reminded her of poetry. Here was a man in his element in the huge, intricately carved Western saddle. The stock of a rifle was visible on one side, while a canteen swung from the other.

"Let's go," he said. "Loop the reins over the

saddle horn, kick Gladys in the ribs and let her have her head. You'll do fine if you stay out of her way.''

With Jason in the lead, they rode into the trees, Diana still puzzling over the interior of his house. It hadn't been a bachelor's paradise at all. Instead, she'd found a snug, comfortable family home, even if it was for a family of one.

He'd surprised her again, once more leaving her off stride. Could there be more to the swinging bachelor than she'd realized?

THEY SAT THEIR HORSES inside a blind created by trees and underbrush on the side of a knoll, looking down on the herd. All dozen of the shaggy beasts, in many sizes and shapes, grazed peacefully in the meadow below.

Diana breathed an impressed, ''Holy cow!''

He had to admit she'd been a good sport about getting here. Obviously, she'd never been on a horse before in her life but was smart enough to take his advice and let the horse do all the work. If she ever wanted to learn to really ride, she'd be an apt pupil.

But this was what they'd come to see, this mass of hulking, humpbacked, shaggy and horned creatures. She glanced at him, her expression filled with awe.

''Wow, this is really something! I thought buffalo were all but extinct.''

''They nearly were, a while back.'' He hooked one knee over the saddle horn and relaxed. He liked looking at her while he explained. Bison he could see anytime. "By the mid 1890s, there were only about three hundred left out of a high of sixty million or so. Today there's probably—oh, 120 to 130,000 in commercial production for meat and hides. There's a few more on public land—probably no more than fifteen thousand or so—but it's the ranchers who've saved the breed."

"They have?"

He laughed at her doubtful expression. "The fact is, nothing people like to eat is going to become extinct. Buffalo meat is better for you than beef— leaner—and a lot of us think it's tastier." He raised his eyebrows. "Although I'm not knocking beef. It's what made the Straight Arrow. But bison's the meat of the future." He hesitated, then added, "You do know they're not really buffalo?"

She grinned, and he thought maybe she was relaxing a little. A relief; he hated to see her so tense and uptight.

"I knew," she said, "but in case I might have forgotten, Blair gave me the lecture."

"Yeah." A grin twitched at his mouth. "Blair knows everything."

"While I know practically nothing." She watched the shaggy beasts graze for a few minutes. "They seem as tame as cows."

"Don't let 'em fool you. These are wild animals," he said flatly. "They'll spook at anything, and once they start running, they don't stop until they drop. You get a two-ton bull shaped like a four-legged battering ram running forty miles an hour and he can do some real damage. On top of that, they're just plain bad-tempered and unpredictable, and humans don't scare them one little bit. They'll trample whatever's in their path, then turn on you when you least expect it.''

''You're not making them sound very attractive,'' she said. ''Why do you keep them? Cows must be much nicer.''

He enjoyed her naiveté. ''Profit. Bison bring in twice what cattle will. On top of that, they pretty much take care of themselves. They're tough as old boots. Even newborn calves can survive blizzards that would wipe out an entire cattle herd. They're also better foragers.''

''All very practical.'' She gave him an oblique glance. ''I take it you're not wrapped up in the romance of the West. It seems to me that's what buffalo—pardon me, bison—represent.''

''Which is a big part of why you're so torn up about Buffalo Bill's disappearance,'' he guessed.

''I suppose.'' A shadow crossed her face. For a moment, she studied the herd and then she smiled. ''Look at that one.''

She pointed toward a half-grown calf following its mother closer to where they sat their horses. The calf stopped to look around, all snorty and nervous.

''You like that one?''

''Of course.'' She gave him a startled glance.

''It's smaller than Buffalo Bill.''

''So?'' She frowned.

He shrugged. ''It's your choice. That's the one you want, you got it.''

Pulling his rifle from its holster, he raised it in one easy motion and sighted in on the animal standing there like a clay pigeon.

CHAPTER FOURTEEN

"WHAT ARE YOU *DOING?*"

Diana—formerly calm, cool and confident Diana—lunged for the rifle, knocking it aside. She almost unseated herself in the process, grabbing the saddle horn at the last second to avoid a tumble.

"I'm about to replace your missing buffalo," he said in a steely tone. He no longer looked or sounded like the proud tour guide. His face and voice had hardened. "I can't give Buffalo Bill back to you because I didn't take him and I don't know who did. But I can give you another one to take his place."

"No way am I going to be responsible for the death of an innocent buffalo—bison, whatever!"

"Then stop accusing me of something I didn't do. I didn't take your damned buffalo, but if you want one of mine, this is your chance."

There. That's what he'd brought her all the way out here to say. In that moment, she hated him.

Or something.

"You've made your point," she said stiffly. "Now *take me home!*"

She didn't wait for him to lead the way, just dug her heels into Gladys's fat sides and rode past him with her chin high and her eyes straight ahead. After a moment, he followed.

THEY DIDN'T STOP at the Straight Arrow on their way back to town. Diana was prepared to do battle on that score, but one look at his grim expression told her he was as annoyed with her as she was with him.

Shoot a buffalo indeed, she fumed. What a grandstand play! And she'd fallen for it. She had to grit her teeth to keep from growling at him.

They didn't exchange a single word all the way back to the Hideout. Pulling up in front, he didn't even kill the engine.

She said through clenched jaws, "Thank you for a very enlightening...adventure."

"Thank *you*." He threw her sarcasm right back in her face. "Just do me a favor and quit telling everybody in town that I stole your damned buffalo."

Hopping out of the pickup, she slammed the door and turned to continue the verbal duel. He thwarted her by stepping on the gas and peeling rubber out of there.

She stomped inside, stomped from the bar to the kitchen, discovering along the way that the Hideout had survived without her for a few hours. She didn't know if that pleased her or annoyed her.

Ryan and Blair came through the back door just as she finished talking to the staff. What a terrific couple they made, both tall and slender and gorgeous and young. Their biggest problem was boredom.

Imagine that.

Diana forced a smile. Still angry at Jason, she was having trouble shaking off a very bad mood. "How's it going, kids?"

They shrugged as one.

"Bored," Blair said. "I can't wait for this summer to end."

"Did you see Jason's buffalo?" Ryan asked.

"I don't want to talk about it." Diana headed out of the kitchen.

Blair nodded wisely. "You and Jason had another fight."

"I don't want to talk about Jason, either." Diana started toward her office, down the hallway behind the bandstand.

The two followed at her heels.

"Diana," Ryan said, "I've been thinking I might look for some kind of job for the rest of the summer. There's still time to pick up a little cash—"

"Oh, Ryan! I need you around here." She paused with one hand on the door. "If it's just a matter of money, I can give you a little more allowance. I know it's selfish of me but I really need you to—"

"What's that?" Blair interrupted with no apparent qualms, pointing at the floor near Diana's feet.

"What's what?" Diana looked down. She was standing with one foot squarely on a folded sheet of paper. The very air seemed to thicken with apprehension while she stared at that paper. After a moment, she sighed and said softly, "Oh, no! Not another one."

DIANA THREW the sheet of paper on Max's desk. "Read it," she commanded the startled lawman. "Just read it!"

Max blinked, frowned, picked up the paper and read,

"'Two million in cash or Bill is buffa-loaf.'"

He followed that with a weak, "Oh, God, buffaloaf!" that only partly covered up the laughter.

"So what do you intend to do about this?" she raged, pounding his desk with her fist. "Somebody's making fools of all of us, and I, for one, am tired of it."

"Diana, I'd like to assure you…" He stopped and swallowed hard, as if to swallow his laughter, as well. His eyes watered with the effort. "I'll get to the bottom of this. You just have to be patient."

"I'm usually a very patient person, but there are forces at work here that make that impossible." Without invitation, she sank into the chair before his desk. Wearily, she buried her face in her hands and added a muffled, "I think someone is trying to drive me crazy."

To her surprise, Max agreed. "Either that or out of town. Who'd want you to leave Cupid, Diana?"

She thought about that. "I don't know," she admitted at last. "Do you think that's the motive?"

He shrugged. "As good a motive as I've been able to come up with. Of course, that'd let Jason out. He wants you right where he's got you."

She grimaced, wondering what the hell that meant. "Nobody knows what Jason wants, including Jason. Max, do you think whoever is doing this will...you know, hurt Bill?"

His mouth dropped open. "Diana, that buffalo's already dead. What more can they do to him?"

"Whatever they do would hurt me more than it would hurt him."

Which, she thought as she walked back to the Hideout, was probably the point. Apparently, she had enemies she didn't even know.

Nevertheless, she had more confidence in Max than she'd had in Jason when he'd been sitting in the marshal's chair. At least Max was neither a cowboy nor a Cameron.

JASON WAS obviously avoiding her. She barely saw him throughout the remainder of the month of July—which was fine with her, of course. He still came into the Hideout occasionally, but often she didn't even know he'd been there until he'd gone again. When their paths did cross, he greeted her with a polite tip of the hat and kept going.

So did she succeed in putting him out of her mind? Did she avoid thinking of him, resenting him, wanting him...to be brought to justice?

In a pig's eye! It soon began to seem as if she thought of him more the less she saw of him. She'd find herself assigning motives, trying to figure out the whys and wherefores, wasting valuable time weaving fanciful scenarios in which she gave him his comeuppance.

August approached with the speed of a runaway train. Time not only flew when you were having fun, it also flew when you were working and worrying night and day, she discovered.

Ryan and Blair told her about the upcoming ice-cream social, the latest in the continuing effort to raise money for the school.

"They're going to rope off Main Street again," Blair explained excitedly, "and everybody will bring their ice-cream freezers and the women will bring pies and cakes and it'll all be auctioned off. There'll be games and balloons and stuff for the kids and it'll be a blast—if you like that sort of thing, of course." She gave Diana an oblique glance. "You're probably not coming."

Diana shook her head. Why on earth would she want to attend such an event? "I'm too busy," she said. "But you kids should have a good time."

Ryan gave her a narrow look. "Ah, Diana, don't be such a drag. All you do is work."

"Leave her alone," Blair said sharply. "If she doesn't want to go, that's her business."

"But—"

"*Think*, Ryan. Jason's sure to be there and you know how much he irritates your stepmother."

His blank look disappeared. "Oh, yeah. If that's what worries you, Diana—"

"Why should it? I just don't have time, that's all. If you'll excuse me, I'm expecting a beer delivery and I need to write a check."

Exchanging significant glances, they watched her go. Jimmy Mosely strolled past.

"Did I hear Diana say she ain't plannin' to come to the big ice-cream social?"

Ryan nodded. "That's the way it looks." He turned to Blair. "Quick thinking. It's better to keep her away from...you know."

The kids ambled off. Jimmy stayed where he was, analyzing the situation. Bottom line: it was better for him, and for his friends, to see that "you know" and Diana Kennedy got together ASAP.

EVERYBODY IN TOWN must have mentioned that blasted ice-cream social to Diana, and she'd told every single one of them the same thing: she simply didn't have the time. Then the employees at the Hideout ganged up to challenge her to spend twenty-four hours away from work whether she went to the ice-cream social or just stayed home.

Dared her, in fact. Bet her that she couldn't. Told her that if she didn't, they'd all start looking for new jobs.

She didn't think she'd been *that* bad, but she did see the handwriting on the wall. So she spent the first Saturday morning in August sleeping late. After a leisurely breakfast with Ryan, she puttered around, even unpacking the final moving box.

Then she found herself wondering.... Was everything all right at the Hideout? Was everything all right with Buffalo Bill, wherever he might be?

Was everything all right with…?

He'd be at that ice-cream social for sure. He'd be the center of attention; he always was. That's why she didn't want to go, not that she wasn't a community booster.

She didn't even want to *see* him. If he made a play for her, she'd be annoyed, and if he didn't make a play for her, she'd be annoyed.

She glanced at her wristwatch. Three o'clock. The ice-cream social had started at two and was well under way by now. When she stood on her front step, she could hear the happy sounds of Cupidians, as Julie called the residents of Cupid in her newspaper.

But if she went inside and closed the front door, all she heard was…the dejected beat of her own heart.

And a knocking on the door. She stiffened. Was it Jason? *Of course it wasn't Jason!*

Grandma Cameron and Ethan Turner stood on the porch, beaming at her. Without hesitation, Grandma opened the screen door and grabbed Diana's hand.

"Come on, girl, we're takin' you to the party," she announced. Ethan nodded agreement.

Diana resisted. "I really don't think that's such a good idea. But thanks for asking."

"Thanks, my eye." Grandma crossed her arms over her chest and glared. "I'm not budging a step unless you come along. You wouldn't want an old lady like me to miss all the fun, now would you?''

The reasoning was convoluted; the big hug from Grandma wasn't.

Diana went.

''YOU OWE ME,'' Grandma growled in Jimmy Mosely's ear.

''Damn straight.'' He nodded emphatically. ''We been tryin' to figger a way to get her to show up all week. We'll take it from here.''

''See that you do.'' Etta May pointed with her chin. ''She's over there with Julie, and *he's* down there with Beau. Now, skedaddle!''

Jimmy skedaddled.

''WAIT A MINUTE, DIANA.'' Julie touched the other woman's arm. ''Do you think that little boy is lost?''

Diana immediately saw the boy in question. He stood at the curb in ragged shorts and T-shirt, looking around wide-eyed at the crowd eddying around him. He didn't appear to be frightened but neither did he seem comfortable with his surroundings.

Julie crossed the street to kneel before him. He turned his freckled face toward her with a kind of tentative little smile. He was adorable, five or six years old with sandy hair and round, freckled cheeks.

''Hi,'' Julie said. ''Are you lost?''

''No, ma'am.''

''Do you know where you are, then?''

"No, ma'am."

Julie laughed and reached out to tilt his chin up. He yanked away.

"You're a stranger," he said simply. But he didn't run away or even step back.

Diana groaned. What a world, when every stranger, no matter how nice, was suspect.

Julie shot her a glance full of agreement, then turned back to the boy. "What's your name, hon?"

"Mikey."

Diana leaned down. "Don't I know you? Didn't I see you at the Hideout with... Is Mrs. Davis your grandmother?"

"No, ma'am. My aunt."

"That's right!" Julie stood up and offered her hand. "I'm no stranger, Mikey. I know your aunt Mary. Now you take my hand and we'll go find her."

He didn't hesitate, tucking his small hand into hers and looking up with perfect confidence.

Julie shrugged. "Sorry, Diana. If you'd like to come along...?"

"No, thanks. I think I'll wander down and see how the ice cream's coming along." And what the crowd gathering at the end of the street found so fascinating.

JASON SAW HER COMING, but he wasn't about to pay her any mind. Deliberately, he sidled away from the makeshift platform where Doc Kunkle held forth as master of ceremonies, his wife, Rose at his side. Doc had pushed right on past middle-aged and into old, but his eyes were still filled with mischief and his smile was wide.

Rose, as always, served as his handmaiden, watching him with adoring eyes even after a half century of togetherness.

Damn, Jason thought, if I could find me a woman like that...!

Doc held up his hands for attention. "My fellow Cupidians!" he orated. "We have a special treat for all you bachelors and bachelorettes—" This was greeted with groans. "Yes, bachelorettes!" he insisted. "In my day... But to get on with it, a special treat—where was I, Mother?"

Rose leaned forward to whisper in his ear. He nodded.

"Right. Now here's what we're going to do. We have two boxes here." He indicated two shoe boxes on a nearby table. "In one box we have the names of all the single boys, in the other the names of all the single girls. Yes, we know who you are!" He enjoyed his laugh before proceeding. "I'm gonna pull one name out of each box. Those two lucky folks will have the honor of sharing a dish of ice cream together—but we're gonna let 'em pay for the privilege! Only, since it's always the fellas that have to pay, this time we'll let the gals fork over a contribution to our building fund."

"I bid fifty dollars for Jason Cameron!" a female voice hollered from the back of the crowd.

Doc tsk-tsked. "No, you won't, Lorrie Purdy! I

happen to know you and that no-account husband of yours are back together again. A big hand for the Purdys!''

The crowd applauded enthusiastically. Jason edged a little farther away. This he didn't need. He was sick of being the center of attention at these things. At least, he was sick of it with Diana watching—although he couldn't be sure she was, the crowd was so thick.

''Lemme at those boxes,'' Doc commanded.

Someone passed them up to Rose, who passed them to her husband. Doc plunged a hand into each and withdrew two slips of paper.

''Why, the first lady drawn is our own Miss Cupid, Melody Stroud!'' Everyone clapped loudly while Melody, pretty if somewhat insipid, made her way to the stage. She watched along with everyone else while Doc opened the other slip of paper and read, ''*'Beau Turner'?*''

''Yo, Doc!'' Beau trotted forward to stand beside Melody. He looked at her with adoring eyes. ''I got me the purtiest woman in Cupid, Colorado,'' he crowed. ''Way to go, Doc!''

Jason held his breath, hoping that no one would say or do anything to bring the big guy down. He really deserved a break.

Melody looked confused. She glanced from Beau to Doc. ''Is this where I pay for him?'' she asked.

''Uhh...'' Doc cleared his throat. ''That's right, Melody. Whatever you think, uh, whatever you think a big ox like this is worth.''

Melody flashed a dimple. "Oh, I don't have *that* much," she said happily, "but I do have ten dollars. Is that enough?"

An awed murmur swept through the crowd. It was more than enough to win Beau new respect.

DIANA LISTENED for a few minutes while several couples were matched up, handed dishes of ice cream and sent off to eat it together. She considered the entire game to be utterly ridiculous. Fortunately, her name wouldn't be in either box. She turned to leave.

"Diana Kennedy!"

"What?" She swung around, startled. Doc stood on the stage waving a piece of paper.

People surrounded her, escorted her forward despite her unwillingness. She appealed to the master of ceremonies.

"There's been some mistake. I didn't—"

"And Diana's ice-cream partner is..." Doc dragged it out as if it were an Academy Award.

In a flash, Diana knew; she'd been set up. Doc was going to say—

"Jason Cameron!"

He'd said it. Jason didn't look any happier about this than she felt. In fact, when his friends surrounded him, he actually took a swing at Jimmy Mosely, striking only a glancing blow, unfortunately. But it took six or eight of them to drag him forward until he stood in front of her, panting, the top buttons of his shirt popped open, his chest heaving.

Looking *good!*

"So what'll you pay for this fine specimen of manliness?" Doc inquired. Somebody twittered. "I mean, of course, for the pleasure of his company," he amended.

Her first impulse was to insult him by offering a dollar—better yet, a quarter. But then she looked around and realized that's what everyone expected her to do. Besides, that wouldn't embarrass Jason.

What would?

She opened her shoulder bag and pawed through the contents with shaking hands. She hated this kind of attention, really, really hated it. She pulled out a handful of bills and shuffled through them, then offered the whole bunch to Doc.

"All I have is forty-two dollars, but it's worth every cent—" she heard the gasp "—to support the school fund." She waved her hands at Jason's captors. "Please let the poor man go. I don't like ice cream anyway."

They let him go, falling back defensively, as if they expected him to turn on them. He straightened and his gray-eyed glance turned from outraged to outrageous in an instant.

"Well, *I* like ice cream," he declared. "You got me bought and paid for, Diana Kennedy, and I am gonna make abso-damn-lutely sure you get your money's worth."

That's when she realized she'd gotten herself into real trouble, trying to beat him at his own game.

CHAPTER FIFTEEN

JASON AND DIANA CARRIED their dish of ice cream over to the park located between Lover's Lane and the businesses fronting on Main Street. Kids ran in and out of the greenery and swarmed over the wooden playground equipment. The picnic tables were crowded with those enjoying their frozen treats.

"Over here!" Tap Wilson waved a hand, then got up from the bench of the picnic table where he'd been sitting with Mary Lou. "We're just leavin'."

"Aren't we the lucky ones?" Jason's tone was borderline sarcastic. He placed his dish of chocolate ice cream on the uneven surface of the table and sat down.

After a moment's hesitation, Diana did, too, sitting across from him with the wooden tabletop between. Ill at ease, she wondered if perhaps he felt the same. Neither one spoke; they simply eyed each other warily.

Finally, he jerked his head toward the sounds of revelry on Main Street. "That wasn't my doing," he said.

"I could tell."

"They set us up."

"I know that, too. I should have realized something was up, as hard as everyone worked to get me here—including your grandmother." She lifted a spoonful of ice cream to her lips. It was delicious...cool and sweet.

He cocked his head and watched her with a question in his eyes. "Forty-two bucks is a lot of money."

He didn't know the half of it. She squeezed every dollar until it cried for mercy. "It's for a worthy cause," she said in an offhand manner.

"Uh-huh." He picked up his spoon. "The school fund."

"Yes, and—" She stopped short, chewing on her lip in uncharacteristic indecision. "Oh, hell," she said, throwing caution to the wind. "It also gives me a chance to apologize to you."

His eyebrows soared and he pushed his hat onto the back of his head. "For what, exactly?" He waited with an expectant gleam in his eyes.

"For being such a grouch the day you took me to see your buffalo herd. I...I know you wouldn't have shot that little buffalo."

"You're sure about that, are you?"

"I was, until this very moment. You *were* trying to make a point, right?" She nodded. "Of course you were. I overreacted and I'm sorry."

Why did he look disappointed? She frowned. "What's the matter? What did you think I was going to apologize for?"

He put down his spoon. He hadn't taken the first

bite of ice cream yet. "For calling me a thief and a liar," he said.

She tried to hedge. "I didn't exactly say *that*."

"The hell you didn't." His tone turned indignant. "You keep telling everybody who'll listen that I stole your buffalo and then lied about it."

"*Somebody* took him," she said defensively. "If it wasn't you, who was it?"

"Don't you think if I knew that, you'd have ol' Bill back in a flash? All I know is that I'm not a thief and I'm not a liar and I don't like being accused of it."

It was hard to doubt him when he looked so offended. "If I'm wrong, then I apologize for that, too," she said stiffly.

"But you're still not sure."

"I'm…" No, she wasn't sure.

"All this over a damned dead buffalo." He shook his head, his expression mournful. "Or is that all we're dealin' with here?"

"What else could possibly—"

"Yeah, what." His face was a study in frustration. "Sometimes it's like…like you blame me for everything that goes wrong, including stuff I don't even know about. Anything to keep me at arm's length."

It was *exactly* like that, she realized in a sudden rush of unwelcome insight. The first thing she blamed him for was reminding her of another man. Then she blamed him because he pushed her into saying and doing things she normally wouldn't, and she blamed him because his very presence made her itchy and uncomfortable and prone to losing control. But what could she possibly say to him that would explain that without giving away too much?

When she didn't speak, he leaned forward. "We got off on the wrong foot from the very beginning," he said. "That *was* my fault."

"When we're together, both feet are wrong." With a burst of honesty, she added, "Mine as well as yours."

"Suppose I'll just have to face the fact that you don't like me?"

She stared at him, astounded he'd think such a thing. He looked back in deadly earnest. "Everybody likes you," she said at last. "*I* like you...when you behave." Even truer. "I don't trust you, though. You make me feel manipulated and maneuvered and—and you seem to think you can grab me any time you feel the urge."

"I see." He looked away, toward children laughing and tumbling around the swings. "Any time I feel the urge, huh? I wish. You don't know the half of it." He rolled his eyes. "I'd like to say I'm sorry about that."

"I'd *like* you to say it, but I'm not sure I'd believe you."

"Too bad. It's the truth—all except the part about grabbing you. Hard to be sorry about that." His smile blinded her. "Since I'm being so honest, I might as well admit it's damned hard for me to keep my hands off you, period."

"Jason..." She said his name helplessly. How was she supposed to keep her wits about her when he said things like that?

He shrugged and stood up, untangling his long legs from beneath the tabletop to do so. "What the hell. We can at least be friends."

She stood up, too, her ice cream forgotten. "I'm not so sure about that. Maybe we should settle for *not* being enemies."

He gave her a whimsical smile. "I'll never be your enemy," he said, "no matter what. But I've got this problem...."

Her eyebrows shot up in disbelief.

"No, really," he insisted. "See, I've got this one-track mind...." He moved around the picnic table to stand before her. He lifted his hands to her shoulders, his manner light and casual.

He didn't fool her for a minute. "Now, Jason!" She put her hands over his but didn't try to push them away.

"Right now," he said, gazing into her eyes, "I have an almost irresistible urge to seal our *understanding* with a kiss. Just a friendly little kiss, a simple peck on the cheek. But I know how you feel about...gratuitous kissing."

Gratuitous kissing? It was all she could do to keep from laughing. "You don't know diddly-squat about how I feel about anything," she whispered, her tone suddenly thick with hidden meanings.

A challenge sparked in his eyes, and something else, too—something powerful and sexy. "Then set me straight,'' he said softly. "*Please,* set me straight...if you've got the nerve.''

"I've got nerve I haven't even used yet.'' It was a rash thing to say. It was even more rash to rise on tiptoe to press her lips to his cheek. She'd intended to dismiss him with what he claimed to want. At least, that's how it started. At the last instant, he turned his head and her lips landed squarely on his.

At the same time, his arms closed around her and she found herself dragged hard against his chest. She lifted her own arms to twine around his neck, her hands twisting through the thick strands of dark hair curling around his collar.

His mouth took hers and her senses reeled. She couldn't believe she was doing this, in public and in broad daylight. The feel of his lean body against hers sent an erotic firestorm through her to settle in a pit of longing at the base of her stomach.

God, she'd missed him.

At last, he lifted his head to stare down at her, his astonishment plain. "Jeez," he muttered, "I guess I *don't* know diddly-squat.''

"You—I—what?" Dizzy, she clung to him.

"Maybe absence really does make the heart grow fonder.''

She gulped in a quick breath of air and sanity. "Don't push your luck.''

"Right.'' He released her instantly and stepped away, swinging his arms around until he could clasp his hands behind his back. "Does this mean we're officially friends again?''

Diana's lips still tingled from his kiss. She licked them nervously, realized he was watching, then gasped, her cheeks burning. "I don't know what it means," she said quickly. "Probably nothing. Let's just try to be civil, okay?"

He grinned, a calculating gleam in his eye. "I can do civil." Leaning toward her, he cupped her chin with one hand and tilted it up. "I don't know about you, but I enjoyed that at least forty-two bucks' worth. See you around, friend." Dropping a last quick kiss on her trembling mouth, he turned and sauntered away.

Diana's knees collapsed and she sank onto the picnic bench again. She was weakening, dammit! She had to keep reminding herself how impossible it would be to get involved with a man like Jason Cameron, no matter how charming and good-looking. He'd chew her up and spit her out. Or would he? Maybe—

"Jeez, Diana, what was that all about?"

She started, surprised to find Ryan standing there with Blair beside him. The boy looked disgusted, the girl speculative. Diana stifled a groan, chagrined to be seen like this by her stepson yet again.

"It's only obvious," Blair said. "Too bad. I thought you were different, Diana."

Diana thought she was different, too. So much for self-delusion. She managed a shrug she hoped looked careless.

"And I thought you were smarter than that,"

Ryan snapped, adding his two cents' worth. "You do know what he's after, don't you?"

Diana's startled gaze flew to Ryan's face. Of course she knew; didn't *he?*

The boy glared at her. "I mean *besides that.*"

"Now you've lost me."

"I'm talking about the Hideout. What else? He wasn't exactly happy when you bought it out from under him. Now it looks like he's come up with some plan to con you into doing what he wants after all."

Diana felt as if she'd been punched in the stomach. "Jason wanted the Hideout?"

Blair gave her a pitying look. "It was no secret around here. I don't think he'd sleep with you just to get it, but maybe—"

"Blair!" Diana and Ryan exclaimed as one.

"Well," Blair said defensively, "I don't. I've got no idea what his game plan is, but if you fall for it, you're not half as smart as I thought you were."

Diana noticed that the girl used the past tense— *thought.* Well, hell, who could blame her? At the moment, Diana sure wasn't *feeling* any too smart.

AFTER THAT, life really went to hell in a handbasket. Each day seemed to begin with another crisis, climaxing on Friday when Diana discovered another ransom note.

"Now we're getting mad. Three million or you'll start getting that buffalo back in shoe boxes."

Attached was a primitive cartoon drawing of Buffalo Bill, a hand holding a butcher knife to the shaggy throat.

Diana saw red. She supposed it had become a familiar sight to the locals, her stomping out of the Hideout and all the way to the marshal's office. Unfortunately, it couldn't be helped.

This time, even Max laughed. "Sorry, Diana," he said, wiping his eyes on his shirtsleeve. "But you gotta admit this is funny."

"I won't admit any such thing." She gritted her teeth. "Any leads since the reward was announced?"

"Oh, yeah, great ones." He rolled his eyes. "A bunch of kids, nine- or ten-year-olds, came in to tell me they'd heard there was a whole bunch of buffalo out at Jason's place and maybe Bill was mixed up with them." He shook his head in amusement.

Diana didn't. "Anything else?"

He rubbed his chin. "Early Biggers told Dwight Deakins that he thought he mighta seen the getaway pickup the night Bill was taken."

"Really?" She caught her breath. A lead, after all this time! She frowned. "Why did he talk to Dwight instead of you?"

"Because he knows Dwight. Unfortunately, Early has a real liking for strong spirits, so we have to take it with a grain of salt."

"Max, we don't have any other leads! When? Where? Who?"

"When was about two in the morning. Where was the gas station across from the Rusty Spur and who was whoever drove past it in the pickup. Seems Early had been sitting in the driveway with a bottle in a paper bag ever since the station closed at ten, so you know what shape he was in." He grimaced.

"What color pickup?"

"In the dark, all pickups look black, at least to Early. Hell, Diana, even if it *was* black, how many black pickups you think we've got around here?"

He was right. She was grasping at straws. "But there must have been something to make him think it might have been the kidnappers."

"Yeah. He said there was something huge in the back. But hell, it coulda been a—a butane tank, a piece of farm or ranch equipment with a tarp thrown over it—anything."

"Heading north," she said.

"That's right."

"Jason lives to the north."

"Dammit, Diana, are you gonna start that again? I'd stake my reputation that Jason's innocent. Hell, I *have* staked my reputation. I sure wish you'd get over this vendetta you got going with him. After what happened in the park—"

"What do you mean, what happened in the park?" But her heart sank with his words for she knew he was referring to the kiss.

"I heard," Max said, "there was some pretty

heavy necking going on over there, that's all. Naturally, I thought you two had buried the hatchet.''

''What a grapevine this town has!'' She banged her temple with the flat of one hand as if she'd just made that discovery.

''Now don't get all worked up again,'' he suggested. ''I'm doing all that's humanly possible to find your buffalo, but I'm not responsible for your problems with Jason Cameron. You're on your own with that, lady.''

Was she?

Not according to the snickers and sly looks she was receiving. And not only at the Hideout: her walk through town for those few blocks to the marshal's office had proven to be a real ordeal. She was beginning to feel as if she was on public display from the minute she stepped out of her house until she closed the door behind her again.

So she'd lost her mind and kissed Jason Cameron in the park! At the time, she hadn't realized what a scoundrel he really was, although heaven knew she should have.

On top of that, she hadn't seen him since the ice-cream social, which gave her an uneasy feeling.

He was up to something. She'd bet on it.

''GRANDMA!'' JASON SLAMMED into the ranch house at the Straight Arrow. ''I'm goin' into town. Wanna come along for the ride?''

Granny walked out of the kitchen, wiping her hands on an apron tied over her jeans. ''You chasin' after that girl again? Ben is gettin' real incensed about all your trips to town."

"Hell, I only chase after her in my spare time," he scoffed. "Gotta pick up some stuff at the feed store anyway, not that it's any of Ben's business. Long as I do my work, he's got no reason to squawk."

"Ben's a worrier." Granny reached around to untie her apron. "Wouldn't mind ridin' along with you at that. I'll just leave a note for Betsy." Bright-eyed, she tilted her head to peer at him. "How're you and Diana gettin' along these days? I hear you two was gettin' real cozy at the park the other day."

Jason's grin threatened to split his face. "You could say that." The grin slipped. "People are talking, are they?"

"Yep."

"I hope Diana doesn't get wind of any gossip. She wouldn't take kindly to it, I can double-damn-guarantee you."

"Ah, pshaw, how could she blame you?"

How indeed? Although he puzzled over that all the way into town, he couldn't think of a single way. They'd parted friends…or something even better, judging from the way she'd ignited in his arms.

Yep, this time, he and the beautiful but prickly Diana Kennedy had reached a whole new plane on the rocky road to love. Because, sure as hell, that's where they were heading.

WHEN GRANDMA CAMERON walked in, Diana was talking to Charlie Gilroy behind the bar. The old lady waited a few feet away for them to finish their conversation.

Diana came around the bar, smiling. "Hello, Mrs. Cameron. It's nice to—"

"Call me Grandma." Etta May gave Diana a hug before she knew what was up. "Just dropped by to say howdy."

"Come sit down." Diana drew Etta May toward one of the small tables ringing the dance floor. At midafternoon, the place was nearly empty, so they had their choice of seats. "What can I get you to drink?"

Etta May considered. "How about…" She grinned suddenly. "I was about to ask for a lemonade, but a nice cold beer would go good right about now."

"You got it." Diana signaled to Charlie. "So how've you been?"

"Fine, just fine. I was down on my back for a day or two but I'm feelin' fine again." Charlie set a napkin and a glass of beer in front of her and she gave him a quick murmur of thanks.

"That's good." Politeness made Diana add, "And the rest of the family?"

"All fine." Her gray eyes narrowed. "Especially Jason."

"Jason?" Diana sat back in her chair. She didn't even want to hear the man's name.

Etta May nodded. "Diana, I am tickled pink to hear the two of you're gettin' so…close. I'm won-

derin'—no, I'm hopin' that there's something serious in the wind.''

Diana stared at her, aghast. "Between me and Jason? My God, where did you get such an idea?"
But she supposed she knew—a suspicion confirmed
by Etta May's next words.

"Honey, everyone knows you two was sparkin'
in the park at the ice-cream social.'' Etta May patted
the younger woman's arm. "There's nothin' to be
ashamed of. He's single, you're single.''

Just then, Jason himself came strolling through
the entryway. Spotting them, he ambled over, the
very picture of nonchalance. Leaning down, he
kissed his grandmother's cheek, then smiled at Diana.

"Hi, hon," he said.

"Hon!" Diana shot to her feet, fury making her
tremble. "I'm not your *hon*."

He looked stunned. "Well...maybe not, but now
that we're at least friends again—"

"Again?" She took an aggressive step toward
him, her jaw jutting out. "Where do you get this
'again' stuff? We've never been friends. It isn't possible to be friends with a man who gets by on
charm!'' And she should know.

"Goddammit, Diana!" Anger brought a tide of
color to his face, a highly unusual reaction for him.
"You are beyond a doubt the most unreasonable
woman it has ever been my misfortune to tangle
with. When I left you in the park, *we were friends*.''

"When you left me in the park, I didn't know

you wanted to run me out of town.'' She stretched up on her toes to spit the words in his face. "When you said I had something you wanted, I never dreamed you meant my business!''

"I didn't. I swear to God.'' He reached for her.

She batted his hands aside. "I'll bet you're the one who's spreading all these rumors. It's part of a plan to make me mad enough to sell out to you and leave town. Stealing Buffalo Bill didn't work, so—''

"If you mention that flea-bitten relic one more time, I—I'll do something drastic!''

"Don't you yell at me!''

"Children, children.'' Grandma, who'd been watching wide-eyed, tried to intervene. "This is all a big misunderstanding. Diana, if I said something to upset you—''

"Not you.'' Hot tears blurred Diana's vision and she blinked them away. Tears? She owed him for that, too. "I apologize, Grandma, but I—I have to get back to work. Please excuse me.''

She whirled away, right into Charlie Gilroy, who was carrying a tray of brimming glasses to a table on the other side of the room. The cold wash of liquid struck her chest, taking her breath away. She leaped back, brushing futilely at her soaked blouse.

Charlie looked horrified. "Ah, hell, Diana, I'm sorry.''

"It wasn't your fault, Charlie.'' She looked down at the wet silk, molded to her breasts like a coat of paint. Her nipples stood out sharply, the result of the sudden assault of coldness. She picked at the fabric, trying to hold it away from her body while edging away. "I've got to get out of these wet things. I'm sorry about the mess, Charlie."

"No problem." He shooed her away. "I'll take care of it. You run along."

Jason watched her go, her cute little rear end swinging beneath the dark skirt with every angry step. He swallowed hard, remembering the way her nipples had peaked beneath the wet silk. Made his palms itch just thinking about it.

Granny patted his elbow. "Set down, boy, and get ahold of yourself."

He sat down but was a long way from getting ahold of himself. "What happened?" he moaned, propping his head on his hands. "What'd I do? Where'd I go wrong?"

Granny shook her head. "You two are at sixes and sevens, I'll grant you that. It's like—it's like you're talkin' different languages."

His head snapped up. "I'm sick of it," he said in a hard voice. "If I want to be insulted, I don't have to hang around here."

"Maybe you do." The old lady's glance turned sly. "I sure don't remember any other gals in town givin' you so much grief. If somethin' or some*one* is worth havin', they're worth a little extra effort. At least, that's what my daddy always told me."

"To hell with that." Jason shot to his feet with fresh resolve. "I'm gonna go have it out with her *now*."

Striding across the dance floor, he heard his

grandmother's soft voice behind him. "You do that, boy. You do that."

IN THE TINY upstairs apartment, Diana stripped off her wet shirt and bra, flinging them on the bed. She was trembling so hard she could barely stand. She had to force herself to suck in deep breaths of air instead of collapsing in hysteria, which was what she wanted to do.

He always made her lose control!

That's what bothered her most. She'd struggled all her life to be in control, thought she'd achieved it years ago, and now this.

Crossing to the chest, she yanked open the top drawer. She'd left a few things here for emergencies when she and Ryan moved to Betsy's house. Snatching a red silk T-shirt from the stack inside, she shook it out.

This time, he would surely understand that there was nothing between them and never could be. Surely. If he didn't, she was uncertain what else she could—

The door to the apartment slammed open and there stood Jason, muscular thighs apart and hands clenched at his sides. "Diana," he grated, "we've got to talk. *Now.*"

Shocked to the core, she watched him cross the small sitting room and barge through the open door into the even smaller bedroom. Too late she realized she was naked to the waist. Awkwardly, she tugged the wadded T-shirt up over her breasts.

"What do you think you're doing, barging in here like you own the place?" she demanded.

He halted beside the bed opposite her...and stared. He opened his mouth to speak, but the sight of her caused words to fail him. Sunlight and shadows streamed past the slats of the blinds, covering the room and the woman with mysterious shadow stripes. Half-undressed, hair in a tangle and eyes half-closed, she emanated such a powerful sexuality that it almost pulled him across the bed.

"Diana..." All the anger was gone from his body, from his voice. In its place blossomed desire so hot and heavy that he thought he might explode.

She licked her lips, mesmerizing him with the rise and fall of those breasts, those wonderful breasts barely concealed beneath the scrap of fabric she held like a shield.

"Jeez," he croaked, "say something. Tell me I'm a jerk. Call the cops. Just...*do* something. Because if you don't, I'm going to have you naked on that bed before you can say Buffalo Bill."

Her lips parted and her eyelids drifted languorously down. She took a shuddering breath and, at the same time, let her arms fall to her sides, the wad of silk dropping onto the bed. "Prove it," she whispered into the heady half-light of the room. "I'm saying it. Buffalo—"

CHAPTER SIXTEEN

DIANA AND JASON came together on their knees in the middle of the bed, drawn there in this sultry atmosphere of light and shadow. Wrapping eager arms around each other, they pressed their bodies together and kissed with a hungry abandon completely free of pretense.

Who am I kidding? Diana wondered, letting her head fall back to expose her throat to his hungry mouth. *I want him as much as he wants me. If I'm going to do this thing, I won't pretend it's against my will.*

Against her better judgment—yes. But not against her will. If she didn't have him now, she thought she'd die.

His hands rose from her waist to stroke her back. She arched her body forward, pressing her forehead into the curve of his shoulder, giving him all the access he needed.

All the access she needed.

His hands touched her breasts, as hot as his mouth on hers. He cupped and squeezed her compliant flesh, fingers tweaking already tight nipples. She moaned, leaning into his hands. When he lowered his head, she whispered an impassioned, ''Yes!''

He thrust his tongue against her nipple, then sucked it deep into his mouth. A spasm of longing shook her, and she fell back onto the bed, dragging him with her. She'd been putting so much effort into fighting the attraction between them that surrender left her light-headed.

The strong sucking pressure of his mouth made her arch beneath him, her fingers clawing at his shoulders. He raked the nipple with his teeth and she cried out, her stomach clenching with desire. Panting, she clawed at his shirt, needing to feel his skin against hers.

The tugging at her breast sent waves of sensation spiraling through her. She closed her eyes, the better to savor what he was doing to her. She'd forgotten how wonderful a man's hands and mouth could make her feel...or perhaps she'd tried to forget, if she'd ever truly known. This was like nothing that had ever happened to her before, both in intensity and the speed with which she'd responded to his touch.

Restlessly, she twisted beneath him while he suckled at her breasts. He touched her thigh and she started as if licked by fire. He slid his hand up beneath her skirt as far as he could go, then cupped his fingers around her, over her panty hose. With each touch, she raised and lowered her hips, her breathing a raw gasp.

With a grunt of impatience, he grabbed the elastic waistband of her panty hose and hauled them down. She bent her knees, willing him to hurry, wild to free herself of all constraints. He pushed his finger-tips into her, and at that first fiery touch, she nearly exploded. Holding her still, absorbing her convulsions, he delved deeper. Groaning, she gave control over to him...completely.

Her orgasm elicited a cry of surprise and pleasure, ending in a groan of fresh frustration. She wanted more, wanted him inside her, making real an image that had haunted her dreams.

But he was still dressed, she realized with some confusion. All she wore was a skirt pulled up around her hips. "Jason," she managed in a voice quivering with strain, "this isn't fair, you dressed and me...not." She tugged at his shirt, which was unbuttoned and hanging outside his waistband. "Take off your clothes."

"Say please." His voice was thick, but even now, he could tease.

She groaned and closed her eyes. "Please!"

"Since you ask so nicely..." He was having more trouble holding on than he cared to admit. Kneeling between her knees, he unfastened his jeans just enough to free his wild erection. There'd be time for finesse later, he soothed his conscience; now he and Diana were united in urgency.

Even so, he dragged out his wallet and extracted the "emergency" condom he kept tucked inside. If this wasn't an emergency, he didn't know what the hell was.

She tried to help him slide it on, but her fingers brushing his turgid length nearly proved his undoing. When he'd regained partial control, he managed to unroll the latex sheath into place. Braced on stiff arms, he stared at her, flushed with passion and crazy with a hunger he understood and shared.

When he didn't enter her immediately, she opened her eyes and met his turbulent gaze. Her full lower lip trembled.

"Do you want me?" he asked in a voice that nearly failed him.

"You know I do." She put her hands on his shoulders and her heels behind his knees, trying to pull him down to her.

"I need to hear you say it. Later..." She surged against him and he choked. "Later when you deny everything and say this is all my fault, I...want to be able...to quote you—"

"Shut up, Jason!" She glared at him. Lifting her hands, she stroked his flat nipples, her gaze locked with his in a kind of insolent challenge.

"Say it!" He groaned with the effort it required to keep from slamming into her.

"Oh, all right." Her voice sounded less in command than the words. She slid her hands between their bodies. "I want you, Jason Cameron." She cupped his heaviness, squeezing a little, lifting, guiding the length of him to the heaven it longed to enter.

And did at last. She gasped and arched her back, hips surging to meet him. Jason drove into her, unable to control the pace as he'd intended, realizing too late that he'd wanted her too much for too long to have complete command now. If he wasn't careful—

"Do you think Diana's in here?"

The voice came from the hallway, just beyond the door—and it was Ryan's. Diana froze in midmotion, her eyes flying wide with terror and disbelief.

"Grandma said..." Blair. *"Grandma said she came up to change her shirt, but maybe she had to go home to do it."*

After the initial shock, Jason began to move inside her again...with exquisite slowness. She jerked beneath him but couldn't escape the throbbing between her thighs. Her entire body quivered with the storm building inside.

But discovery lay just outside the door. "Are you crazy?" Her hoarse whisper burned her throat.

"I...couldn't stop now if I wanted to." But he did manage to hold himself still, filling her. "And I don't...want to."

"Nah, she keeps stuff in here for emergencies." Fists banging on the door made both Diana and Jason flinch. Even then, he resumed his deliberate stroking. The possibility of discovery was very real but somehow seemed merely to add an extra erotic thrill. He could sense her struggle not to respond; she dug her fingers into his biceps and held on, refusing to match his deliberate rhythm.

"Quit pounding on the door. I told you, she isn't here."

Diana couldn't hold out any longer. With a muffled groan, she lifted her hips to meet his. Her eyes closed and she chewed on her lower lip, but he knew she was still listening to the voices outside. Her breath was an agonized gasp.

"Maybe the door's unlocked. We could just..."

Diana bucked beneath him like a wild thing and he knew why; if those two kids opened that door, they'd have an unobstructed view of the bed and everything going on there.

Diana shoved at him and he caught her wrists with his hands, managing to pin them to the bed beside her ears. Feeling diabolical and on the very edge of control, he lowered his lips to hers, kissing her with slow thoroughness while his hips ground into hers. She was his. Nothing could stop him from taking her—

The doorknob rattled and Jason froze. Then Blair restored his faith in her—or would, when he had time to think about it.

"Ryan Kennedy, nobody's in there. You're just trying to get me to go inside an empty apartment with you—in your dreams! I knew we wouldn't find her and Jason there anyway. She doesn't even like him. You can't make me..."

The voice faded away. Jason wanted to reassure Diana that they'd dodged that bullet, but he was losing it—fast. "So you don't even like me." He punctuated his words with fancy movements.

She groaned. "Not...even a...*little bit!*"

She clenched on the last word and her climax brought his own crashing and thundering through him. He collapsed onto her, rolling immediately to one side with her still in his arms to avoid crushing her. Spasms of sheer delight quivered along his nerve endings and he closed his eyes on a guttural sigh of pure satisfaction.

He was therefore completely unprepared for the fist that came crashing down on his chest.

IF SHE THOUGHT he'd made her lose control *before*...

She sat up and glared at the astonished man staring at her as if she'd lost her mind. Well, maybe she had—but this wasn't proof of that theory.

"They almost walked in on us!" she wailed. "How could you *do* that to me?"

"Excuse me? You *wanted* me to do that to you."

"No, I meant..." She chewed on that poor abused lip. "Why didn't you stop when they started talking just outside the door? They could have heard us, they could have walked in and seen us, which would have been worse."

"They didn't." He touched her breast, lifting the beautiful shape in his palm, admiring the coral tip. It made his mouth water just looking at it.

She caught her breath and shoved his hand away but didn't look pleased about doing it. "They could have, though. And you just kept right on...doing what you were doing."

"Did it ever occur to you that I couldn't stop?"

She looked surprised. "No." Jumping out of bed, she looked around for her panty hose. Snatching them up, she sat on the edge of the bed and began pulling them on.

Disappointed, he could still take pleasure in watching her naked breasts jiggle in time to her movements. She had beautiful breasts, full and lush but also high, standing out from the wall of her chest. And her nipples... He nearly groaned, remembering the pleasure he'd taken in them.

But all that, apparently, was past tense. Shucking the condom, he lifted his hips off the mattress and tucked himself inside his jeans. "What's your rush?" he asked plaintively. "That happened so fast that I thought we could take our time on the next go-round."

She darted him a quelling glance. "There's not going to be a next go-round. I lost my head, but that will never happen again."

"Wanna bet?" It took considerable effort not to laugh. After all *that,* she thought they could just forget the whole thing and get on with their lives? The woman really *was* nuts!

Locating the bra on the floor near her feet, she picked it up and slipped the straps over her shoulders. Leaning forward, she settled her breasts unerringly into the lacy cups. How in hell did women do that?

"I do *not* want to bet," she said primly. "Nor do I want to continue this relationship."

"Which one? Are we talking friendship or sex here?"

"Both." The red T-shirt was crumpled up on the

bed between them. She shook it out, then pulled it over her head.

"Nope. No way." He shook his head vigorously. "Don't you know it's impossible to go back after doing what we just did? Everything's changed."

"My mind is made up." She stood up, smoothing the T-shirt into place. "Look, I'm going to my office. Wait a few minutes and then try to..." For the first time, she let him see past the icy facade but only for a second. "For God's sake, *try* to get out without arousing any more attention."

"You mean sneak."

"Okay, I mean sneak."

"I don't sneak."

"And I don't rip off my clothes and throw myself at every guy I meet." She glared at him, high color flooding her cheeks. "Just do it, okay?"

That's when he knew he'd gotten to her, big time. He waited until she'd gone, then spent a few minutes tidying up the room. He flushed the condom down the toilet, stuffed the telltale foil in his pocket, picked up his boots and carried them out into the hall.

After walking to the bottom of the stairs, he sat down on the last step to pull on his boots. When he'd accomplished that task, he stood up—and saw that two waitresses and a cook had been watching him.

So much for sneaking.

THE NEWS FLASHED from ear to ear, covering the entire town of Cupid in less than twenty-four hours:

The Queen Bee and the Cowboy King *did it!*

"This is great," Jimmy Mosely enthused. "Man, if they'd just get married, all our troubles would be over."

Diana's troubles were just beginning. By the time the gossip reached her days later, it was far too late to do anything to scotch the rumors.

Stalking to her office to grapple with the question of rumor control, she saw the folded sheet of paper right away. Hell, she didn't even want to pick it up. She knew what it was.

And she was right.

"Four million dollars or Bill's a goner. This time, we mean it!"

The accompanying drawing showed a cartoon Bill with a gag tied around his muzzle and a rope around his neck.

Beleaguered on all sides, the normally calm, cool and controlled Diana sat right down at her desk, laid her head on her arms and wept. That buffalo's saga had become a symbol of her entire life: out of control.

Nobody was ever going to find Bill, and nobody was ever going to understand what had happened between her and Jason—or why it caused her such grief. Jason...damn him. She hadn't seen him since the day they hit the sack and she hoped she never would. Because she didn't want him less, she wanted him more. Since she'd never in a million years give in to her baser instincts again, it was far better if they avoided each other entirely.

God, she hated charming men!

Grandma Cameron found Diana in the office, still sniffling. "Good heavens, girl, what's the matter?" the old lady demanded. "You look like your dog just died."

Diana managed a wry smile. "It's not my dog, it's my buffalo." She offered the note for Granny's inspection.

Etta May heaved a relieved sigh. "There for a minute, I thought you were cryin' over that Jason. If he did anything to harm you, I'd tan his hide good, even if he is all grown-up."

"I'm ignoring Jason." Diana brushed at her damp cheeks. "Nobody's going to find Buffalo Bill," she went on unhappily. "Every time I get one of these notes, it just makes me miserable all over again."

"Well, hon, if you could start lookin' at it with a little humor the way everybody else does, it'd be easier to take." She patted the younger woman's hand. "You'll get your buffalo back, just wait and see. When you stop reacting the way those miscreants want you to react, he'll turn up and everybody will have a good laugh."

"I hope." But she really didn't believe it. She drew in a deep, wavering breath. "Thanks for trying to cheer me up."

"Don't give it a thought."

"D-did you drop by for any special reason? Is there anything I can do for you?"

"Well..." Granny looked embarrassed. "I got some news and I don't want you to take it wrong when you hear it."

This sounded interesting. Diana cocked her head and waited.

"I, umm, I'm gonna be movin' to the Lazy T."

"You're moving in with Ethan Turner?" Diana stared at the old woman with astonishment, unable to believe her ears.

Etta May frowned. "Not the way you mean, missy! I'm gonna be cookin' for Ethan and his grandson, that's all. They need me, and the Straight Arrow don't anymore. It's as simple as that."

"I don't think it's all that simple for Mr. Turner," Diana said gently. "He cares for you a great deal. You know that, don't you?"

"I don't know any such blamed thing. I'm just mentioning this so that if any of my kin gets on their high horse, you'll know the truth of it."

Any of her kin, meaning Jason—oh, and Ben, of course. "I don't expect to be seeing much of Jason," Diana said stiffly. "I'll go further and admit that I've never been able to set him straight about *anything.*"

Granny just smiled. "You got more influence with that boy than you know," she said.

Remembering the comment later, Diana sighed. Little did Etta May know....

"A COOK," BLAIR said scornfully. "Like anybody's gonna believe that."

Several days had passed and word of Etta May's intentions had gotten around. Now even Blair seemed moved to comment. Sitting across from his niece at one of the small tables at the Hideout, Jason glowered at her. This was the first time he'd come back to this place since making love to the beautiful owner before being summarily tossed out on his...ear. He was in a bad mood because she hadn't even spoken to him since he'd gotten here.

"Yeah, well." Jason swallowed a big bite of his hamburger. "I'd say nobody in the family believes it anyway. Surprised about you, though. I sorta figured you'd be on her side."

"I am," Blair agreed. "I'm just not falling for that 'cook' song and dance. So they want to live together—big deal! They're of age."

"Several times." But Jason was shocked. His grandma was eighty-something if she was a day. Much too old for what this flippant teenager was suggesting.

"We'll solicit an impartial third opinion." Blair waved. "Yoo-hoo, Diana! Can you come here a minute?"

She came, Jason thought reluctantly. Nevertheless, he was delighted to see her...someplace besides in his dreams. She looked even better than usual, now that he knew what delights lay beneath that demure exterior.

Blair plunged right in. "Diana, what do you think

of Granny's plans to move in with Mr. Turner? Be honest now.''

Diana's smile didn't look easy to Jason. "I'm always honest," she said. "I think it's wonderful."

Jason bristled. "Ah, c'mon. What good can possibly come from this?"

Her hazel eyes narrowed fractionally. "They'll be good for each other. Haven't you been paying attention? They adore each other. It's called love, Jason."

"It's called crazy. They're old enough to know better."

"They may be old," Diana said calmly, "but they're not dead. They deserve any happiness they can find together."

"You're saying everybody deserves happiness, then?"

She looked discombobulated. "I—yes, of course."

"In that case..." He shot a quick look at Blair, who pretended to eat a French fry while actually watching with avid attention. "What time are you getting off tonight? Maybe I can, uh, drive you home and we'll see if *we* can find a little happiness, which God only knows *I* deserve."

"Jason!" She gave a warning glance at Blair before rounding on him again. "What do I look like—stupid?"

"No, you look..." But he, too, was handicapped by the presence of the teenager. "Blair, don't you have somewhere to go?" he asked pointedly.

"No." Her expression was clear and untroubled, not to mention intensely interested.

"Where's Ryan? Maybe you should go find him."

"He's out back helping unload crates or doing something manly." She wrinkled her short, straight nose. "Besides, I like it here. You two are more fun to watch than television."

"Oh, for—"

"Hey, here comes Grandma and Ryan now." Blair stood, waving madly to get their attention.

Etta May approached without visible enthusiasm, Ryan at her side. "Blair," she said. She nodded at the other two but didn't smile.

"Have a seat," Jason said quickly, feeling ashamed of himself when he saw how tired she seemed.

Ryan held her chair, then took his own seat beside Blair.

Granny glanced around. "Been talkin' about me, I see."

Jason said, "Now, Grandma..."

Blair said, "That's right."

Diana said, "I'm very happy for you and Mr. Turner."

Granny's shoulders slumped. "You're all makin' this out to be something it ain't. The man needs a *cook*."

"What do you need, Granny?" Blair's expression conveyed nothing but love and concern.

"I need... I guess I need to feel needed."

"Hell, Grandma, we all need you." Jason hoped he didn't look as uncomfortable as he felt.

"No, you don't," the old lady said. "None of you do anymore. Ben's got Betsy, Maggie's got Chase and you've got..." She darted a somewhat guilty look at Diana.

"So what's the difference?" Blair demanded of Jason. "Grandma Cameron and Grandpa Turner have as much right to be together as you and Diana do, Jason."

"Now wait a minute," Diana protested. "Jason and I aren't together—not the way you mean."

"I get it. You just fool around occasionally."

Jason surged to his feet. "Blair Britton, you apologize for that crack!"

"It was no crack, just the truth. Everyone in town knows." She appealed to Ryan. "Isn't that right?"

He managed to nod and shrug simultaneously while going to great lengths to avoid his stepmother's gaze.

"Right." Blair nodded for emphasis. "So what's the difference between Granny and Mr. Turner shacking up, Jason and Diana doing it upstairs at the Hideout, and—" she eyed everyone around the table with a challenging expression "—me and Ryan?"

CHAPTER SEVENTEEN

"YOU AND RYAN *WHAT?*"

Diana had never seen Jason so upset. He leaned on the table, his attention riveted on his niece.

Even the irrepressible Blair looked taken aback. "W-why, nothing about us. I mean, we're not doing anything we shouldn't but—but if we did—I mean, everybody else..." She stumbled to a halt.

Diana found her voice at last. While she'd been worrying about the Hideout, Ryan could have been doing *anything* and she'd have been the last to know. "Ryan—"

"Ah, she's just making a point," he said. "Jeez, Blair, you trying to get me grounded for life?"

Grandma banged a fist down on the tabletop and startled the lot of them. "Pipe down and let me have my say," she ordered. "This is all my fault anyway."

"Ah, Granny—"

"Hush!" She took a quick, hard breath as if steeling herself for an unpleasant task. "The child's right. It's more important for me to set a good example for the younger generation than to go gallivantin' off pursuing my own selfish way."

Jason frowned. "Which means what?"

"That I won't be movin' in at the Lazy T." She said it with complete finality.

Everyone was caught by surprise except, naturally, Blair. Who smiled and patted Granny's veined hand. "Maybe it's for the best," she said with eighteen-year-old certainty. "If he loved you, he'd marry you. Or at least, that's what you've always told *me*."

Laughing, Granny pulled Blair close for a hug, but Diana thought she saw a sheen of tears in the old lady's eyes.

SOMEHOW DIANA ENDED UP in bed with Jason again that night. She told herself she'd agreed to talk to him after the Hideout closed at ten simply because she was upset about the gossip going around about them—ninety-nine percent of it true. What she told herself, unfortunately, was a lie.

It didn't take him fifteen minutes to get her up those stairs and flat on her back in the second-floor apartment. "This time," he said, unbuttoning his shirt and looking at her with the light of conquest in his gray eyes, "we're going to do this right!"

Diana closed her eyes and bit her lip to keep from groaning. The last and only other time they'd made love hadn't exactly been chopped liver! She sat up on the bed and started on her own buttons, but he stopped her.

"Let me." He covered her hands with his. "I've wanted to undress you since the minute I saw you. Humor me...."

She did and he did. They kissed, working at the fastenings of their clothing, wiggling out of garment after garment. They teased and played, rolling around the bed with a kind of sensuous abandon, taking their time...taking their pleasure. When he finally entered her, she breathed a heartfelt *"Yes"* and gave herself up entirely. Pressure built and climbed until she clung to his shoulders with straining fingers, to his hips with trembling thighs, her breathing harsh and urgent.

Matching his.

Then all self-control disintegrated into an explosive climax that lifted her and sent her sailing, and to her joy, he sailed with her.

NATURALLY, SHE HATED herself the moment her wits returned. She couldn't believe she was so weak! Even lying there on the tangled bed, still intimately joined with him, she had to finally admit that she was just as crazy about this man as every other woman in this part of Colorado—a sorry state of affairs.

She cleared her throat and his eyes blinked open, so close to hers on the pillows that she could see past the long, dark lashes into their clear depths. He looked as open and innocent as Blair always did.

Blair.

"Jason—"

"Diana—"

"You go first."

"No, you."

He was smiling and relaxed; she wasn't. She had too many issues to thrash out, issues pertaining to what had just happened between them but must never happen again. Everybody knew about them, even the teenagers.

When she didn't say anything, he reached out to touch her tender lower lip with a gentle forefinger. She resisted the urge to draw it into her mouth and—

"Blair's right," he said suddenly, transferring his attention from her lips to her right breast. "If Ethan loved Granny, he'd make an honest woman of her." Beneath his clever fingers, her nipple peaked instantly.

She felt an enormous surge of relief, mixed with an equal, if unwelcome, surge of desire. "Blair's... pretty sharp for a kid," she managed to say.

"Yeah. And so was Granny when she said that adults need to set a good example."

"Yes." Was she responding to his words or to the gentle tugging of his fingers? Both, maybe...

"Great." He rolled over until he covered her naked body with his. "We're adults. Let's do it."

"Do what?"

"Get married."

She stiffened, no small accomplishment with him doing his best to keep her moving. "How dare you insult my intelligence!" she cried.

He blinked, lifting his head higher so he could see her face. "Whoa! That was a marriage proposal, on the off chance you missed that part of it. I don't think too many women consider that an insult."

"You should know." She bucked beneath him, shoving him away. She'd never been so shocked in her life. He was such an obvious love-'em-and-leave-'em type of guy; everybody knew it. Even Blair, who'd warned against him. She sat up and swung around to the edge of the bed. "Blair *is* right," she said. "You never mean half of what you say."

"The hell I don't!" The very picture of righteous indignation, he sat up in the middle of the bed, pushing back the black hair falling over his forehead. "I meant every word I ever said to you, Diana Kennedy. Hell, I…" His gray eyes went wide as if with shock and his lips parted on a quick sharp breath. "Hell," he began again, "I *love* you."

"Yeah, right." She started grabbing for her clothing, strewn from door to bed. "I'll bet you say that to all the girls." In her experience, charming men would say anything to get what they wanted.

"As a matter of fact, I've never said it in my life, at least to anyone who wasn't blood kin."

Yanking on her skirt, she made a sloppy job of tucking in her blouse before buttoning the waistband. That done, she straightened to look him directly in the eye. Even sitting naked on the bed while she confronted him fully dressed, he didn't appear to realize he should have been at a disadvantage.

"Jason Cameron," she said, "you have no

shame. Apparently, you'll not only steal a person's buffalo to get your own way—"

"I didn't steal your damned buffalo!"

"You'll even make love to the buffalo's rightful owner."

"That's a damned lie." He scrambled to the side of the bed and swung long, muscular legs over the edge.

"Really? Is it also a lie that you wanted to buy the Hideout yourself and got bent out of shape when I beat you to it?"

He frowned. "Sure I wanted to buy the Hideout. So what? Everybody knew that. It's old news."

"Not to me, it isn't! I notice you don't deny being bent out of shape when I—"

"Woman, will you give me a chance?" He pulled his jeans up his legs, then rose and hiked them into place. "I took one look at you and forgot all about an entrepreneurial career as a conveyer of fine food and spirits." He moved so quickly she had no time to avoid his hands clasping her upper arms. He hauled her up close. "Hell," he said, "if I'd been *that* serious, I had plenty of time to put the deal together. After seeing how hard you work at it, it's a good thing I didn't do any more than talk."

"That's what you say *now*." Her jaw felt tight to the point of locking. "Silly me! When you said I had something you wanted, I thought you meant *me*."

"I did. I do."

"Forget it, Jason." Her heart grew heavier with

every word she uttered. "You're nothing but a common buffalo thief. Now will you kindly take your hands *off* me?"

For a moment, he didn't react. Then he slowly let his arms fall to his sides. He gave her a woeful look. "Does this mean you don't want to marry me?"

Oh, she did! But he was playing games, manipulating her shamelessly. She wasn't fool enough to fall for that kind of line. She shoved her feet, minus stockings, into black pumps.

"Go away, Jason." She spoke with a flat indifference she was far from feeling. "I never intended anything like this to happen." She cast a significant glance at the rumpled bed. "Since I have no intention of selling the Hideout any time soon, I'd say you've been wasting your time and...talents."

His square jaw hardened. "I said I love you and I meant it. I also said I had nothing to do with the disappearance of your damned buffalo—I thought I explained all that. Dammit, Diana, I'm not accustomed to having my word doubted."

She managed to shrug but it wasn't easy. "I'm not accustomed to tumbling into bed with the first pretty face I meet. Do you have any idea how cheap it makes me feel, to know I fell into bed with you not once but *twice?*"

"Yeah," he said as if he really did understand. "You're a control freak. I'm willing to live with that."

"You," she said, "are out of your mind. What I'm telling you here is that we're finished—done, over, *through*. I'm not going to sleep with you again and I'm not going to sell my business to you and all I want is for you to go away and leave me alone."

"Forever?"

"If not longer!"

So he went. Boots in hand, he stomped out of the door and got all the way to the front steps before slowing down long enough to realize he was in stocking feet. Sitting on the top step, he hauled on his boots.

Then he just sat there, glaring out at the streetlight halfway down the block in front of the gasoline station.

He'd made an awful fool of himself, but dammit, he'd do it again. He did love her, coldhearted though she might be. But no longer would he try to defend himself from her crazy accusations. No way. She either believed in him or she didn't. Ha! No contest there. She was bound and determined to blame him for the disappearance of that friggin' buffalo—like he needed a dead bison. Okay, Cameron, he told himself, you proposed to her and she spit in your eye and told you to get lost. *Do it.*

It damn sure was over between them. He wouldn't bother her again. Hell, miserable as he was, he wouldn't bother *anyone* again. He headed toward his truck. Somebody in a dark-colored Jeep Cherokee drove past, honked, waved through the open window. Jason barely glanced up.

Screw 'em. Screw 'em all. He was going home to lick his wounds.

WITHIN A WEEK, all Cupid was buzzing about the change in Jason Cameron. He was moody, broody, short-tempered and abrupt—and those were his good qualities.

"It's the Queen Bee, for sure," Jimmy announced over a chicken-fried steak sandwich at the Rusty Spur. "He's been seduced and abandoned, sure as hell. Poor ol' Jason. Maybe now he knows how the rest of us feel every time he makes off with one of our gals." His smile was evil.

"Hang on a doggone minute." Tap helped himself to a French fry off his friend's plate. He'd already eaten all his own. "It kinda makes me nervous to see Jason actin' more like his big brother than like hisself. Remember what happened that time when Ben turned all lovesick? He shot ol' man Turner, that's what happened."

"Jason's not gonna shoot anyone," Jimmy said.

Lorrie Purdy, on her way to the cash register, stopped. "Either of you guys seen Jason lately?"

They exchanged significant looks.

"The Queen Bee done him dirt and he ain't takin' it real well," Tap said.

Lorrie sighed. "Yeah, that's what I think, too. Jeez, guys, I know most of Cupid wanted revenge, wanted to see him get his comeuppance. Jason just makes life look so bloomin' easy while the rest of us are strugglin'. But I never dreamed it would completely change his personality."

"Yeah," Jimmy agreed. "For the worse."

"Maybe we could get 'em back together," Lorrie suggested hopefully.

"Maybe we could mind our own business," Jimmy countered. "We helped get him in this mess." He brightened. "But hell, he's a big boy. He'll get over it."

Lorrie sighed. "Maybe," she said.

EVERYBODY WAS just full of advice and Jason wasn't buying any of it.

"Take her flowers."

"Send her candy."

"Find her buffalo."

Go to hell.

He was about to take woman-advice from Jimmy Mosely and Tap Wilson? He'd give up women before he'd do that.

Actually, he *had* given up women. He might as well be a damned eunuch for all they meant to him now.

Then the family got down on him.

Ben, being the oldest son, threw the first lick. "What the hell you doin' hangin' around that ranch day after day? You're gonna go stir-crazy if you don't get out more often. Come over here and eat with us at least once in a while."

"Two weeks ago you were bitchin' because I

spent all my time in town chasin' women,'' Jason countered.

"Make that *woman*." Ben's look narrowed. "What'd you pull on Diana to put that burr under her blanket?"

"Me? Me? I didn't pull a goddamn thing. She's thrown my ass out for the last time, that's all."

Sweet Betsy tried to smooth troubled waters. "Ben, I'm sure this isn't all your brother's fault. I like Diana, but she's quite capable of taking care of herself."

From Ben's expression, he didn't believe that for a minute.

Sister Maggie took the next shot. "Everybody in the family tells me you're acting like a big baby," she began.

Jason groaned. "Thanks, Maggie. I can always count on you to phrase it delicately. Next to you, Ben's the soul of sensitivity."

Her laughter lit up her face. Marriage had certainly improved her; she was almost always happy now, and Jason remembered when that hadn't been the case at all. Her first husband had been an invalid and his death had been hard for her to handle.

Then she'd met Chase Britton—and don't forget his daughter, Blair, the little troublemaker.

Who now jumped into the fray. "Why don't you marry Diana instead of just sleeping with her, Jason? You're not getting any younger, you know. It's time you settled down while you're still young enough that you can find somebody who'll have you. Everybody says so.''

Jason glared at Maggie. "You hear how she talks? You're her mother. Wash her mouth out with soap or something.''

"Sorry," Maggie said serenely, not looking sorry in the slightest. "In this case, she happens to be right.''

"Oh, yeah?'' He wanted to say something about Ryan Kennedy, throw Blair's friendship with the boy in Maggie's face, but all he had there was a feeling. A feeling...that the kids were getting too close. And remembering back to the days when he'd been eighteen himself, Jason wanted to groan. He didn't think Ryan and Blair had been intimate, but the smart money said most kids their age were sexually active.

If so, damned kids were better off than he was. He hadn't slept with anyone except Diana since she came to town.

Life sucked.

Then Julie got ahold of him.

"Diana's miserable and it's your fault," she said, launching her opening salvo.

"Don't give me that," he snarled. "I'm doing exactly what she told me to do—staying out of her life. What do you women want—blood?''

"Yes," Max said.

"Stay out of this, Cosmo," Julie warned. "My brother is about to cut his own throat and I'm trying to save him.''

When Julie had gone to put supper on the table, Max gave his brother-in-law a sympathetic glance. "Don't mind her," he said. "She's kinda tense these days. We thought she might be pregnant but it was a false alarm."

"I never mind her." Jason sank lower on his spine in the easy chair, filled with sympathy for his twin. She wanted kids so bad she could hardly stand it. Jason, on the other hand, would be afraid they'd grow up to be like Blair. Suddenly, he sat up straight. "Max, you got any leads on Diana's damned buffalo?"

Max shook his head. "None to speak of. It's gotta be kids, Jase. Big ones, maybe, but kids. It's a joke. If she'd just ease off, they'd bring that blasted buffalo back. But the way she keeps carrying on about it, she just may never see Buffalo Bill again."

"She still thinks I'm responsible."

Max cocked an eyebrow. "Feelin' sorry for yourself, are you? She's a city gal, so what do you expect? If you recall, I came here from a big city, and in retrospect, I'll admit I had a little to learn, too. Fortunately, Julie was willing to take me on."

"Diana isn't interested in taking me on."

"Don't be too sure of that, Jason." At Julie's call from the kitchen, Max rose. "Sometimes you've got to take chances to keep from missing out entirely. Now come on in to dinner and let Julie take her best shots at you."

And that's exactly what happened.

JASON DIDN'T HEAD back home until after eleven. Julie had taken her shots all right, but nothing she said had made any difference. Something Max had said might, however.

Sometimes you've got to take chances to keep from missing out entirely.

With that on his mind, he turned right on Lover's Lane instead of left. He'd take the longcut through town and drive past the Hideout. There was always the chance that Diana would still be there, and if she was, maybe...

The saloon looked dark at his approach. Pulling into the parking lot, he drove slowly toward the back. If she was there, he might see a light in the upstairs apartment or even in the kitchen. If he did...

He rounded the corner and the first thing he saw was light—but not the light of electricity and not in the second-floor apartment.

Fire! Flames curled through the kitchen windows. Braking, he leaped from his pickup and started forward at a run.

The moon sailed out from behind a cloud at that moment to reveal a sight he couldn't have conjured up in his wildest imagination.

Beau Turner and Ryan Kennedy struggling to drag a hulking shadow—Buffalo Bill, Jason knew instinctively—out the back door and down the delivery ramp. Off to one side, Blair Britton fumbled with a garden hose draped over a faucet on the side of the building.

And behind them, flames threatened to engulf the Hideout entirely.

CHAPTER EIGHTEEN

JASON REALIZED INSTANTLY what must have happened.

Ryan and Blair had heisted Buffalo Bill as a lark and big, dumb Beau Turner, out of some mistaken sense of loyalty, had followed their lead. Now the teens were trying to end the game by returning Bill to his rightful place before they left for college.

Call it summer fun.

The fire had to be some damnfool accident—an accident that could ruin their lives. If they were busted by the law for this prank, it could get Ryan and Blair booted out of college before they'd even started. For Beau, the repercussions would be even greater. He was already on probation for horse rustling and this stunt could send him to jail.

The futures of all three were at stake.

Blair glanced up, saw her uncle bearing down on them and screamed. "Jason! Oh, my God, it's Jason!" He ignored her, leaping up the ramp to help drag Buffalo Bill to safety.

"Shit!" Beau heaved mightily on the furry hindquarters of their unwieldy cargo. "Shit, Ryan, you said nobody was gonna—"

"Shut up and push!" Ryan, his arm around Bill's neck, was busy pulling.

The addition of Jason made the difference. Once they got Bill to level ground, it was simple enough to haul him out of harm's way.

The three thieves huddled around Jason, shaking with well-deserved terror.

"Oh, God," Beau groaned. "Oh, God, I'm goin' back to jail for sure."

Jason knocked the big man's hands away from his face and spoke harshly to cut through his dread. "No, you're not. Tomorrow I'm gonna give the three of you the verbal hiding you deserve, but now we've got other things to worry about. Blair, get your cell phone on the double so I can report the fire. Then here's what we're going to do..."

DIANA KNEW. She didn't know how she knew, but the minute she heard the fire alarm, she leaped from bed and started throwing on her clothes. She hadn't been asleep anyway. She wasn't sleeping these nights, hadn't had a good night's sleep since that final scene with Jason.

She should have believed him. If life was going to be this miserable without him, what was the point of being "right"? Tomorrow Ryan would leave for college and she'd be all alone...

Rounding the curve in Lover's Lane in front of the marshal's house, she saw flames shooting out of the back of the Hideout and her heart stopped beating. She spotted the town's only fire truck already parked in back, people milling around it in the parking lot.

Leaving the minivan on the fringe of all that activity, she rushed toward the orange glow of flames. Someone grabbed her arm to halt her panicky flight.

"Easy, girl." It was Doc Kunkle, who lived next door to Max and Julie. "Nobody's been hurt yet and I'd like to keep it that way."

"Oh, God," Diana moaned. "What happened?"

Doc shrugged, his expression sympathetic. "Danged if I know, but it's an ill wind that doesn't blow somebody some good. Look who's come home." Taking her elbow, he turned her toward the rear of the lot.

Buffalo Bill stood there like a sentinel watching over the efforts of the volunteer fire crew. With a little cry of joy, she rushed toward her buffalo.

Throwing her arms around his neck, she burst into tears. Now that she had Bill back, she might not even have a place to put him.

"...the right to remain silent. Anything you say can and will be used against you..."

She recognized Max's voice and it brought her bolting upright. Had Max caught the thieves? Could it possibly be that someone was actually going to pay for this outrage?

Swinging toward the sound of his voice, she saw him slip handcuffs on a tall man who stood with his back to the flames. "Marshal Mackenzie!" She started to head over to him. "Does this mean—" she began.

Max turned at the sound of her voice and so did his prisoner.

His prisoner was Jason Cameron.

JASON HAD KNOWN it would be hard, but nothing could have prepared him for the sickening rush of disappointment in Diana's face. Although he didn't know what she had to be disappointed about. She'd suspected him all along, hadn't she?

"Max?" She stepped closer, her gaze darting from one to the other. "What's going on here? This can't possibly mean what I think it means—can it?"

"It means," Max drawled, "that I've arrested this man for stealing your buffalo and then starting a fire in your place while trying to return him."

"No!" She swung on Jason. "This isn't true. It can't be true!"

He kept his face expressionless, which wasn't all that difficult. He couldn't imagine that he would ever smile again, even if the occasion arose.

Which didn't appear likely.

She grabbed the lapels of his shirt. "Tell the marshal you didn't do it!"

Jason had trouble forcing out a response. "He caught me red-handed. He's got to do his duty." He couldn't resist adding, "Don't act so surprised. You said all along—"

"I don't care what I said all along!" Distraught, she wrung her hands, looking around for support.

Dwight Deakins, the volunteer fire chief, caught her eye. He held up one hand in a thumbs-up gesture. "We 'bout got it," he yelled. "Don't worry, Di!"

"Don't worry." She repeated it like a death sentence. Squaring her shoulders, she faced the marshal. "What happens now?"

"Well, I'm gonna take our buffalo bandit over to the hoosegow for the night. Tomorrow we'll try to sort all this out." He took Jason's arm and steered him toward the street.

Diana stepped into their path. "Do you have to arrest him? He won't go anywhere." She glanced at the prisoner. "Will you?"

That's when he knew she had nothing but contempt for him. "You had to ask." Hell, he'd welcome a night in jail. At least he'd be alone.

MAX UNLOCKED the handcuffs, then opened the door to one of the two cells in the jail. Stepping aside, he gestured for his silent prisoner to enter. "I figured you'd be right at home in here," he told Jason.

Who rolled his eyes and grunted noncommittally. Walking inside, he sat down heavily on the narrow cot against the far wall. Jason had been in this tiny cell before and so had his brother Ben. Max had threatened at one point to put a plaque over the door designating it the Cameron Family Cell. Hell, you'd think the whole lot of 'em were nothing but desperadoes the way they came and went here. Elbows on his knees, he let his head sink into his hands.

Max leaned against the bars, his gaze assessing.

"So who you covering up for?" he asked pleasantly.

Jason jerked his head up and glared at his brother-in-law. "Nobody. Why would you—"

Max laughed. "You think I just fell off a turnip truck? You didn't steal that friggin' buffalo and you sure as hell didn't set any fire. For one thing, you didn't have time after you left my house, unless you had old Buffalo Bill stashed in my barn."

Jason glared. That was the only reason Max could think of? There wasn't *time?* "You caught me red-handed," he reminded the marshal self-righteously.

"That's right. I also have reason to believe you made the call reporting the fire. Somebody did. And who the hell else would have even noticed, until it had burned all the way to the front of the building? Hell, Jason, if you hadn't been there, it could have burned to the ground."

"I'm a hero," Jason agreed sarcastically.

Max looked unperturbed. "The way I figure it is, you happened by and saw something going on— maybe saw the fire—and decided for whatever reason to let the perpetrators off the hook and take the blame yourself. Am I getting close?"

"Not by a country mile."

"Now who do you like enough to take the fall for 'em? There's Granny, but I don't figure she had anything to do with this."

"Naw," Jason agreed. "It couldn'ta been Granny." Even in his current predicament, Jason was beginning to enjoy Max's perceptive approach to crime solving.

"And I figure we can rule Ben out. He's not exactly strong in the practical-joke department, and besides, Betsy would skin him alive."

"This is true."

"It wasn't Julie. I have it on good authority that she was just starting to cuddle up to her husband when the alarm came in. She was already in her nightie, shall we say, or she'd have come along." A sudden grin broke out on the marshal's face. "In fact, I'd hazard a guess that she's not any too happy this is taking so long."

"That rules Julie out, then."

Max looked thoughtful. "Guess all that leaves is Blair."

Jason reared back. "She's not big enough to handle that buffalo. Besides, she's way out on the Straight Arrow."

"Wrong." Max straightened away from the bars. "She's spending the night with us, but she's out with that Kennedy kid. Said there was a dance one or two towns over."

"See? She's accounted for."

"Maybe. Maybe not. That Kennedy kid is goofy over her, you know. If she told him to steal a buffalo, he'd steal a buffalo."

"But the two of them couldn't handle Bill," Jason argued. He hoped he was only imagining sweat popping out on his brow.

"Probably not. That's the only flaw in my theory.

Now if I could just figure out who among their friends is strong enough and dumb enough..." He shook his head. "Guess I'll worry about that tomorrow. Now I gotta go home and tell your sister that I've thrown your sorry ass in jail. That'll probably put the kibosh on *my* plans for the evening." He paused at the door that led into his office, his expression disgusted. "I'll be back in the morning. In the meantime, try to stay out of trouble."

"You're not worried about lynch mobs?" Jason called after him. "You're not worried my gang will bust me out? You're not worried...?"

The hell with it. The die was cast. Jason, for one, wasn't going to think about any of it.

IN THE HARSH LIGHT OF DAY, the back of the saloon looked awful. Diana stared at the charred wood and soggy floor, a sick lump of despair gathering in the pit of her stomach. She had insurance, of course, but how was she going to come up with the deductible? Not to mention the inevitable increase in her insurance rates.

Worst of all, how was she going to survive Jason's betrayal? Apparently, everything Blair and Ryan had said was true: Jason wanted to make her quit and he'd steal her buffalo or sleep with her or burn her business with equal callousness.

Ryan jogged up. "Why didn't you wake me?" he asked, stretching out his hamstrings.

"What for? There's nothing you can do." She reached out to brush the hair from his forehead.

Blair had dropped him off last night from the dance at just about the same time Diana had returned from the fire, so she'd told him what had happened. When she said that Jason had been arrested, Ryan and Blair hadn't reacted at all, just looked at each other blankly.

She supposed their attention was focused on their own plans for the following day. Ryan was catching his flight to Texas in midafternoon at Denver International Airport. Blair had begged to be allowed to drive him there before she went home to Aspen to make final preparations for her departure to Colorado University in Boulder.

Now Diana realized that Ryan looked pale and drawn, with unfamiliar dark shadows beneath his eyes. "Are you all right?" she asked with concern.

"I'm fine." He spoke impatiently, stepping beyond her reach. "Look, there's something I have to do. Will you be okay here?"

"Run along." God, she was going to miss him!

"Are you going to hang around here much longer?"

She shook her head. "I have to go talk to the fire chief and then I'm going over to the jail to find out what's being done about Jason."

Ryan started, his eyes going wide. "He didn't do it, Di," he said.

She smiled at his tense young face. "I know he's your girlfriend's uncle, but we'll have to leave his guilt or innocence for the law to decide," she said. "It's nothing for you to worry about."

For a moment, he looked as if he might argue. Then he sighed. "No," he said, "I suppose not."

A GROWING BABEL OF SOUND finally penetrated, and Jason sat up groggily on his cell cot. Running his hands over his face in an effort to wake up, he looked around for the source of the noise.

It'd been late before he'd gotten to sleep—only a few hours ago, in fact. The lights bothered him but his situation bothered him more.

He'd done the right thing. He'd get his pound of flesh from the three "desperadoes," but he simply couldn't let them get in trouble with the law because of a stupid prank. The fire, though—that worried him more.

And then there was Diana.

Well, hell, she'd suspected him from the beginning. He had to put her out of his mind and get on with his life.

A pounding at the single small barred window brought him swinging around. Beau stood there, gesturing madly. Jason pointed to the door, trying to tell the big guy to come on inside for a visit.

The door leading to the marshal's office swung open. Max stood there, looking harried and none too happy.

"Shit," he said explosively. "I got half the town out here raising hell because I locked you up and the other half raising hell because I didn't figure out you were the guilty party and arrest you weeks ago. I'm damned if I do and damned if I don't."

Julie shoved past her husband. "No, Cosmo, you're damned if you do. Let my brother out of that cell this instant." She actually stamped a foot. "He's not guilty and you damned well know it."

Jason spoke before Max could respond. "I am guilty, Jewel."

Her jaw dropped. "I don't believe it. You didn't have time to do all you're accused of between the time you left our house and the time you got caught behind the Hideout."

"Obviously, you're wrong."

She grabbed hold of the bars of his cell. "Jason, what are you trying to pull here? You don't seem to realize how serious this is."

Hell, yes, he realized it, but it wasn't as serious for him as for the three perpetrators. "Butt out," he told his twin. "That's my story and I'm stickin' to it."

She glared at him. "We'll see about that after I sic Grandma on you. I'm going to the Arrow *right now* and you can bet the whole family's gonna be on your case once I tell them what you're doing."

Max watched her go. "She's right," he said. "They'll be on you like ugly on a gorilla." He gave his brother-in-law a narrow glance. "Sure you don't want to change your story?"

"Not a chance."

The door opened and Beau stuck his head through. "Can I come in, Marshal?"

Max glanced at Jason, who gave a slight nod.

"Sure. Anybody else you wanna see while I do the paperwork and talk to the injured party in all this?"

"Not a soul," Jason said. "Keep 'em all away from me, will you, Max?"

"I'll try, but I wasn't kidding—the whole town's gathering out there. I don't know if the majority wants to lynch you or break you out."

He left, closing the door firmly behind him. Beau edged closer to the bars, looking about half-scared. "Jeez, Jason, I hate to see you in there when it was me—"

"Shut up, Beau, and listen."

"But, Jason, I want to stand up and take my medicine like a man. Why can't we just tell the truth? We stole that buffalo and hid him at the Lazy T."

"Because you're on probation and you'd go to jail, my man. And those two stupid kids would have a record and probably get expelled from school. You don't want that, do you?"

Beau groaned miserably. "No, but you—"

"I've got less to lose," Jason cut in. "Actually, I don't have jack to lose, so here's the deal. I want you to take a message to those two dumb kids..."

MAX WAS SURPRISED how easy it was to strike a deal with Diana. She'd been determined all along to blame Jason for the theft of Buffalo Bill. Now that she had him dead to rights, she seemed almost relieved and not at all vindictive.

"The fire chief says it wasn't arson," she announced, her voice heavy with worry. "He thinks it was an electrical malfunction but he'll know more later.''

''Then that means...''

She nodded wearily. ''Jason may have saved the Hideout from even worse damage by calling the fire department.''

''He says he didn't make that call.''

She shrugged. ''He said he didn't steal Buffalo Bill.'' She glanced toward the door leading to the cells. ''Why don't you let him out, Max?''

''Can't. The law's already involved. Besides, I thought you'd want to throw the book at him.''

''What good would that do?''

''It might make you feel better.''

She gave him a horrified glance. ''It would make me feel *worse,* if that's possible.''

Max pulled a large key ring from his desk drawer, then stood up. ''I'd guess your feelings will have some bearing on all this. Maybe we can get the judge to just give him a fine and umpteen hours of community service.''

''Whatever. That would be okay with me.'' She chewed on her lower lip. ''Could I—could I see him for just a minute?''

''Sure, if it's okay with him.''

Max unlocked the door and gestured her through, then stood back to watch.

She walked to the cell door and stopped. Jason, who was facing away to look through the small barred window, turned slowly toward her.

Their gazes met and locked on. Max shivered, feeling the sizzle passing between them.

"Why are you doing this?" Diana asked in a trembling voice. "Why?"

Jason held her gaze for another ten seconds, then turned to Max. "Get her out of here. I've got nothing to say to her, now or ever."

Max frowned. "Don't be so hasty. We've just done a little plea bargain here, assuming you don't screw everything up, you ungrateful bastard."

"Like what?"

When Diana didn't answer, Max did. "Apparently, you're not responsible for the fire." He thought Jason sagged with relief, then caught himself. "If that holds up, all you're guilty of is the usual—felony stupid in the form of buffalonapping. Diana's ready to settle for a fine and community service."

Jason was shaking his head before Max finished offering the deal.

Max's temper broke loose. "You dumb bastard, you're getting off easy."

"Too easy." Jason did not look impressed. "Here's *my* deal. I'll pay the fine and do your community service, but I'm also going to make restitution to the Hideout. Once it's up and running again—"

Diana finally found her voice. "You don't have to do that, you know. Dwight says you had nothing to do with the fire."

Jason looked at her again and his chilly glance

softened, became vulnerable. "God, Diana, I'm sorry. You don't deserve any of this. Once everything's the way it was, the way it should be, I'll get out of your life for good."

"But, Jason, why?"

He straightened and his expression grew remote. "I'm not going to talk about this anymore. I regret everything that's happened but I won't make excuses." He hitched up his jeans. "Okay, Max, let me out of this cell and I'll go see if I can disperse that mob out there."

BLAIR AND RYAN MET BEAU in Lover's Lane Park, the three of them hunched over a wooden picnic table. Blair supposed they must look guilty as sin but there didn't seem to be anyone around to notice. The whole town was over at the jail.

Beau licked his lips anxiously. "Jason give me hell," he said, "but I'm supposed to pass it on to you guys. He said what in the hell did you hope to accomplish, stealing that buffalo? How could you put someone you're supposed to like through that? He said..." Beau frowned. "I forget the rest but he really lit into me and I'm supposed to light into you."

Ryan glanced at Blair. Reaching out, he closed his hand over hers. "We've got to tell the truth," he said.

She nodded, although the thought almost made her sick. "I feel awful, letting him—what *is* it, Beau?"

Beau was shaking his head violently. "He said if you did, he'd skin you alive. He said I'd go to jail if Grandpa didn't kill me first."

"Jail!" Ryan looked confused. "Why? We didn't set the fire. We just borrowed a buffalo."

Blair knew why. "Because Beau's on probation for horse stealing," she said. "That's it, isn't it?"

Beau nodded. The big man looked completely miserable.

Ryan squeezed her hand. "We won't implicate you, Beau. We can take the blame."

"Her pa'd kill her," Beau predicted, nodding at Blair. "Then Jason says she'll get kicked out of college and you, too. And you'll both have a record and your lives will be ruined."

Ryan's jaw jutted out stubbornly. "Diana wouldn't press charges."

"Too late, Jason says. Law's already involved. He's ready to make restitution, but how would we do that if I'm in jail? Naw, he says to keep our mouths shut or he'll make us wish we had. And he says if you feel guilty, *good.* Learn to live with it."

Blair didn't cry until Beau had departed and then she let the tears flow. "I *hate* this!" she said, sniffling.

"Me, too." He put his arms around her and held her gently against his chest. "Life sucks. I don't want to leave you."

She realized how much she enjoyed the comfort of his arms and sat up, pushing him away. "Yes, and I know why. *If you love me, you'd let me.*"

"I never said any such thing," he declared indignantly. "But I do love you." He grinned. "And I do wish you'd let me."

She smeared the tears over her cheeks with both hands, struggling to get hold of her emotions. "Jason's protecting us. I feel like shit."

Ryan's head drooped. "Me, too. How can I leave for school with everything so up in the air, like a rat deserting a sinking ship?"

Blair stood up. "Diana's ship won't sink. Jason will see to that." She added passionately, "But I wish I'd never seen that damned buffalo!"

"Me, too." He stood beside her, took her gently in his arms and kissed her. Lifting his head, he managed a strained smile. "You taste salty." He licked his lips.

"Oh, Ryan!" This time, *she* kissed *him,* which she'd never done before. She even slid her tongue into his mouth, awkwardly, but determined to show him how she felt. When the kiss ended, she stood with her cheek pressed against his shoulder, breathing hard. When she could speak again, she whispered, "I wish I'd let you, and now there isn't time."

He didn't have to ask what she meant.

CHAPTER NINETEEN

A NEW, TIGHT-LIPPED JASON emerged from the Cupid Jail.

Everybody noticed; everybody talked about it—but not to him. He had only one thing to say and he said it in front of the jail the morning he was released, afterward refusing to discuss anything relating to the case.

What he said was, "I'm responsible and I'm prepared to make it right again no matter what it takes."

Then he turned, walked the couple of blocks from the jail to the Hideout and went to work.

He wasn't alone for long. Diana watched with growing astonishment as most of Cupid joined him. Those who thought he did it and those who thought he didn't all pitched in to help him clean up and repair the Hideout.

This time, Diana accepted their help because she had to. And in so doing, she discovered that it didn't really hurt. These were her friends after all. They'd do the same for any among them.

When official word came that the fire had been caused by an electrical problem, they cheered and then went back to work. Many of them might think

Jason capable of stealing a buffalo, but nobody thought he could be a firebug, even by accident.

It took almost two weeks, but eager volunteers didn't let up until the job was done. Jason paid for all materials; Diana was out the income from those days but nothing more. When he tried to give her a check to cover even *that,* she tore it into little pieces and let them drift to the floor.

"You've done more than enough already," she told him, her heart aching because of the void between them. "The only thing I want from you now is an explanation."

"That's the one thing you'll never get," he said curtly.

The new Jason was often curt; she couldn't remember the last time she'd seen his infectious smile or heard his coaxing laughter. "Talk to me," she pleaded. She reached for him, but her hands barely brushed his sleeve before he pulled back as if from danger.

"Give it up, Diana." He sounded weary. "I've already groveled. What else do you want? Blood?"

"No! I want..." But she couldn't go on because she didn't know what she *did* want. To go back, to start over, to sell Buffalo Bill to a junk dealer before any of this ever happened?

Jason turned and walked out of the Hideout. She watched him go with a horrible sinking feeling that she'd never see him again.

Of course, she did, but only at a distance. He'd retreated to his ranch and pretty much stayed there.

He didn't even emerge for her grand reopening although everybody else for miles around did.

She concealed her disappointment as best she could, but Grandma Cameron saw right through her. The old lady put her arm around Diana's shoulders and gave her a hug. "You okay, hon?"

"I'm fine. Everyone's been so wonderful to me..."

And the tears started. Grandma led Diana back to her office and closed the door behind them. "If you want to cry, now's your chance," she said. "Then I'll give you some there-there and you'll feel just fine."

But Diana brushed away her tears and squared her shoulders. "I don't want to cry. Why should I?"

"Well," Grandma observed, "your boy's off at his first year of college and your beau—"

"Jason was never my beau."

"Honey, that's just my old-fashioned word for lover. He was your lover—now don't deny it, he was. You're missin' him is all, no matter what you call him."

Diana's shoulders slumped. "I'm so confused," she moaned. "I *do* miss him. I don't get it—I've never minded being alone before. In fact, I've always enjoyed my own company. I've prided myself on my independence, and now all of a sudden, I feel as if I'm about to fall apart every time I'm alone." She searched the old woman's face for encouragement. "Do you think Jason will ever talk to me again, Grandma? I've begged him to and he simply refuses."

She wanted Grandma to reassure her, to say that perseverance would carry the day. Instead, the old lady sighed. "I wish I knew," she said at last. "I've known that boy from the day he was born and I've never seen him like this, all withdrawn and kinda cold."

Diana uttered a little groan filled with frustration. "If I could only find some way to make him talk to me—but what would I say? 'I'm no different from all the other women who've chased after you—'" She stopped short, struck by the rest of that thought: *Except that I love you, I really do love you.*

And she did. Buffalo be damned, she did. Too bad she had to lose him before admitting it.

"Furthermore," she announced, "I know he didn't steal my buffalo."

Granny gave her an oblique glance. "Then who did?"

"I don't know and I don't care." And she didn't. It was the most wonderfully liberating thought. Sudden realization flashed on her: she'd used Bill's disappearance as a means to keep a distance between herself and Jason and her new neighbors.

Not that it had worked. She'd fallen in love with Jason and had let him and the town rescue her when her back was to the wall. They hadn't even made her ask.

The theft of the buffalo *was* a joke, as everybody

else had seen from the beginning. Where was her sense of humor? Where was her *sense?*

"Is it too late?" she asked Grandma, her heart threatening to burst with a mixture of hope and hopelessness.

Granny considered. "While there's life, there's hope," she said finally. "I'd say give him a little time and then try again." She turned toward the door, adding almost as a throwaway, "By the way, me'n Ethan are gonna get married before I move out to the Lazy T." She grinned. "All nice and legal."

"That's wonderful! I'm so happy for you." Diana's own grief was swallowed up in a rush of happiness at the news. "When's the big day?"

"Soon as Ben comes down off the ceiling." Granny reached for the door and paused with her hand on the knob. The glance she gave Diana over her shoulder sparkled with mischief. "By the way, Blair was right. If they love you, they'll marry you."

JASON THOUGHT SPRING would never arrive. Holed up in Paradise Valley with only buffalo for company and diversion, he lived like a hermit, avoiding everybody including his own family.

Which wasn't easy when one or the other of them kept showing up every time the snow melted enough to let them in. Most of the time he could handle them, but when Julie showed up, there was bound to be fireworks.

But not immediately, because she wasn't alone.

"Who's the kid?" Jason asked.

Julie laid a protective arm across the little boy's shoulder. "This is my buddy, Mikey. He's Mary Davis's nephew. I baby-sit him once in a while."

The boy's lower lip thrust out. "I'm no baby!"

"Figure of speech." Julie patted his shoulder, her brown eyes softening. Jason hoped her goodwill would carry over to him.

It didn't. Once she'd found a cracker and a glass of milk for the kid, she lit into her brother.

"Diana's been asking after you," she announced.

"No kiddin'," Jason said.

"Sarcasm doesn't become you." She spoke in her most superior manner. "I don't think she believes you're the one who took Bill anymore."

"Look," he said impatiently, "I've paid my debt to society. Wanna get off my back?"

"She misses you."

He groaned. "You're out of your cotton-pickin' mind. Diana Kennedy doesn't miss anybody, never has and never will. She's one self-contained, self-satisfied woman." He tossed another armload of fuel into the woodbox beside the fireplace. Mikey glanced up briefly from a copy of *Bison Journal*, then went back to looking at the pictures.

Jason continued in a calmer voice. "Even if she does, I don't miss her. As a matter of fact—" he beat on his chest in an approximation of a bull gorilla "—I don't miss anyone and I like it that way."

"You lie!"

Mikey gasped. "You said a bad word, Miss Julie!"

She looked properly chastised. "Honey, it's only bad when it's not true. Jason *did* tell an awful, barefaced lie."

Jason sneered. "Got any proof?"

"I've got woman's intuition, which is better." Her tone changed, grew coaxing. "But moving right along..."

He didn't like the gleam in her eye but refused to rise to the bait. He just waited, jaw out and arms folded over his chest.

She gave him a tentative smile. "Spring Fling's coming up in a few months. Everybody wants to know if—"

"No way, not a chance, forget it."

"But you don't know what I'm going to ask."

"No kissing booth and no dunk tank."

She let out an annoyed *harrumph*. "C'mon, Jason," she wheedled. "Everybody's worried about you. If you don't do any of the things you've always done—"

"My mind's made up. Hell, I'm not even going. How d'you like them apples?"

"Not very damn—" She glanced at Mikey, watching and listening with rapt attention, and changed it to "—not very doggoned much. Besides, if you don't even show up, everybody will think— well, they'll think you're in even worse shape than the gossips claim."

"What do I care what anybody thinks?"

"Even if they think you're a victim of unrequited love?"

"That's the stupidest thing I ever heard in my life." But his heart pounded a mile a minute. Shit. It *was* unrequited.

It was also love. But no way was he going to put his neck in that noose again. He'd proposed to her once—hell, he'd said he loved her and that obviously packed no gear with her. As long as he lived, he would never lay himself open like that again.

"Tell them," he ordered his twin, "that Jason Cameron has retired as the village idiot."

And although she and Mikey hung around most of the afternoon, and she wheedled and coaxed and threatened, that's all she got out of Jason on the subject.

BUSINESS AT THE HIDEOUT had hung in throughout the long winter months and Diana had no cause for complaint on that score. Once she'd come up with "the plan," however, she could barely wait for spring to come, and with it, the Spring Fling.

Betsy Cameron, one of the most ardent supporters of the Cupid Elementary School fund drive, had said that the May Day event should put the building fund over the top.

"Will Jason be there?" Diana asked as casually as she could manage.

"I'd think so," Betsy said without much conviction. "Actually, we haven't seen much of him this winter. But he always helps out, even if we have to send Julie to bully him into it." She changed the subject abruptly. "So what do you hear from Ryan?

Blair seems to be having a bit of trouble adjusting to college life...''

So was Ryan, Diana thought as Betsy talked on. When he'd refused to come home for Christmas, she'd flown *there* and found him a bit tense and withdrawn but happy to see her. They'd spent five days together and then he'd gone to a friend's house for the remainder of his vacation.

She didn't know what his plans were for the summer but realized she'd have to trust his judgment. He was a young man now, not a child. When they'd parted, he'd put his arms around her and kissed her cheek.

"Thanks for everything, Di," he'd said. "I hope I never disappoint you again."

She'd laughed because he never *had* disappointed her.

"So," Betsy said now, "we're lining up people to work the kissing booth. Think you might sign up to kiss a few frogs?"

"I'd rather slit my wrists," Diana said with heartfelt sincerity. But later when she was alone, sudden inspiration struck.

When Jason started his stint in the kissing booth, she could muscle her way to the front and keep handing him five-dollar bills and kissing him until he *had* to talk to her. And he would. He'd know how difficult it was for her to make such a spectacle of herself. His sense of humor would eventually kick in. He wouldn't be able to turn her down if he was laughing, right? Oh, please, God, make it right!

Those who'd seen him lately swore he'd lost that
sense of humor along with the special something
that made him *Jason,* the most popular man in this
part of Colorado. Diana didn't believe it for a minute, didn't *dare* believe it.

And May 1, she'd prove it.

"JASON, OL' BUDDY! Good to see ya!"

Tap Wilson stuck out his hand and Jason felt
obliged to shake it. Even in the middle of the Spring
Fling mob, his friends had quickly spotted him and
descended en masse. Hell, he already regretted giving in to family pressure.

"So where you been all winter?" Jimmy wanted
to know. "We wuz beginnin' to think you'd turned
mountain man or somethin'."

"That's about it," Jason agreed. "Excuse me, fellas, but I've gotta go see a man about a horse."

"You gonna be at the dunk tank later?" Jimmy
inquired, following along for a few steps.

Jason shook his head and kept walking.

"How 'bout the kissin' booth?"

Jason just kept shaking his head and walking.

"Well, hell." Jimmy stared after his friend.
"Looks to me like the Queen Bee has done ruined
that boy entirely."

"Yeah," Tap agreed darkly, "with a little help
from his friends. I'd say Cupid's revenge has back-
fired—big time."

LEAVING CHARLIE GILROY in charge at the Hideout,
Diana spent her morning working the ticket booth

and later assisting at the cakewalk. But always she watched...watched for Jason Cameron.

She saw him only from a distance. He never came close to her, and being tied up with volunteer duties, she couldn't very well track *him* down.

But that was okay, she reminded herself. When he entered the kissing booth, she'd be first in line. The next time Betsy hustled over to see how sales were going, Diana asked casually, "So what time will Jason be selling those expensive kisses?"

Betsy seemed surprised. "Didn't you know? He won't be doing that this go-round."

"But—why not?"

Betsy shrugged. "Who knows? Even Julie couldn't get him to change his mind." She sighed. "Poor Jason."

Diana leaned across the counter in alarm. "What's wrong? Is he ill?"

"Oh, nothing like that!" Betsy laughed. "I guess you'd say he's...depressed. But then, who wouldn't be, holed up all alone for most of the winter?" She glanced around as if searching for someone. "You haven't seen Julie, have you?"

"No. What's up with her?"

Betsy's smile blossomed. "She and Max think they've found a child they can adopt. She's absolutely beside herself, she's so thrilled."

"Oh, Betsy, that's wonderful. I'm so happy for them. If I see her, I'll tell her you're looking for her." But Diana's thoughts had already returned to

Jason. Her plan was a bust; now what was she going to do?

"Thanks." Betsy sighed. "Guess I'll just have to tell them to close the kissing booth when Miss Cupid gets tired of puckering up. I hate to do it but—"

"Maybe you won't have to."

Oh, God, did I really say that? Diana stifled a groan, then squared her shoulders with purpose. If I can't get to him one way, she told herself, I'll get to him another...if he cares for me at all, that is.

"HEY, FELLAS, YOU SEE who's about to set up in the kissing booth?"

Jason, who'd been searching for a way to shake Jimmy and Tap and the rest of the bachelor herd, looked around at the sound of Beau's excited voice.

"Who?" Tap asked in a disinterested tone.

"The Queen Bee, that's who!"

A stunned silence settled over the little group and they all turned as one to look at Jason.

If they were stunned, *he* was stupefied. There had to be some mistake. Diana would never put herself on display that way. Never in a million years...

He realized they were all staring at him. "Hey," he said, "it's your money and her lips. I got nothin' to say about this, nothin' at all." He added for good measure, "Nothin'!"

"In that case...!" Jimmy took off at a trot and the others fell in behind him, except for Beau. The big guy wore a worried expression.

"Heck, Jason, why don't you just go talk to her?"

Jason frowned. "What the hell are you cater-wauling about, Beau?"

Beau nodded toward the kissing booth, nearly concealed by the crowd. "I ast her. I said, 'Why you doin' this, Diana?' And she said, bold as brass, "cause Jason won't talk to me. It's suicide by kis-sin'.'"

Jason choked off surprised laugher. She was try-ing to manipulate him and he wouldn't have it. She could kiss cowboys 'til the cows came home and he still wouldn't have a word to say to her. They were through, finished, done for. He'd learned to live without her.

Okay, it wasn't fun, but life was full of tough choices—and he *hadn't* stolen that friggin' buffalo! Even if she was willing to "forgive" him for that, he wasn't going to sacrifice his honor for her or anybody else.

But he wouldn't mind edging over a little so he could witness her embarrassment because she *was* going to be mortified. He was sure of that.

In fact, he knew her well enough to doubt she'd be able to go through with it. Yet there she was, standing behind the thin partition with its narrow waist-high counter designed to maintain at least a little decorum.

Her smile looked shaky but determined as she stared out at the dozen or so men already in line. She held up her hands for their attention. "Okay, guys," she said in a voice at once unsteady and resolute. "I've never done this before so...be gentle, will you?"

That earned her a hoot of knowing laughter from the line and a groan from Jason. He clenched and unclenched his hands, absolutely sure she wouldn't do this stupid thing.

Jimmy stepped up and slapped a dollar on the counter. He cast an impish grin over his shoulder. "I been wantin' to do this ever since she come to town," he announced. Turning back to the wide-eyed Diana, he threw out his arms. "You're available, I'm available. Come to Papa!"

And she did. Goddammit, she did! She closed her eyes and leaned right over that counter and Jimmy grabbed her like she was a Hostess cupcake.

The sonuvabitch kissed her—he *really* kissed her and she let him. With a roar of protest, Jason sprang from his partially hidden vantage point. He had Jimmy by the scruff of the neck and was yanking him away before anybody knew what was happening.

Diana opened her eyes and blinked in surprise. Up this close, Jason could see that she was pale and looked almost faint, as if it had taken every ounce of her considerable willpower to do this idiotic thing.

Snatching out his wallet, he began flinging bills at her. She made no move to catch them or stop him. The money floated to the ground.

"Okay," he yelled, "you win! Get out of there and I'll listen—but you can't make me talk!"

She looked at him. She didn't smile, just looked at him with an expression he'd never seen from her before.

"I haven't won yet," she said softly, "but now I know I'm going to."

Reaching for him, she curved her hands around his neck and pulled his head down. Her lips were cool at first but quickly warmed beneath his, opening in an unmistakably poignant welcome. And he tasted something he'd never encountered before.

It was love.

She pulled her lips away just enough so she could speak in that soft, vulnerable voice. "I was wrong and you were right. We should have gotten married the first time you brought it up."

"Jeez!" The new voice belonged to Tap, and Jason realized without caring that the kissing line had moved up to surround them. "He proposed!" Tap went on. "Jason proposed and she turned him down. Did you ever hear of such a thing?"

"Shut up, Tap," Jason growled. "Diana—"

"I love you," she said.

Hearing that knocked all the air out of him. He stared at her, probably stupidly.

"If you're any kind of gentleman," she added, "you'll give me a chance to make amends."

Jason had been hurt too badly and had brooded too long to sweep their differences aside this easily—even though he did love her and knew damned well he'd never love any other woman. Still, he had to say, "That could take a while."

She flinched, then lifted her chin in that characteristic gesture of defiance. "In that case, we'll just have to risk setting a bad example for the younger generation—and heaven knows, they get into enough trouble without that. The bottom line is, I'm not going to let you get away from me again, Jason Cameron."

"Even though you think I'm a thief and a liar?"

She caught her breath on a sigh. "I never thought that—never, not really. And now I know I was totally wrong. Are you going to make me grovel? I won't like that, but if I have to, I will."

From that he deduced that she knew. Beau, Blair or Ryan had told her *they* took the buffalo. She hadn't realized on her own that he wasn't the kind of man who'd do a thing like that.

But looking at her with love shining from her eyes, he knew that none of that mattered. He loved her and *something* had to give before he became an unredeemable curmudgeon.

Hell, he could already feel the "old" Jason resurfacing. Throwing back his head, he let out a "Yah-hoo!"

All of Cupid breathed a sigh of relief.

After the ceremony, Diana asked her husband for his understanding and when they finally ended their honeymoon, would she be allowed to finish her new novel... the one she had begun just for him? Because only she knew how it would end, he had to let her...

EPILOGUE

DIANA KENNEDY and Jason Cameron were married at the Hideout Saloon during Cupid's Fourth of July celebration. Among those looking on with approval were most of Cupid, including Buffalo Bill and all the Camerons—even the newest. Julie and Max had brought along their son, seven-year-old Michael Davis Cameron. Mikey's aunt Mary had finally realized she was unable to care for him properly and, when faced with losing him to the social services system, had begged Julie to take him.

Begged? Julie would have gladly given her life to have that boy, and Max was quickly as enamored of Mikey as was she.

Also new to the Cameron clan was Ethan Turner, who couldn't seem to stop smiling at his bride, the former Etta May Cameron, now Turner. Married only a couple of weeks, their pleasure at being a couple in the eyes of God and man was something to aspire to, Jason thought.

He looked at his own bride and *he* couldn't stop smiling, either. At the reception, he finally tore himself away long enough to track down Beau, Ryan and Blair to thank them for telling Diana the truth, even if he had sworn to kill them if they did.

After the congratulations and the smiles, he put his arms around the kids and grinned at Beau. "I don't know which one of you spilled the beans, but I want to thank you," he said with heartfelt sincerity. "Otherwise, I'm not really sure—"

"Tell!" Beau glowered at the kids. "One a' you told?"

Blair's hand flew to her throat. "Not me! My God, Jason, you told us you'd kill us if we ever breathed a word."

"Well, it wasn't me." Ryan looked royally peeved. "You think I'm crazy? You said *death*. I believed you!"

"Me, too," Beau chimed in.

Across the room with her arm around Grandma Cameron-Turner, the matron of honor, Diana heard her brand-new husband's roar of laughter. Following the sound, she spotted him with his arms around Ryan and Blair. Then Beau stepped into the circle and they all hugged.

Grandma noticed, too. "That Jason," she said admiringly. "He can charm the birds off the trees with a smile."

"That's the truth," Diana agreed. "Wonder what's so funny?"

"Heaven only knows."

True, Diana thought, but I'll find out. *I've got a lifetime to do it in after all.*

She also had ways of making him talk... wonderful, wonderful ways.

When her own laughter soared, it was his turn to look...and wonder.